THE LAND GIRLS AT GOODWILL HOUSE

FENELLA J. MILLER

Boldwood

First published in Great Britain in 2022 by Boldwood Books Ltd.

Copyright © Fenella J. Miller, 2022

Cover Design by Colin Thomas

Cover Photography: Colin Thomas

A CIP catalogue record for this book is available from the British Library.

Paperback ISBN 978-1-80162-856-3

Large Print ISBN 978-1-80162-854-9

Hardback ISBN 978-1-80162-853-2

Ebook ISBN 978-1-80162-855-6

Kindle ISBN 978-1-80162-857-0

Audio CD ISBN 978-1-80162-848-8

MP3 CD ISBN 978-1-80162-849-5

Digital audio download ISBN 978-1-80162-851-8

Boldwood Books Ltd
23 Bowerdean Street
London SW6 3TN
www.boldwoodbooks.com

For my wonderful son, daughter-in-law and grandson, Lincoln, Karyn and Charlie

1

GOODWILL HOUSE, AUGUST 1940

Joanna, Lady Harcourt, was touched by the response from the village to the near disaster of the fire in the Victorian wing of Goodwill House. The morning afterwards, not only did one tender from the base turn up but also an engine from Ramsgate. There was an absolute army of willing volunteers from the village.

She'd found a pair of slacks, not something she often wore as she thought it rather fast for a woman to be wearing trousers, and had been outside to greet and thank everybody. There were heavy canvas hosepipes trailing across the once shiny parquet floors in the grand hall as the engine from Ramsgate did its best to pump out the gallons of water that had been pumped in last night.

Joanna's adopted children, Joe and Liza, were up and dressed in their oldest clothes, ready to muck in as they always did. Jean, almost a member of the family, had every available kettle and saucepan boiling ready to make tea and toast for all the helpers.

'I'm not surprised the three of you are wearing your gumboots,' Joanna said. 'I fear the parquet flooring will never recover from the soaking it got last night.'

Jean replied as she made the first pot of tea. 'Better a wet floor than a house going up in flames. Liza's going to take over here whilst I help your mother-in-law. She was fast asleep when I came down – too much excitement isn't good for someone her age.'

Jean had come to Goodwill House to be a personal maid for Joanna's mother-in-law, Elizabeth, but over the months had become first a seamstress and now housekeeper. She was an excellent cook, efficient and a good friend, but she'd never really replace Betty, who had died so recently of measles.

Joanna blinked back tears as she thought of her friend and how shocked she'd be to know that her own husband had possibly set fire to the house in an act of revenge. Bert had been dismissed and lost his home because of her intervention.

Lazzy, the enormous dog Joanna had found and rescued from the Victorian wing a few months ago, nudged her leg, almost sending her from her feet. 'Stop that, silly boy, I know you haven't had your breakfast but then neither has anybody else.'

Joe came in from the yard where he'd been taking care of the chickens, ducks and geese as well as checking that Star, the only horse they still had on the premises, had sufficient water for the day.

'I'll feed him now, Ma, and then I'll go next door and see what I can do to help. There's a sergeant from the base wants to speak to you.'

Her pulse skipped a beat. 'I'm coming, I think it must be the young man who was in charge last night. He's called Sergeant Sergeant – isn't that amusing?'

'He didn't tell me who he was, but he's definitely the bloke in charge. I'm surprised Manston has let him come a second time. What if a plane crashes whilst he's here?'

'I'm sure they've thought of that, Joe. I expect if a squadron's scrambled then they'll return immediately. It's only two miles to the base and they could be back in ten minutes.'

Why was she standing here talking when she could be outside meeting the handsome young firefighter who had made her feel like a girl again? She smiled wryly as she headed into the yard. Joanna had never had the opportunity to enjoy just being young, to fall in and out of love with a series of handsome young men. There hadn't been the opportunity, as her late husband, David, had snatched her up as soon as she'd left school.

Sergeant John Sergeant was giving orders to a couple of his men when she emerged into the early-morning sunlight. This gave her the opportunity to look at him in daylight. Last night, she'd only noticed his odd eyes – one green and one brown – and his flashing smile. Now she could see that he was a head taller than her, had an athletic build and thick, wavy black hair but, as he had his back to her, she still couldn't see his face.

He finished his conversation and turned. Instead of striding across to her as she'd expected, he remained stationary for a moment, staring at her, as if he too wanted to get a better look at a person who'd made an impression on him last night.

She could see now that his complexion was darker than hers; perhaps he had Mediterranean ancestors. Then he smiled and came to join her.

'Good morning, my lady. It won't take the blokes from Ramsgate long to remove the surface water from your home but it's going to take weeks for it to dry out completely. You'll need to leave the windows open. Better to let it dry naturally.'

It was fortunate he'd carried on talking, as for a few moments she was unable to gather her thoughts. He was even better looking, more attractive, more interesting than she'd thought last night and he was having a very strange effect on her breathing – on everything, really.

'Thank you, Sergeant Sergeant, we do appreciate you coming back, as there was no necessity for you to do so. Did you ask the local firemen to return?'

'I did. Our tenders aren't equipped to remove water, only to pump it, and foam, onto a fire.'

'Of course. You don't deal with house fires,' Joanna said. 'Why did you come last night, then?'

'I was on duty, my lady, and saw the flames. None of our kites were up so it made sense to come and help.'

'I'm glad that you did. Thank you. If you hadn't been here to help the Ramsgate crew, it would have been even worse.' She found herself mesmerised by his eyes, and the way they seemed to reflect the sunlight somehow. She forced her mind back to a more sensible topic. 'My son's worried that there'll not be enough tenders to take care of any incoming aircraft whilst you're here.'

He grinned. 'We've three others, we'll not be missed for an hour or two. I'm afraid the news from next door isn't good. I thought the upper floors relatively unscathed by the fire but, on closer inspection, I think the entire structure could now be unsound.'

'Are you suggesting it should be demolished?'

'I am. There's plenty of salvageable materials that can be used by builders repairing bomb damage.' He took her arm and moved her aside as two firemen emerged from the door, rolling up one of the hosepipes as they did so. 'Look where you're going, you cretins, there are civilians on the premises.'

This sounded harsh but was said with a smile and the two men took it in good part. They nodded at her and apologised for almost sending her flying.

'I'm in the way out here, Sergeant, I just came out to thank you and to say that there will be tea and toast arriving shortly.'

He chuckled and shook his head. 'We were talking about

knocking down a third of your stately home and you offer me toast and tea?'

'I've always hated the Victorian wing, it's not been used this century. I'll be glad to see it gone and the house will look much better for it.'

'Don't take my word for it, after all, I'm more familiar with aircraft than houses. Someone from Ramsgate fire station will be in touch in due course.'

Joanna couldn't think of a way to prolong the conversation, of any legitimate reason why she could invite him back, but she really wanted to get to know him better.

Liza emerged, carrying a tray with a dozen mugs of steaming tea, and Jean was close behind holding a second tray with plates piled high with toast. From the smell, it was dripping and salt, not butter and marmalade. Not her favourite combination, but no doubt these hard-working men would appreciate it.

Joanna retreated to the safety of the kitchen, deliberately removing temptation. What was wrong with her? Was it possible she'd become infatuated with this young man after just two meetings? This was the sort of behaviour one would expect from a girl of Liza's age, not a mature, sensible woman of thirty-six.

She hid in the safety of her small sitting room until the men from Manston and those from Ramsgate had departed. Elizabeth came in search of her.

'There you are, my dear, why are you hiding in here?'

'I needed time to come to terms with what happened last night. The house is in chaos, everywhere smells of smoke and I expect the furniture and carpets are beyond hope.'

'Are you worrying about the cost of replacing them?' her mother-in-law said. 'Surely David would have had some sort of insurance against fire damage?'

'I've no idea, as he didn't share that sort of information with me. The young man from the base said that in his opinion the entire wing should be demolished, but I'm waiting until this is confirmed by a senior person from Ramsgate before I do anything.'

'Instead of sitting here moping, Joanna, why don't you look through the pile of documents that Mr Broome sent over a few weeks ago?'

'I hadn't thought of that. Thank you for reminding me. To be honest, I just put them on a shelf and forgot about them.'

Elizabeth frowned and looked around the room as if she didn't know why she'd come in. 'I came here to ask you something, but I can't remember what it was.'

This was happening more frequently but as long as this mental decline manifested itself as forgetfulness, Joanna wasn't particularly bothered. Hardly surprising that Elizabeth was a bit confused after the drama of last night.

'You came to find me, Elizabeth, and I'm glad that you did. I'm hoping there's a cup of coffee available in the kitchen. Shall we go and see?'

Her mother-in-law beamed. 'That's why I was looking for you. Jean has just made the coffee and Liza has made some sort of cake to go with it.' The old woman grimaced. 'I know there's a war on, that butter and sugar are rationed for good reason, but cake just doesn't taste the same nowadays.'

Joanna agreed and, taking Elizabeth's arm, she escorted her out through the damp hall and out onto the terrace where they'd taken refuge from the flames last night. It had been agreed earlier that as long as the weather held, they would spend as much time out here as possible.

The twins and Jean were there already, as was the dog. The table had been repositioned so they had their back to the house and couldn't see the fire-damaged Victorian wing.

'We were about to send out a search party, Ma,' Joe said as he hurried across to his adopted grandmother to lead her to her seat.

'I'm sorry, I must have dozed off. I didn't get much sleep last night.'

Elizabeth cackled. 'No one did, Joanna, so going to sleep is no excuse.'

Once they were settled, Joe lifted the heavy silver coffee jug and filled three cups. There was a second jug containing cocoa made with milk for the twins, who didn't like coffee.

The cake, despite its provenance, was in fact delicious and even Elizabeth approved. They chatted about the weather, enjoying the unexpected quiet of a day so far not destroyed by the noise of aircraft taking off from the base.

'I'm surprised we haven't had a visit from the police, aren't you?' Jean said. 'Didn't that sergeant from Manston think the fire was set deliberately?'

'I do hope that isn't the case,' Joanna said. 'That it doesn't mean there's a lunatic trying to dispose of us all.' Elizabeth was upset by this suggestion, but the twins just looked interested and waited for her response.

'I'm not sure he was trying to commit murder. Setting fire to the Victorian wing was going to cause us inconvenience and expense but was unlikely to do any more than that.'

'It's irrelevant what his motives were, isn't it, arson is a very serious offence,' Jean said.

'It is, of course, but it could have been accidental.'

* * *

John Sergeant preferred to drive the tender, although he could have delegated this task to one of the others. Driving meant that none of his blokes expected him to chat and this suited him just fine.

He preferred his own company, avoided the sergeants' mess, and what free time he got – which was precious little – was spent reading or playing the harmonica. His dad had taught him how to play when he was a nipper and he'd become an expert over the years.

On the return journey to the base, he'd plenty to think about. The only reason he'd taken the tender to Goodwill House this morning was to see if his reaction to the owner of the property, Lady Joanna Harcourt, had been imagined or genuine.

He tuned out the jovial conversation of his men and thought about this second meeting with a woman so far above him socially that to even contemplate a relationship with her was like suggesting he invited Princess Elizabeth to afternoon tea.

'Oy, Sarge, what do you think?' Percy, a corporal and therefore his right-hand man, shouted above the noise of the Crossley tender, which rattled and banged, making normal conversation almost impossible.

'I'll think about it,' he yelled back, thinking this would cover most eventualities. It seemed to satisfy his men, who continued talking amongst themselves and left him to his thoughts. No doubt he'd discover what he was supposed to be considering at some point during the day.

Joanna. He refused to think of her in any other way, as he didn't hold with titles – he wasn't a communist but was certainly a socialist. He believed that nobody had the inalienable right to be in charge of the country just because they'd been born with a silver spoon in their mouth.

His aversion to the upper classes was why he'd refused to become an officer, as most of those were a group of chinless wonders in his opinion. He could have trained to be a flyer, but again he'd refused as he didn't want to kill anyone himself. He'd been tempted to declare himself a conscientious objector but had decided that Hitler and his Nazis had to be stopped and sitting around on the sidelines didn't seem right.

Therefore, he'd volunteered to be an RAF firefighter. They were now actually training men to take on this vital role, but he'd had to learn on the job. Once he'd understood whether to use foam or water on a fire, could get into one of the asbestos suits and be ready to walk into a fire and try and pull out the poor bugger trapped in his cockpit, he was considered proficient.

Three minutes was all they got to rescue the pilot or the crew when a plane crashed. He wasn't surprised that fire was the biggest fear of any flyer. He'd seen with his own eyes what a horrific way to die it was.

He parked the tender in its designated place. His men knew to check all the equipment was in working order, and all tanks were filled, before they retreated to the area at the back of the hangar where they could get a cuppa and a wad.

He took care of the paperwork – not that there was any, as the visit hadn't involved them doing any actual work – and being efficient, he'd already filled in the reports for last night's event.

The fire crews, like the flyers, were on duty night and day. However, unlike the Brylcreem boys, his blokes had a regular twelve-hour shift – they either worked from midday to midnight or midnight to midday. His crew, and the others that had accompanied him last night, were on the latter shift.

He had a Thermos in his cubbyhole so didn't need to join the others. Someone had put a greaseproof paper-wrapped spam sandwich on his desk and he smiled. He might bark at his men, was tough on them, but he was a good leader and, under his watch, no one had died so far. He looked after them and they did the same for him.

As John sipped his tepid stewed tea, he wondered how Joanna would react if she was aware of his interest in her. He grinned. She'd be horrified, disgusted that someone of his class had the temerity to even consider her as a possible partner.

The phone jangled noisily and he picked it up. He dropped it back on the cradle and was on his feet in an instant, all thoughts of romance forgotten.

His crew were already looking in his direction. They would have heard the telephone themselves. 'Crippled Wellington on its way. Wireless on the blink, so no idea if anybody bailed out or is injured. Percy, you and me into the suits.'

A Vickers Wellington was a medium bomber with a crew of six. A pilot, wireless operator, a forward and rear gunner, a bomb aimer and the navigator. It was highly unlikely that all six of them would escape unscathed; in fact, if any of them got out alive, it would be a good day.

The two ambulances were ready, they held the driver and a medic, and he was sure they'd both be needed this morning. He hoped the three tenders would be sufficient. It was unpleasant and suffocatingly hot inside the asbestos suit, but it meant that he and Percy could go into a burning wreck if necessary.

The unmistakable sound of the damaged bomber approaching meant they should start moving. The fire crews and ambulances weren't the only ones heading for the main runway. The ground crews were appearing from the hangars, temporarily abandoning their crucial work keeping the Blenheims, Hurricanes and Spitfires airborne.

The kite was flying low, smoke pouring from the left engine, but the right prop was still functioning. John's breath hissed through his teeth. It mightn't be as bad as he'd feared, as the landing gear was down – this wasn't going to be a belly flop – possibly not even a crash landing.

The fire trucks and ambulances raced alongside the runway so they could be in action the moment it touched down. There were bullet holes in the fuselage and John couldn't see the rear gunner, but that didn't mean he was dead or injured – he could just have made his way to the front of the kite to be ready to bail out if necessary.

Obviously, he wasn't driving, as that would be impossible in his unwieldy fireproof suit. The bomber was travelling fast and it hit the deck hard, the landing gear buckling and pitching the kite onto its nose. There was the horrendous screeching of metal tearing and he watched, aghast, as the Wellington broke apart on impact.

The front half continued to slide forwards, flames now licking the fuselage beneath the cockpit. The rear half slewed sideways, ploughing up the grass that ran beside the runway. He was off the tender and racing to the front section where the crew were most likely to be. Percy was close behind him.

His men didn't need telling to get the foam directed at the flames – water would make the conflagration worse in this case.

Two of his men had a metal ladder up against the open end and John scrambled up it. Doing anything in the asbestos suit was more difficult, but he'd become used to the cumbersome clothing. Without it, he wouldn't be able to go into the heart of the fire and rescue any of the poor sods that were still alive.

Three figures staggered towards him through the smoke, stumbling over the various pipes and pieces of equipment, desperate to get out.

'This way, quickly now. Down the ladder. There's someone there to take care of you.' He didn't wait to see if they got out, he was pretty sure somebody would be there to assist them. There were still three others unaccounted for somewhere ahead.

His voice was muffled and he needed to save his breath, as it was becoming difficult to breathe. Smoke was as likely to kill you as the flames in this sort of fire.

John grabbed Percy's arm and pointed. There was no need to say anything else. The front gunner had gone for a Burton, too late to do anything for him. However, both the navigator and pilot were still alive and, so far, no more than a little singed.

'I'll take the pilot, you get the other bloke. Don't dawdle. We've got no more than a minute before the whole lot blows up.'

He reached down and slung the pilot over his shoulder, paused for a moment to make sure that Percy had done the same with the other injured man, and then they picked their way carefully through the debris, heading for the safety of the runway.

Eager hands removed his comatose patient from his shoulder and then he slid down the ladder. The same was done for Percy and he too arrived safely on the ground.

John pulled off his helmet. 'Get back, everybody, get back. There's still fuel in the tanks and it's going to explode at any moment.'

No one needed telling twice and he was hauled headfirst onto the rear of the nearest tender and then had to cling on for dear life as it raced away, not a moment too soon.

2

Sally O'Reilly, who only answered to Sal, had changed into her smart land girl uniform in the ladies' room on the station at Romford. If Den, the bloke she was trying to get away from, had seen these clothes, he'd have stopped her leaving and sold the lot on the market.

She reckoned not even her own ma would recognise her now. Being of medium height and build, everything fitted just lovely. She stuffed the things she'd been wearing into an old sack, intending to dump it at the earliest possible opportunity. Her battered cardboard suitcase now held the dungarees, beige short-sleeved shirts, and a spare pair of socks, a mackintosh and overall coat, as well as some smashing brown leather shoes.

She was supposed to bring two spare sets of underwear, a nightdress and house slippers as these weren't supplied. Imagine having two sets of spare knickers and bras – one on and one off was how it went in her family.

Lil, her best friend, had joined the WAAF and she'd got every-thing given to her. Sal had been tempted to sign up herself but didn't fancy being bossed about all day by snooty officers. She knew nothing about the countryside, wasn't keen on animals, but as a land girl, she'd just be working like she had sewing frocks in the sweatshop and could leave if she wanted.

She viewed the gumboots with dislike. She couldn't shove them into the suitcase, so she'd have to wear them despite the fact that it was blooming hot today. When she'd collected her uniform, the lady had said she'd be issued with winter wear in the autumn.

The breeches were a bit baggy, but the shirt and green pullover fitted all right. She wasn't too keen on the hat – but at least it hid her very distinctive hair. She patted her curls; she didn't have to use peroxide to make it this colour, she was a natural blonde.

The train to London steamed in and Sal marched out, head held high, proud to be in uniform but even happier to be getting away from Poplar, her rotten family, and her even worse boyfriend. He thought she was visiting her nan who lived in Romford, otherwise she wouldn't have been able to sneak away.

By the time she arrived at this Newton Abbot place, she was knackered. It had taken all day to get to Devon, she'd had nothing to eat, only one cup of tea to drink and her feet were squelching in her boots.

She'd managed to dump her civilian clothes and only had her overfilled suitcase and her mac to carry. She emerged into the sunlight and immediately spotted two other girls dressed the same as her. One was a brunette, she looked like a model in one of those posh magazines; her uniform might be the same colour, but it certainly wasn't the same as Sal's.

The other girl was a bit older, probably in her twenties, with red hair and a lovely smile. She looked just the ticket.

'Come and join us, we're hoping to find a taxi as it's more than three miles from here to Seale-Hayne Agricultural College.' The speaker was the brunette and she was ever so posh but seemed nice enough.

'Cor, ta ever so, I need the bog first and I'm gasping for a cuppa.' Sal smiled at both of them and they laughed.

'Dump your things, we'll take care of them. There wasn't a ladies' room on the platform, but you could nip behind those bushes. I don't think anybody will notice.'

This suggestion from the red-haired girl was quite unexpected, but suited her down to the ground. 'I'm Sal, I expect you've guessed I'm from the East End.'

'I'm Daphne and I come from Colchester,' the red-haired girl said.

'I'm Charlotte, but you can call me Lottie or Charlie, I answer to both. I'm from Guildford.'

'Fair enough. I won't be a tick.'

Sal was glad she'd been wearing her gumboots as these were easier to wipe clean on the grass. She'd been that desperate her aim hadn't been good. She dashed back to find the two of them smoking – not Woodbines, but something posh like Senior Service. This was one vice she didn't have – she liked a bit of how's your father and enjoyed a tipple or two but had never taken to fags.

'Right, I'm going to take these bleeding boots off. Me poor feet are swimming in there and I reckon I can wring out me socks.' She looked at their luggage – they'd both got two suitcases so didn't have the same problem.

'If you put your spare socks on, you can tie your boots together and wear them round your neck like a very smelly rubber necklace,' Charlie suggested as she blew a perfect smoke ring.

Sal had been about to apologise for using bad language but neither of them seemed bothered by her swearing. She'd fallen on her feet, and she reckoned that these two were going to make good mates.

She hooked her boots off, the socks followed, and it was lovely to have fresh air on her bare toes. 'If I open that bugger, I'll never get it closed again.'

'We'll manage. Come on, get a move on. We've got a long walk ahead of us,' Daphne said cheerfully.

The stout brown leather brogues were ever so comfortable and looked a treat with her brown corduroy breeches. 'I'm parched and me stomach thinks me throat's been cut. I've got a couple of bob and if we can find a caff, I'll treat you to a bun and somethink to drink.'

'That's the ticket, there's bound to be somewhere we can get a cup of tea, at least,' Daphne said as she picked up a suitcase in each hand. They looked heavy but she carried them as if they weighed nothing at all.

With her smelly boots slung over a shoulder – she'd almost gagged when she'd hung them round her neck – Sal picked up her case and followed Charlie, who'd gone first.

They found the perfect place as far as she was concerned, but Charlie wasn't impressed. Daphne was happy with it, so they went in. A jolly old geezer, with a pair of false teeth that moved up and down when he spoke, greeted them.

'Welcome, girls, my lady wife has just made a fine batch of scones. I'm afraid we can't offer butter or cream, but there's plenty of marge and jam.'

'Thank you, that sounds perfect. A pot of tea and scones for three, thank you,' Charlie said with her posh accent.

'Put your luggage in the corner, girls, it'll be out of the way.'

They did as he asked and took the only vacant table. They got one or two funny looks from those already there, but mostly it was nods and smiles. The place was busy and they'd been lucky to get a table.

'You've got plenty of time to eat your tea before the bus goes,' he said as he vanished through the bead curtain to give their order to his wife.

'A bus? That's a hoot – we'd have looked very silly if it had sailed past us as we were trudging along the road with our suitcases,' Charlie said. 'He didn't say when it was going but I reckon some of them at the other tables will be catching it too.'

Daphne swivelled in her chair and spoke to the nearest customer. 'Excuse me, could you please tell me what time the bus that passes the agricultural college leaves here?'

'Four o'clock, then there's not another one until six. You can't miss it, as it pulls up right outside this café and most of us in here will be getting on it.'

'Thank you, that's very helpful.' Daphne turned back and smiled at both of them. 'Do you know what time we're supposed to report?'

'No, my letter just said I had to be here today. What about you, Sal?'

'I didn't take no notice of all that writing and such. I'm not too clever with reading and writing.'

'Then being a land girl is the perfect place for you,' Charlie said, not at all shocked by Sal's revelation.

'I'm not so sure about that. I've never seen a cow, I ain't keen on fresh air and I don't like the cold.'

The other two laughed and Sal joined in, enjoying being a part of the group. She'd never had many friends and hoped these two might one day become hers.

* * *

Joanna put out all the ledgers, folders and files that had arrived in an official-looking cardboard box from the solicitor's office a few weeks ago. So much had been going on in the house that she'd not got round to looking in them.

Even the household accounts had been handled by David, so she'd absolutely no experience dealing with the things she was looking at. However, it shouldn't be beyond her capabilities to find evidence that there was some sort of valid fire insurance on the house.

She'd only looked through a fraction of the things on her desk when Elizabeth joined her. 'I thought you might like some help, my dear. I might be decrepit and rather forgetful nowadays, but my eyesight's still excellent and I can read as well as I ever could.'

'I didn't want to ask you, it's a very tedious task, but having you sharing it with me will make it less onerous.' Joanna pointed to the pathetically small pile of files that she'd examined. 'Those are done; I'm afraid that all the rest of the stuff on the desk has still to be looked at.'

Elizabeth nodded and began to flick through the items and, for a moment, Joanna thought she wasn't actually reading anything.

'Right, my dear, you're making this far more difficult than it needs to be. These files are carefully organised and labelled with the contents. There's no need to look in half of them.'

If her mother-in-law had announced she was a devil worshipper, Joanna couldn't have been more surprised. 'Good heavens! How stupid of me – I just started at one end and didn't actually read what was written on the front. Thank goodness you came in and pointed it out to me.'

'Then let's put what we don't need back in the boxes. The task will seem less daunting, my dear, once we've done that.'

They worked well together and in less than an hour, Elizabeth had found the paperwork that proved the buildings were insured against fire.

'There you are, you have your answer. Perhaps it might be best to ask your solicitor to deal with this?'

'I certainly won't,' Joanna said. 'I'm Lady Harcourt, I think that carries enough weight to get a favourable response, don't you?'

'Let's hope so, my dear. I thought I heard several cars coming down the drive. Are you expecting anyone?'

'Yes, actually, I am. The police from Ramsgate have to investigate the arson and also someone from the fire department must confirm that the young sergeant is correct about having to demolish the Victorian wing.'

'I think the insurance company would prefer you to do that as it would be cheaper for them than rebuilding it.'

This remark puzzled Joanna. 'Surely it doesn't matter which I choose to do. If the building is insured, then I should be paid the value of that wing.'

'Things might have changed over the years, my dear, but when I was living here, the newly installed indoor plumbing proved unsatisfactory and the ceiling above the drawing room fell in. My husband, not a particularly pleasant man nor someone who shared anything unless forced, on this occasion was so incensed by the insurance company's decision that I would have to have been both deaf and a simpleton not to have known what happened.'

'What did happen?'

'He was forced to accept a lesser settlement, just repairs to the ceiling and replastering when he'd wanted the entire ceiling removed and replaced, as what remained was definitely damaged by the water.'

'Let's hope the company I have to deal with isn't the same one.'

Jean appeared at the door. 'Excuse me, my ladies, but the same two policemen, the unpleasant ones who came before are here. Also, there are two police cars with several uniformed men heading for the Victorian wing.'

'Would you be kind enough to direct the detectives here? The study seems an appropriate place speak to such people.'

To her surprise, Elizabeth wandered off, saying she needed to fetch something from the garden. Fortunately, Jean had overheard this vague remark.

'Don't worry, I'll go with her.'

'Thank you, that's kind of you,' Joanna said. 'I really don't understand what's going on with her – the past two hours she's been sharp, absolutely wonderful sorting out these papers and now she's drifted off into a world of her own.'

'I'll go after her and send the inspector and his sergeant to you. Shall I ask Liza to make tea or coffee?'

'No, I want this meeting to be as brief as possible. I don't suppose this chief inspector will be any more accommodating than he was the last time.'

An hour later, the sergeant had written down, laboriously, a report of what had happened. Bert Smith was being searched for but hadn't been found so far.

'I can assure you, my lady, that we take arson very seriously. He'll go away for years.'

'Are you not being rather premature, Chief Inspector?' Joanna said. 'It could have been a vagrant; it might not have been Bert at all. Am I not correct in thinking that there has to be conclusive evidence in order to charge a person?'

The obnoxious man stared at her with dislike. 'My lady, I can assure you that my men are searching at this very moment for the necessary evidence.' He smirked and nodded at her as if she was too stupid to understand the legal processes involved. 'Smith will be apprehended and charged. Circumstantial evidence is more than enough in this case. That man made threats to you and has now carried them out.'

She decided to end the conversation. 'Thank you for your time. Please keep me informed about anything you discover from your investigation. Good morning, gentlemen, and thank you for coming.'

They had no option but to depart but did so with bad grace. Joanna watched them drive away faster than was safe and was relieved when their car vanished onto the road at the end of the drive. The two police cars remained, but there was no sign of the men who'd arrived in them. The telephone jangled while she was watching through the grand hall window.

'Goodwill House, Lady Harcourt speaking.'

'Good morning, my lady, Mrs Dougherty here. I just wanted to let you know that there's been a slight delay in sending your contingent of land girls. The young ladies we had earmarked for your billet have now gone elsewhere.'

'I see. Does that mean I won't be getting anyone or is there just a delay?'

'My word, of course you'll be getting girls. They're now training at an agricultural college in Devon. They'll be with you by the end of the month – only a week or two after the others would have come. I'm sorry for any inconvenience.'

'Actually, Mrs Dougherty, we've had a few problems this end, so the delay will suit us perfectly. We had a fire in the disused wing and, although nothing was damaged on this side, it will take a week or so to get the house dried out and ready.'

'Excellent, you'll be given twenty-four hours' notice of their arrival. The girls will be expected to make their own way to Goodwill House. One of the reasons it's ideal to have girls living with you is that it's on a bus route and central to the farms and market gardens that we wish them to work on.'

After a few further pleasantries, the call ended. Joanna could smell coffee being brewed in the kitchen and headed that way. Elizabeth was sitting at the table, talking to the twins, and seemed quite unaware that less than half an hour ago she'd been distracted and not herself at all.

Having land girls wouldn't be any different from having WAAF and both Joanna and Elizabeth so enjoyed the laughter and bustle of a full house.

That night, as she was brushing her hair prior to retiring, Joanna examined her reflection more critically than usual. Her hair was lustrous, not a single strand of grey, eyes bright, her lashes long and her teeth white and even. She stood up and flattened her nightgown against her naked form.

Her breasts were still pert, her waist small and her hips satisfactorily rounded. She smiled at her daring. Was she really contemplating having a liaison with the handsome sergeant? Why else would she be so interested in her appearance – especially her figure?

John considered his day a success. Five of the six crew had been saved – three completely unscathed and the other two had minor burns and concussion, but not so serious that they'd be out of action for long.

After any incident like this, he felt obliged to join his men in the mess for a jar or two before they headed for their billets. The runway was already cleared, the holes filled in and the only sign that there had been a crash was the blackened patches on the concrete.

His men hadn't been required again before they finished their shift. He now had to clean up, snatch a few hours' kip, get some scoff and then be back on duty at midnight.

When he arrived at the hangar that night, he was told the four squadrons had been scrambled twice that afternoon. He'd learned to sleep though any noise and hadn't heard them go or return. Two poor bastards in a Blenheim had been shot down in flames over the Channel, but all the other kites had returned safely.

'Let's hope for a quiet night, lads, more than enough excitement yesterday,' he said as he filled his Thermos flask.

'Billy said some posh bird rang and left a message for you. Going up in the world, are you, Sarge?'

'It'll be Lady Harcourt about the fire we went to the other night. I can't ring her now, so I'll do it in the morning.' He glared at the speaker, an erk, the lowest rank, and a nasty bit of work. 'It's none of your bloody business. You shouldn't be poking about in my office. If you do it again, you'll be on jankers.'

The man muttered something obscene under his breath, but John decided to ignore it. If he put all the blokes who swore at him, or about him, on a charge, there'd be nobody left to fight fires. Everybody swore and apart from this one individual, it didn't mean anything. He prided himself on having a happy team but was tempted to put Travis on a charge just to get rid of him.

The note was left prominently on the desk but could only have been read by Travis if he'd actually been in the office, which was out of bounds to all but NCOs. Joanna hadn't left a number – it didn't do to bandy that around – and hadn't even left her name. She must have guessed that he'd know who it was.

He screwed the paper up and tossed it into the cardboard box put aside for paper waste. This was recycled somewhere – nothing went to waste nowadays, and paper was in short supply, like everything else. As soon as it was light enough, he got the men to clean the tenders – the engines would have been checked when the tenders weren't in use.

He'd ample opportunity to think about the phone call he had to make. In fact, he'd done nothing but think about Joanna since he'd met her. He wasn't stupid; he knew that nothing permanent could come of it, but there was something about her that made him put these doubts aside.

He was probably delusional to even think she might consider having an affair with him. It could be nothing more than that and, for him, it wouldn't be enough. That said, if that's all that was on offer, he'd take it happily.

He smiled wryly at his crazy thoughts. She'd hardly telephone the base for personal reasons – it could only be something to do with the fire. However, a bloke could dream, couldn't he?

3

Sal stared out of the bus window, eyes wide and mouth open as the place where she was to spend the next four weeks became visible over the hedge. 'Blimey, would you look at that? It's like a blooming palace, that's what it is. I've never seen nothing like it.'

She was sitting next to the window and her two new friends were sitting together in front of her. Her battered suitcase, barely holding together, was on the seat next to her, not in the luggage space at the front. Sensibly, she'd left her gumboots with the suitcases as she didn't want them next to her.

'It looks impressive,' Charlie said as she turned round to speak to her. 'I can't imagine why the benefactor who founded this place wanted to build an agricultural college looking like this. It should be more functional, in my opinion.'

'Will we be living in that building...' The bus rocked to a halt and the conductor shouted down to them that they had to get out here. Sal clutched her suitcase in both arms, terrified it would fall to bits before she got off.

'Here you are, I don't suppose you'll even notice the smell

after a few days,' Daphne said as she hung the boots over Sal's shoulder before picking up her own suitcases.

It was quite a hike from the bus stop to the building and, as they approached, she saw there were other girls dressed the same as them, all of them smart as paint and looking just as new.

'None of them have their luggage,' Charlie said. 'I think that's the main entrance over there. Shall we announce ourselves and find out where we're billeted?'

Neither Sal nor Daphne argued as Charlie seemed a natural leader – it was something to do with her posh voice, Sal reckoned.

They were directed to the far side of the huge building and told that their dormitory was on the first floor. They would be sharing it with nine others.

'It appears that all twelve of us will be going to the same place when we finish our training, so the powers that be want us to get to know each other,' Charlie told them.

'Makes sense,' Sal replied. 'If the others are as nice as you two, then I'll be as happy as Larry.'

Fortunately, she made it to the room without spilling her belongings on the stairs. There were three vacant beds at the far end of the room which were obviously for them. Everybody else had unpacked, so they did the same.

'Do we have to wear these thick pullovers? It's blooming hot today. I'm not wearing this horrible hat whilst I'm here. I'll put it on when I'm out, but that's it.'

'I agree,' said Charlie. 'None of the girls out there were wearing them so I assume it's all right to abandon the hats. I'm going in search of the WC and bathrooms. Are you coming with me, Daphne?'

'I am. I suppose we'll have to get used to nipping behind a bush like you did, Sal, when we're working in the fields.'

The two of them dashed off, leaving her to get her bearings and unpack without her tatty knickers and bra being seen. She didn't have house slippers and her nightie had seen better days too.

The two of them came back smiling. 'It's just at the end of the passageway. I think we must be the closest. There are two bathrooms and three lavatories,' Charlie said as she unpacked her things.

Sal watched enviously. Nothing tatty or cheap about anything Charlie had and even Daphne's knickers and such looked new – not as expensive as Charlie's, but a lot better than hers.

She visited the bog on the way past and it was spotless, not like the outside privy she and her family had shared with two other families. She went into the bathroom to check her appearance, ran her fingers through her hair and gave herself a general tidy up.

Daphne put her head around the door. 'Goodness, you've got short hair. It suits you and must be so much easier than having to pin it up every day.'

'It grows ever so quick and it'll need cutting again in a couple of months. Me ma said it was me crowning glory – it's been nothing but trouble and I wish I had mousy-brown hair so blokes would take no notice of me.'

'It's certainly lovely, but even with brown hair, you'd still be beautiful. At least you don't have to worry about being bothered by unwanted attentions whilst we're here.'

* * *

The next morning, they were up at dawn, no breakfast, not even time to grab a cuppa and a piece of toast, before being sent to the dairy to learn how to milk a cow. There were just the three of them; the other lot were already in groups and were sent to do other things.

The man in charge of instructing them showed them a rubber udder filled with water. This was a revelation to Sal as, until then, she'd not really thought about how milk got from the cow to the kitchen table.

'Blimey, this is a lark,' she said as she tugged as instructed on the rubber teats. 'I reckon I'll be able to milk a cow if it comes out as easy as this.'

All three of them mastered the technique and were then led to the dairy. The cow she'd been allotted was a right comic and squashed her against the bars of the stall.

'Give over, you rotten thing, give us a chance. I ain't even seen a cow before today.'

Having her face pressed up against the hot, smelly side of a huge animal wasn't something Sal enjoyed. The cow swung her huge head round and mooed and then attempted to kick her.

The instructor appeared beside her. 'This won't do, young lady, you won't be passed as fit to work on a farm until you've completed each section of your training satisfactorily. I expect that bucket to be full by the time I come back.'

Sal tried again. After perching herself on the three-legged stool, she grabbed hold of the dangling teats and attempted the same technique that had been so successful on the rubber udder.

The next thing she knew, she was on her arse, the bucket and stool on top of her, and she was covered in muck. The cow returned to her feed as if nothing had happened. Daphne called from the other side of the shed.

'What happened? Are you all right?'

'Blooming marvellous! I'll give it another go and then that's it. If I get chucked out, too bad. I don't reckon I'm cut out for this farming lark.'

She scrambled to her feet, brushed off the worst of the muck from her once clean breeches, righted the stool, recovered the bucket and was about to try again but realised her hands were filthy. No point in washing the underneath of the cow if she then put her dirty hands on it.

'I'm going to wash me hands. I won't be a tick.'

There was a pump outside and Sal heaved on the handle a few times with one hand and managed to wash the other in the stream of icy water and then reversed the process. She kept an eye out for the grumpy instructor, but he'd gone – at least for the moment.

Her heart sank when she stepped back into the cow shed and saw him standing at the end of the stall that she should have been in. She was in for it now.

'Well done, Primrose isn't usually so generous with her milk. Take it to the dairy and then you can go and get some well-deserved breakfast.'

Sal could hardly tell him the full bucket of milk had nothing to do with her. It was a mystery, a miracle really, not that she believed in all that religious stuff. She was baptised Catholic but had stopped going to mass and confession when she'd left home and moved in with Den after being bowled over by his charm, his good looks and his money.

She'd only been living with him a few weeks before she discovered his true character and, for the past six months, she'd been trying to get away from him. Her family wanted nothing to do with her – she was a fallen woman, as far as Ma was concerned – and she'd nowhere to go until she'd seen a poster asking girls to volunteer for one of the services. And now here she was, milking cows and filling up buckets of milk without even trying.

The dairy was across the yard and she carried the brimming

bucket over. It didn't smell like the milk she was used to and it was all warm and frothy.

'There you are. You got the short straw, Sal, even I found it difficult to get any milk and I'm a bit of an expert,' Charlie said as she walked in. 'I milked her for you whilst you were cleaning yourself up.'

'Ta ever so, I thought I'd had it. I hope I don't get sent to a dairy farm as I'm not cut out for that. He said we can go and have breakfast now – I'm starving. I ain't used to working before I get anythink to eat.'

'I'll give your jodhs a wipe down. They're a bit whiffy at the moment.'

Whilst her two new friends did their best with the smelly patch on her backside, she asked Charlie how she knew so much about farming.

'I thought posh birds like you walked around in mink and silk and ate caviar – whatever that is.'

'Don't be fooled by my voice, Sal. I do come from a very rich family, but when my mother died, my father handed me over to a distant cousin. I grew up on a farm, worked with horses and most other animals.'

'Then why would you want to come here to be trained if you already know it all? In fact, why didn't you stay with your family?' Daphne had asked exactly what Sal was thinking.

'It's a long story, maybe I'll tell you both one day,' Charlie said. 'Come on, let's eat. If the breakfast's as plentiful and as delicious as last night's supper, then I'm going to enjoy being here.'

Charlie looked ever so sad and Sal wondered what had happened to her.

* * *

Joanna had left a somewhat cryptic message for John yesterday afternoon. She couldn't think of him as Sergeant John Sergeant any more – though they'd only met twice, for some reason, he filled her thoughts in a way that was quite novel.

She'd never have telephoned the base on the flimsy pretext that she needed his advice about the fire damage if she hadn't had an extraordinary conversation with Elizabeth, who she'd discovered had led a racy and exciting life in the south of France! It had been a revelation for Joanna.

She ignored the fact that Elizabeth had said it was one thing to have lovers where you were an anonymous, rich English-woman living abroad and quite another to do the same when you were living in a small village where everybody knew you and you were expected to set an example.

'Ma, there's a truck turned up with some blokes in it,' Joe yelled from the kitchen.

'Please don't shout, my dear, I do so dislike hearing loud voices in the house.'

Joe appeared in the hall where she she'd been dithering by the telephone as if expecting it to ring at any moment and for John to be on the other end of the line. He would be off duty now and must have had her message.

'Sorry. Are you going to come and talk to them, or do you want me to handle it?'

'I'll come. Have they identified themselves?'

'No, they just said they wanted to speak to the lady of the house.'

She could see the vehicle parked a short distance from the front door so decided to go in search of these mysterious visitors that way. The door was open and two men were standing under the portico – one grey-haired and possibly in his fifties, the other a little older than Joe.

'Good afternoon, I'm Lady Harcourt. How can I be of help?'

'It's like this, my lady, we're general builders and heard that after the fire the end of the house has to come down. We'd be happy to demolish it for you and clear the site, in return for salvaging all the materials.'

'I see. I'm still adjusting to the new reality. I can't decide immediately; I need to think about it and take advice. If you'd like to leave me your details, then my son can bring you a note if I take up your offer.'

'Fair enough. We can't do anything until it dries out anyway.' He handed her an envelope with an address on it, presumably his, nodded and then he and his silent companion returned to their lorry.

Joanna was delighted to have this offer, as it now gave her something legitimate to ask John if he did contact her. No sooner was this thought in her head than the telephone rang. She ran to answer it and was about to snatch it up but took several deep breaths before she lifted the receiver.

'Goodwill House, Lady Harcourt speaking.'

'John Sergeant here, returning your call.'

She rather liked the fact that he didn't address her by her title. 'Thank you for getting back to me so promptly. If it's not too much trouble, I'd like your advice about something.'

'I'm off duty now. I've got a motorbike and could be with you in five minutes.'

That was stretching it a bit, but she liked his confidence – in fact, she liked everything about him. 'That would be splendid. It will be so much easier to talk in person. Would you please come to the Victorian wing? Don't come to the main part of the house. I'll meet you there.'

'Got it.' He hung up without saying goodbye and she wasn't sure if that was deliberate or because he was so eager to come.

Elizabeth was dozing in the small sitting room; Jean was busy in the kitchen and Liza was helping her. Joe was outside doing something in the vegetable garden with the old chap who came in every day to take care of it. Even her dog was out with Joe, so she didn't have to worry about him either.

This meant she didn't have to tell anybody where she was going and wouldn't be missed until one o'clock when luncheon was served. Joanna looked at the staircase, sorely tempted to rush upstairs and put on some lipstick, perhaps change her frock, but didn't do so. If she came in for luncheon wearing something different, that would certainly raise eyebrows and cause comments.

The smell of wet wood, crumbling plaster and smoke still lingered in the house. All the doors and windows were open, curtains pinned up from the floor, and the parquet still had dark patches where it was wet. The panelling, which had been soaked to stop the fire coming through, was cracked in places, but she was hopeful that in a week or two, everything would be restored to its usual appearance.

She slipped out through the front door and then hurried along the terrace to the Victorian end. She was shocked by the charred doors and window frames, broken windows, and the puddles of black water everywhere. The overwhelming smell of fire almost made her gag.

It wasn't safe to go in and she really didn't want to hover in the doorway. Then the quiet summer's day was ruined by the roar of a motorbike as John sped down the drive. When he skidded to a halt in front of her, all hope of his visit being a secret was gone as everybody in the house had come out to see who'd arrived on a loud, powerful motorbike. Her pulse quickened. There was something about this man that made her want to do things she shouldn't. He was so different from David in every imaginable way.

'Sorry, not my finest moment,' John said with a grin.

'Don't worry. I need your advice.' She quickly explained about the offer from the local builders and he nodded.

'Sounds fair. You must get the builder to make good the adjoining wall, the one the wing is attached to. Also, he must brick up the entrance. There might be things in there you've forgotten about. I'll have a look around for you just to confirm my thoughts.'

'I've never been in there apart from to rescue Lazzy so have no idea what might be lurking in a corner. I can't believe there's anything of value.'

'You'd be surprised. Saucepans and so on are impossible to buy, so it would be worth checking the kitchens.'

'Shall I come in with you?'

'No, it's not safe. Give me a few minutes.' He nodded toward the interested family watching from the terrace. 'Might be a good idea to let them know what I'm doing here. Don't want to give them the wrong idea.'

Before she could react to his remark, he'd vanished inside the burnt building. She was warm all over at the very thought that he might be finding her as attractive as she found him. She made her way to the terrace – this didn't extend to the Victorian part of Goodwill House – and by the time she reached her family, and Jean, she was composed.

'The young man from the RAF has kindly come to assess the value of the contents next door. Before I agree to the builder's offer, I wanted to know if it was a sensible thing to do.'

'What does an RAF fireman know about buildings?' Elizabeth said sharply. 'He spends his time with aircraft.'

'That's true, but he's the only person I could think of to ask.

He's having a look to see if there are any things we could remove before the wing's demolished.'

'Saucepans, cutlery and so on would be good. We're going to need them with so many girls coming in a week or two,' Jean said.

'That's what the sergeant suggested. If there's a safe way in, then we could have look ourselves.'

'There are at least two doors at the back. One of them might allow safe access, my dear,' Elizabeth said.

'Why don't Joe and I go in? I reckon we'd be safe in there,' Liza said.

'If the sergeant agrees, then by all means do so,' Joanna said as she turned and made her way back to the charred front door. It had always puzzled her that this wing had been built as if a separate house, with its own kitchens, entrances and so on. Had it been intended for guests or for use as a dower house? She would be happy to be rid of the eyesore and so would Elizabeth.

4

John had seen Joanna's reaction to his casual remark and began to think that maybe his wildest dreams were not so wild after all. He'd give the situation further thought before he said anything that could be misconstrued or ignored. His elation fizzled out when he considered just how difficult it would be to have any sort of relationship with the most important woman in the neighbourhood.

They couldn't meet in public, obviously – hiding it from her family was also essential. They were all heavily invested in each other's lives, which would make any sort of secret affair all but impossible. He'd do nothing to jeopardise her position or cause her embarrassment or distress, so maybe it would be better to forget all about it.

He picked his way carefully over the charred wood and broken glass in the entrance hall, which was where the fire had started. He looked more carefully at the seat of the fire and something about this puzzled him. Why would an arsonist start a fire in the centre of a large, tiled area, as far away from the flammable materials as possible? Maybe this was, as Joanna had suggested, a vagrant who'd lit a fire to cook himself something.

After searching, he discovered a few singed duck feathers and the bones and skin of what was once a rabbit. His theory was correct. He was about to make his way to the kitchens when he heard a sound from the first floor. Someone was hiding up there.

He didn't hesitate; he was sure whoever it was wasn't dangerous. 'Come down, mate, no one here to arrest you.'

There was a slight scuffle and then a dishevelled man made his way down the dangerous staircase. 'I didn't mean to set the place on fire, I was cooking my dinner and had a call of nature. I think when I opened the side door the wind must have blown the sparks against the curtains.'

'I'm sure that's what happened. Don't worry, I'll speak to the local constabulary and make sure they know this wasn't deliberate. I'm John.'

'I'm Bert Smith, I came back to see my wife's grave and to apologise to Lady Harcourt and the others that loved my Betty for the way I behaved when she died, but I didn't have the courage, so decided to camp out here for a few days.'

Joanna appeared at the door. 'Bert, I heard what you said. I'm afraid the police are convinced that you tried to set fire to Goodwill House deliberately. It won't matter what the sergeant or I say, they like to have a neat solution.'

'Sorry, my lady, for everything,' Bert said. 'I loved my Betty, it was grief that made me behave like that. I deserved to be thrown out after what I did.'

'I accept your apology, and I'll make sure that everybody knows. But you can't stay in Stodham, however much you might want to.'

'I've got a suggestion,' John interrupted. 'If you can find him some decent clothes, get him tidied up, I'll take him to Hastings and he can enlist. I don't suppose they've heard about this fire fifty miles away.'

Joanna nodded immediately. 'That's the perfect solution. Betty wouldn't want you sent to jail for something you did by accident, Bert. I've still got my husband's clothes in the attic and I'm sure they'll fit you well enough. Have a bath and a shave, and after that, Jean can cut your hair for you.'

John knew nothing about the circumstances they were both referring to, but it was obvious the poor bloke had not only lost his wife but his job and his home as well. The least he could do was to get him away from the coppers.

He wasn't sure, but he thought someone found guilty of arson could get a life sentence and this Bert Smith didn't deserve prison at all. He could smooth things over with the Ramsgate Fire Department, but he doubted the police would be so ready to accept his explanation.

'Fortunately, there's nobody from the village working here today, as it would be better if only the family sees you,' Joanna said. 'Quickly, Bert, let's get you inside and cleaned up.'

She flashed John a warm smile and he thought giving up his kip and making a round trip of over a hundred miles, with a bloke he'd only just met, would be worth it just for that.

'I'll get back to my inspection of the house. I'll call in and tell you what I find.'

'Thank you, I really appreciate you helping us like this. The children said they could come in through the kitchen door if there's anything worth salvaging in there.'

Bert pointed to the upper floors. 'There's bedding, decent furniture, boxes of material, trunks with all sorts in the attic. I don't understand why it wasn't properly shut down if no one was living in it.'

'I'll have a dekko right through the building. It'll probably take an hour to get Bert ready to leave.'

'Thank you, Sergeant, for a second time. You're giving up your much-needed sleep to help us out. I do hope that won't put you at risk when you're working tonight.'

'No, ma'am, we're a tough lot in the RAF and frequently work a double shift. The flyers, when things get hot like they did at Dunkirk a few weeks ago, are lucky if they get a couple of hours' kip in between sorties.' For some reason, he didn't mind addressing her as ma'am but refused to use her title.

'There'll be a hot drink and something to eat when you come to the house. Be careful, those stairs look about to collapse.'

She and Bert walked off to the main house, leaving John to continue his investigation. The bloke had been right to say there was a lot of decent furniture, boxes of miscellaneous items – memorabilia from what could be the Boer War – but no silver and no artwork on the walls. He thought the family must have removed everything valuable and just left behind what they didn't need or want.

Things were different now and everything was in short supply. Even the faded, somewhat moth-eaten curtains and bedding would be of use. John headed back to the kitchens and there was a positive treasure trove of useful cutlery, pots, pans and crockery. Even if the Harcourts didn't want it, when the bombing began, there'd be folk desperate for items like this.

He exited through the back door, which opened easily as it had been in use recently. He checked his watch – he'd been about half an hour. Whatever they were going to give him to eat should be prepared by now.

Although the park – now ploughed up and with spuds planted – surrounded the entire building, at the back, there was a brick wall dividing the Victorian part from the rest. He discov-

ered a wooden door which moved after he put his shoulder
to it.

As he stepped through, he was knocked flat by a huge, hairy
dog. The animal planted paws on his chest and, although he
wasn't growling, he didn't look particularly friendly. From his
prone position, he got a good view of the massive head and fear-
some teeth.

'Lazzy, get off! Sergeant Sergeant is a friend, even if he did
come in through a strange door.' John recognised the speaker as
Joe Harcourt.

The dog released him and he scrambled to his feet. 'Bloody
hell, I thought I was going to be his dinner.'

The boy grinned. 'Lazzy's a gentle giant. He only bites bad
people.'

'That door in the wall leads directly to the back of the Victorian part of the house. It's safe enough in the kitchen to collect
whatever you want, but don't attempt the stairs as they're unsafe.'

Joe nodded in response. 'There's corned beef hash, plum
crumble and custard waiting for you.'

'Good show. I didn't stop to eat before I came here.' John
regretted having revealed this, as the boy might wonder why he'd
been in such a rush.

There was no sign of Joanna and he thought that might be
deliberate. Whatever the attraction between them, and it was
definitely there, she'd made the sensible decision and removed
temptation from his sight.

'There you are, Sergeant, I'm a dab hand at corned beef hash.
Bert Smith ate two helpings but there's still some left for you,' the
girl, Liza, said.

John devoured the meal with enthusiasm. The food at the
sergeants' mess was good, but this was excellent. He drained two
mugs of tea and felt ready for anything.

'Ma said to go through when you're finished as Bert's ready to leave.'

John pushed his chair back, ruffled the hair on the dog's head, and stood up. 'That was the best meal I've had in months. We could do with you at our mess, Miss Harcourt.'

She giggled. 'Call me Liza, I'm not used to being called Miss Harcourt.'

This intrigued him but it wasn't something he could ask her, and he certainly wasn't going to ask Joanna as it was none of his business.

'There you are, Sergeant, Bert's unrecognisable now. I think if anybody sees him on the back of your motorbike, they wouldn't know it was him.'

Joanna was right. Smith was wearing clothes way above his station, was clean-shaven, smelled fragrant, and had a decent haircut.

'If you're ready, mate, we need to get on. I have to be back on duty at midnight and want to get a couple of hours kip if I can.'

Sal was so tired after working all day in the dairy, finding out how to make cheese, cream, put the milk into washed bottles and so on, that she headed for bed and ignored the recreation room where the other girls were going. She wanted to be first in the bathroom as she reckoned the cow muck had soaked through her breeches to her knickers. If anyone saw the brown stain when she was undressing, they'd think she'd had an accident.

She ignored the black line painted round the inside of the bath, indicating the five inches they were supposed to have, and filled it half-full. This was a posh place, there'd be plenty of water for the girls who came later. She'd taken her underwear into the bath with her and the nasty marks came out a treat with a good scrub.

Sal lay back, revelling in the luxury. Even when she was living with Den, they'd not had proper indoor plumbing. He might have worn swanky clothes and swaggered about as if he was something special, but this hadn't extended to his living accommodation.

He'd just wanted her to be his skivvy; unpaid, and one he could poke whenever he wanted to. She'd not enjoyed the bedroom part of it – if she was honest, she'd not enjoyed any of it apart from getting out of the family home where there had been eight of them squashed into a two up, two down.

The novelty of living in a terraced house with just one person, the same size as the one her parents had for eight, had soon worn off, but she'd made her bed and had to lie in it. She reckoned he'd have thrown her out if she'd got in the family way, but she'd been lucky and hadn't caught on. If he hadn't started knocking her about when he'd had a few drinks, then she'd probably still be there.

But Sal was nobody's punchbag and she wasn't married to him so could leave and find herself somewhere else to live. She'd moved twice already, but he'd found her and dragged her back – threatened to kill her if she ran away again.

It was no good thinking about that now. She was safe in the Land Army, surrounded by people who'd look out for her. When she'd heard that the twelve of them in this dormitory would be going to the same place, she'd been pleased. The book that she'd been given about the Land Army had said they could be billeted on their own in the farm they were working at, in a cottage with a couple of girls, or in a hostel with twenty or more.

* * *

Sal was jolted awake by the loud clang of a bell in the doorway. She sat up, muddled and not sure where she was. She rubbed her eyes, blinked and her heart stopped thudding. It was just someone waking them up, she was safe with eleven other girls in a dormitory in Devon.

'It's scarcely light,' someone at the far side of the room complained. 'I don't think even the cows, chickens or pigs will be awake yet.'

Sal looked across at Charlie, who was already out of bed. 'Blimey, you're quick. Do we have to work with cows again, do you reckon?'

'No, I think we're with the chickens today.'

'That's a relief. If I never see another cow again in me life, I'll be happy. Don't have nothing against chickens, though.'

She'd scrubbed the seat of her breeches and they'd come up lovely. Her knickers were dry, but the corduroy was still a bit damp. She was dressed in a flash – something her cramped upbringing had taught her – you only had a couple of minutes to get decent before someone would be awake and gawping at you.

'There's tea in the canteen but no breakfast until nine o'clock,' Daphne said.

'It's downright cruelty, making us work for hours without food. Them soldiers and such get a good breakfast before they go out.'

Charlie laughed. 'We don't have to kill anybody or be killed ourselves, so stop whingeing, Sal, and hurry or there won't even be any tea left. The three nearest the door have already gone to the bathroom.'

'Cor, them others were quick. We ain't going to be last, that's somethink, I suppose.'

The three of them had a lick and a promise, cleaned their

teeth, returned their stuff to their chest of drawers and were off to the canteen like rats out of a drainpipe.

The room was already half-full and the queue at the tea urn was long. Eventually Sal had a lovely cuppa, no sugar, as she'd learned to do without when rationing came in, and she retreated to a quiet corner to drink it with her friends.

'Charlie, you're the expert on all this farming lark, ain't you? Do they expect us to be able to do all the jobs what we're being shown and learn them in a day?'

'Haven't the foggiest. The new intake, of which we're a part, are housed in this section. I'm hoping we'll bump into someone in their final week and they might be able to elucidate.'

Sal didn't understand a lot of what her friend said, but she liked to hear the long words. She'd never had an educated friend before and maybe she'd pick up a bit herself and come out of this not looking quite so stupid.

A tall, sturdy girl sitting at the next table overheard this remark. 'This week, it's a day in every section to get a feel for it. Then they choose who they think is most suitable for dairy, arable, market gardening, timber work, mixed farming and so on. You then spend a week in the three sections they select.'

'Thank you, that makes perfect sense,' Charlie replied.

'Thank gawd for that, I'll not be chosen for dairy work,' Sal said. 'I wasn't any good at churning butter nor cheese making.'

'I'm hoping I'll get to work on a farm with horses, I love them and much prefer to plough with a team of horses than use a tractor.' Charlie drained her mug and stood up. Immediately, Sal and Daphne did the same.

The chickens were shut up overnight but let out first thing. They had an outside area to wander about in, where they could pick up insects and such.

Their instructor this time was a woman. She had grey hair

scraped back in a bun and was almost as broad as she was tall. Sal thought all fat people were supposed to be jolly, but this wasn't the case with Mrs Simpson.

'Now then, girls, pay attention. You let the chickens out, feed them, make sure they have water in their trough, collect the eggs, grade and wash them and put them on the trays, pointy side down, then clean the shed. Is that clear?'

'Yes, Mrs Simpson,' all three of them chorused.

'Good. Get on with it. I'll be keeping an eye on you, and you can't move on to the next part of your course if you don't get a satisfactory grade from me.'

Then she waddled away, no doubt to stuff her face with breakfast. Sal reckoned the woman must spend all day eating to be the size she was.

'Is that it? I thought she was supposed to show us what we do. I hope you know what chickens eat, Charlie, as I certainly don't,' Daphne said.

'Nor me. Do you reckon these are the only chickens? Don't seem enough to produce eggs for market or to feed us lot,' Sal said.

'Don't panic, ladies, I told you I grew up on a farm. Before we let them out, we need to go into the fodder store and see what's in there.' Charlie pointed to a small shed. 'That'll be where the grain and so on is stored. There can't be more than a couple of dozen hens here so, to answer your question, Sal, I expect that there are hundreds more elsewhere. These unfortunate fowl are for beginners to practise on.'

Under the capable guidance of Charlie, the hens were fed, watered and cleaned out in record time. Then the eggs were wiped clean with a damp rag and sorted into size. Cracked ones were put separately from the others.

'No sign of that woman, but it's nine o'clock so we can go for breakfast. There's nothing more to do here anyway, so I wonder what we're going to be doing after we've eaten.'

'As long as it's not cows, I don't care. I'll race you there,' Sal said and set off at a run.

5

John dropped Bert at the recruiting office in Hastings and then left him to it. He returned at speed to Manston, parked his bike and headed for his billet. He fell onto his bed fully clothed and was asleep in seconds. An orderly woke him at 11.30 with a welcome cup of tea.

'It's peeing down out there, Sarge, it's going to be a quiet night for you.'

'Thanks, good to know.'

He gulped down his tea and headed for the sergeants' mess. There'd be hot drinks but no hot food in the middle of the night. He helped himself to a corned beef sandwich and what passed for a sausage roll. He shoved both of them in his pockets for later.

He was a lucky bloke and had a pushbike as well as a motor-bike and tended to use the former at night. No need to wake everybody up if he didn't have to. He pulled an oilskin over his uniform and pedalled cautiously from the sergeants' quarters to the far end of the airfield, where the fire tenders and ambulances were kept.

As always, he was the first of his shift to arrive, as it was his job to speak to the sergeant of the other fire team before he clocked off.

'Nothing to report, John, not a dicky bird. A taxi-Anson had a near miss, but apart from that, all quiet. It'll be even quieter for you lot, you lucky blighters. Everything's grounded in this weather, even the bleeding Germans.'

'Hope you're right, mate. See you later.'

His team of twelve men trooped in, binding about the weather and shaking themselves like wet dogs as they stepped into the comparative warmth and dryness of the hangar. John had already filled his Thermos and put his sandwich and pallid sausage roll safely out of sight, away from the thieving mitts of his men.

The only drawback to a quiet shift was that it gave him too much time to think. He had, as always, a book to read, but this new Agatha Christie didn't hold his attention. There was no routine maintenance to do as the other shift had already done it.

The drum of the rain on the tin roof was a welcome reminder that, for the next few hours at least, they wouldn't be needed to put out any fires or rescue any airmen. Like the rest of the blokes, he took the opportunity to put his feet up. He tipped his chair so the back was resting safely against the wall and then dozed off.

The NAAFI van called in between six and seven so they could grab something to eat. Wasn't the same as a fry-up, but they could get bacon butties with brown sauce and that was good enough. The rain had stopped some time ago, the sun was out, everywhere gently steaming and it was hard to believe that at any moment, death could be dropped on their heads.

John rubbed a hand over his bristly chin, wishing he'd taken the time to shave before he'd fallen asleep on the bed last night. Now he'd have to spruce himself up before visiting Joanna. It was a feeble excuse to go, just to tell her that Bert had been delivered safely, but it would have to do.

He was enjoying his breakfast when, in the distance, he heard the bell ringing where the fighter squadrons were parked. This indicated they were being scrambled – usually the sirens wailed immediately afterwards, but this time they remained silent.

He checked his watch and within four minutes of hearing the bell, the fighters were airborne, screaming out to sea on whatever sortie they'd been given to deal with. Must be something going on in the Channel. It couldn't be the invasion, or all hell would be breaking loose, and it was quiet on the base.

'Everything's ready to go, Sarge, if needed. Let's hope it's not,' Percy said cheerfully as he finished the last of his bacon sandwich.

'I expect it's something to do with the shipping in the Channel needing protection.'

An hour later, all the kites were back safely and none of them had refuelled and taken off again. Whatever the emergency had been, it had been dealt with and didn't require the services of the fire tenders.

John was back, shaved, washed and ready to leave before one o'clock. He wasn't going to warn Joanna that he was coming and give her the opportunity to put him off. He drove at a more sensible speed and throttled back as he turned into the drive so that he coasted the last couple of hundred yards.

The dog was sitting on the terrace with the old lady but had the good sense to wait until the motorbike was stationary before racing over to greet him.

'Good afternoon to you, boy,' he said. 'I've come to see your mistress. Do you think that she'll agree to speak to me?'

He almost stepped back, knocking his precious bike from its

stand, when the old lady spoke from just behind him. For an old bird, she certainly moved swiftly.

'Are you in the habit of speaking to animals as if they understand what you're saying, young man?'

'I don't have much interaction with them, ma'am. I was hoping to see your daughter-in-law in order to give her an update on Smith.'

'Is that not what the telephone is for? I cannot see that a personal visit was called for, unless there's another reason for your being here?'

The old lady fixed him with a beady eye, and he ran his finger around his collar, which had become unaccountably tight. 'I was able to offer her some advice about the Victorian wing...'

'Indeed? I think, young man, that whatever plans you might have with regards to my daughter-in-law should be abandoned forthwith. Depart immediately, unless you wish me to contact your superiors at the base and say that you've been making a nuisance of yourself?'

He was tempted to tell the old bat to mind her own business but thought it might be wise to do as she said. He'd been mad to even consider pursuing Joanna and better that he was sent away with a flea in his ear than cause them both embarrassment later.

How could the old Lady Harcourt possibly have guessed what he was hoping to do? He didn't even know himself if he was going to risk everything and pursue the impossible. He rather thought the old biddy was a lot sharper than he'd given her credit for.

John nodded but didn't reply and was back on his bike and out of the drive in seconds. He joined his fellow NCOs in the mess. Nobody flinched or commented when the kites took off for the third time. Then, as he was halfway through his meal, the siren wailed.

He ignored it, as did everyone else, and carried on eating.

Food wasn't left to congeal in this mess. Then someone sitting closest to the window jumped to his feet. 'Bloody hell, boys, get to the shelter now. Three German buggers have got through. Our guys are after them, but I reckon it'll be a close-run thing.'

John was already at the door. If there were going to be bombs dropped on the base, they would need every available firefighter working. He was on his motorbike and about to roar off when Percy jumped on the back.

'I'm coming too, Sarge, they'll need all of us. Tally ho!'

This was what flyers yelled when going into a dog fight – hardly appropriate but he understood the intention. He covered the distance to the hangar in seconds and as he kicked the bike onto its stand, he could see the Me 109s approaching. The menacing drone of the engines made the hair on the back of his neck stand up.

He watched from the open doorway of the shelter; no one wanted the door shut in case they were needed. If bombs started dropping, the door would be closed, but until then, they watched.

'Blimey, two of our boys have got one of the bastards,' Percy yelled.

'Here come four Spits, they'll get the other ones,' someone else shouted in John's ear.

He was watching the damaged bomber closely. Smoke and flames were belching from the engine. The kite was coming down. It was going to crash on the runway.

'Back, get this bloody door shut.'

He and Percy reacted as one. The door slammed shut and they herded the dozen men to the far end of the shelter. Not a moment too soon, as something huge hit the door and they were thrown backwards by the force onto the concrete floor in a mêlée of arms and legs.

* * *

Joanna had sent Joe into the village with a letter accepting the offer from the builders with the proviso that they did what John suggested to the adjoining wall. The twins had reclaimed an impressive number of kitchen items, which were now stored in an unused outhouse in the yard. They then ventured, very cautiously, they'd assured her, to the attics and brought down several trunks full of interesting items. These were also in the storeroom, waiting to be looked at one day when she had the time and inclination.

John hadn't come back to tell her if Bert had successfully enlisted, and she wasn't sure if she was relieved or disappointed. Probably best not to venture down that dangerous path. If only Elizabeth hadn't told her about the affairs she'd had when she was younger, then she wouldn't even have contemplated such an action.

The physical side of marriage had always been something she'd endured and had never enjoyed. When David had stopped coming to her bedroom, it had certainly been a relief to her and, with hindsight, she thought it might have been to him as well.

Having her pulse race at the very thought of being kissed by a man, any man, was a novel experience for her. She'd lived without physical passion all her life and could continue to do so. There was a war on, she was Lady Harcourt of Goodwill House, and to even be contemplating having an affair with a sergeant – not even an officer – was both scandalous and impossible.

* * *

The following day, the planes from Manston screamed overhead and Joanna was certain it was all four fighter squadrons.

Moments later, the wail of the siren on base filled the air and then this was followed by the one in the village.

This had happened several times over the past weeks, and they'd worked out a system for getting everybody down to the shelter in the cellar with the minimum of fuss. Her task was to find Elizabeth.

'There you are, I thought you'd be on your way to the kitchen and ready to go downstairs.' Elizabeth, who was still sitting staring somewhat vacantly into space, looked around, startled by Joanna's sudden appearance.

'Siren? Goodness me, I must have been asleep. I'm ready, I'm coming. I do so hate being down in the dank cellar, but I suppose we have no choice.'

Liza raced around locking the French doors onto the terrace, checking the front door was also secured and all the windows were shut – that was her job. Joe had to find the dog and take down a basket of whatever was available in the kitchen. Jean filled the four Thermos flasks with boiling water. There was tea, sugar and so on stored safely in a tin box in the shelter so that rodents couldn't get to it.

Despite the fact that it was a very warm day, the cellar beneath the house was always unpleasantly chilly. Joanna kept her arm firmly through Elizabeth's and they negotiated the steep stone stairs safely.

Joe was already there and had lit the Primus – they didn't actually need to heat anything but doing so would soon warm the shelter up.

'Here we are, Elizabeth, your chair's ready,' Joanna said. 'I'll just go back and collect the cushions and blankets with Liza.'

'Why don't you keep them down here and save yourself all the fuss?'

'Things get damp in here and it's better to keep them in the hamper in the boot room.' This was a conversation they had every time, and it was becoming increasingly obvious that Elizabeth's short-term memory was failing.

The sirens were still howling when Joanna closed the door that led down to the cellars behind her. With her arms full of rugs and blankets, if she did trip over, at least she'd have a soft fall.

Once they were all settled, Jean made the tea – there was no longer any coffee available, apart from the disgusting liquid which pretended to be coffee. Camp was made mainly from chicory and tasted like it.

'Ma, where are all the land girls going to sit if there's an air raid?' Liza asked.

'If there's a raid during the day, then none of them will be here. If there's a raid at night, then we'll just have to manage. We can bring in another four small chairs and put them along the wall by the WC.'

'Then I sincerely hope that nobody has to use the facilities, as it will be most embarrassing for the person in the cubicle and unpleasant for anyone sitting outside,' Elizabeth said.

'The girls will be a lot safer in the fields than they would be in this shelter, Grandma,' Joe said, hastily changing the subject, as he handed her plate with a slice of plum pie.

'Then I think that I'll go and sit under a hedge when the siren sounds next time. I really don't like being incarcerated down here.'

Joanna was about to protest but then thought about it. 'Actually, I don't see why we couldn't go and sit in the summerhouse during the day. The honeysuckle and clematis growing over the roof must make it invisible from the air. It's only a brisk five-minute walk from the house and would be far more pleasant than being shut down here for an hour or more.'

Jean pushed over a mug of tea. Joanna shook her head at the

offer of plum pie. 'If we set things up in the summerhouse, I think it's a good idea, my lady.'

Jean always used her title when Elizabeth was there, but they were now on first-name terms when they were just with the twins.

There was a chorus of agreement from the other three and they spent the next hour happily working out how to make this new arrangement work.

'I don't walk as fast as I used to, my dear, but if we make our way along the hedge, I don't think even the sharpest-eyed German bomber would see us.'

'Those German blighters won't be looking over here, Grandma, they'll be dodging our boys in the sky and trying to drop their bombs on Manston.'

Sal wasn't that fussed about chickens and was happy to spend the rest of the day with the main flock and four other girls cleaning out the chicken houses, collecting eggs and getting them ready for market. It was a relief not to be asked to butcher any, as although she'd skinned and gutted rabbits – the neighbour had kept them in hutches for eating – she didn't fancy actually killing anything.

Picking spuds was backbreaking but she soon got the hang of it and by the end of the week had got ticks in all the right boxes from all the instructors. After supper, she and her friends found themselves a comfortable spot on the grass and were joined by the other nine from the dormitory. They'd become friendly with most of them.

'I could do with a nice half of shandy,' Daphne said as she stretched out her feet.

'It's a great shame that we're so far away from civilisation, or we could walk into the nearest village and buy ourselves a drink,' Charlie said.

'I'm whacked out, I couldn't walk half a mile even for a beer,' Sal said.

'Do any of you know what we're likely to be concentrating on for the remaining three weeks?' Jill asked.

Nobody knew the answer to this, but Sal thought as long as she wasn't put with the cows, she'd be happy. The blooming big cart horses had been gentle giants and with Charlie's guidance, she was now a dab hand at harnessing them and had even managed to steer them more or less straight.

'I like the market gardening,' Daphne said as she wriggled her toes in the late evening sunshine. 'Tomatoes in a greenhouse smell heavenly, and it'll be much nicer working in a glasshouse in the winter than being out in a field.'

'None of us had anything to do with timber – I suppose that's because wherever we're going, that particular skill isn't needed,' Charlie said. 'Hang on, one of the senior instructors is heading our way.'

'Right, ladies, good news,' the instructor said. 'Every one of you has passed every section of this week's courses and we decided that we're going to send you to your posting at the end of next week. You'll be going to Kent and billeted at Goodwill House with Lady Harcourt.'

'That sounds a bit of all right,' Sal said happily. 'What sort of work will we be doing?'

'Dairy, mixed arable, pigs, poultry and market gardening. There'll also be hop-picking in September, but the majority of that work will be done by the invasion of Londoners and their families.'

They were all on their feet now and eager to ask questions. They were told that the lists were up in the admin building so they could see which three areas they were to concentrate on for the remaining week. A list would also be up showing which farms they would be sent to first.

They trooped across and Sal was delighted to find she'd be working on a farm with horses, doing general work but no dairy.

'Cor, love a duck – would you look at that? The three of us will be working together,' she said with excitement.

Everybody seemed to be happy with what they'd be doing. When they went to bed that night, Sal, who'd hidden her disquiet, was able to mull over the worrying news that the one place in England where she might be recognised was on the hop fields of Kent. Still, that wasn't for a few weeks yet, so no need to worry now.

6

John and Percy were on top of the pile of men, so the two of them untangled themselves and got to their feet. The room was full of dust – hopefully from the ceiling, not from outside – but apart from that, the shelter remained intact. The cursing and swearing coming from the heaving mass meant that apparently nobody was seriously hurt.

'Get some light on this tangle, Percy, whilst I try and get everybody back on their feet.'

'My bloody torch's kaput, Sarge, reckon I fell on it.'

John tossed his own in the general direction of the voice and by some miracle, his corporal caught it. The powerful beam illuminated the blokes pulling themselves from the muddle of limbs. Everybody was on their feet, apart from three who seemed to be a bit worse for wear.

'Anything broken, Dickie?'

'No, all tickety-boo, thanks, Sarge.'

'What about you two?'

'We're fine. We were at the bottom of the pile, but nothing to worry about,' one of them replied.

That was one thing sorted, now John needed to investigate at the other end of the shelter. 'I can't smell smoke. But something hit the door. We'll probably have to wait to be let out.'

There were now several torches lit and it was easy to see his way to the door. This was metal and had proved effective against the blast.

'Crikey, look at that, Sarge. The door's all but caved in,' Percy said, pointing at the central bulge.

'It did its job.' He put his hand out but didn't touch the metal. 'It's hot. There's definitely a fire on the other side. From the impact, I'm pretty sure at least part of that German kite is on the other side of this.'

'Better stay there too, Sarge, or we're all done for.'

John couldn't see who'd spoken but the bloke had just said what everybody must be thinking. 'None of that crap, thank you. If we were going to go for a Burton, it would have been a few moments ago. Just a matter of waiting now.'

He turned to Percy. 'Check how much water there is in the cans. We need to ration it. Now, listen, everybody. Our biggest risk is going to be lack of oxygen and water. Make yourselves comfortable, have a drink, and then try to sleep. No talking, sit still, that way we'll conserve what air we've got. Take off your jackets and use them as pillows.'

Nobody argued – not that they would have, as he was the man in charge. Percy went round with half a mug of water for all of them and then put the two containers under the bench. John wanted to touch the door again and see if it was getting hotter, but there was no point in alarming his men.

'Okay, if everybody's settled, then torches out.'

'What if we need a leak, Sarge?'

'There's the bucket at the end of the shelter. Just be grateful it hadn't been used when you fell on it, Tommy.'

The wooden benches that ran down either side of the shelter were probably less comfortable than sprawling on the floor but there wasn't room for everybody to do that. His hope was that, as all of them were permanently fatigued, falling asleep in the dark warmth of the shelter wouldn't be a problem.

Soon it was quiet, apart from the deep breathing indicating that most of his men were sleeping. As he and Percy had been at the end of their shift, it should have been easy for them to sleep, but he knew his corporal was as wide awake as he was.

Under normal circumstances, even with the door shut, you could hear the all-clear. But there was no noise from outside at all and this was bothering him. The only explanation was that the entire shelter was submerged by debris of some sort.

Had the adjacent hangar collapsed on top of the shelter at the same time as the Me 109 had collided with the front? There was sod all he could do about it, and he was confident that a highly efficient team would be working frantically to get them out.

It was noticeably warmer, but breathing was still relatively easy. Thank god for small mercies. If they got out of this alive – if he got out of this alive – he'd ignore the warning from the old Lady Harcourt and make a direct approach to Joanna. It didn't matter that their relationship had to be transitory; she could never marry someone of his class, and he could be posted anywhere at any time.

That didn't matter. He didn't believe in God. You only got one shot at life, and he wasn't going to waste time agonising over the rights and wrongs of having an affair. They were consenting adults, there was a war on, you had to take whatever life offered you, as you could be dead the next day.

Having made his decision, John dozed off like everyone else in the shelter. He wasn't deeply asleep, was aware what was going on, and after an hour, he had Percy take around another drink.

'Bloody hell, Sarge, it's hot in here now.'

'That's only to be expected, Tommy, there's twelve of us and no fresh air. I checked the door and it's no hotter than it was before. Although we can't hear the sound of a rescue, we all know the blokes outside are going to get to us eventually.'

There was no need to remind them to stop talking. Three of them needed to use the bucket, which caused a short-lived ripple of amusement. He just hoped nobody needed to do more than pee before they were released.

The air was definitely thinner, he could feel a slight tightening across his forehead, but nothing dangerous yet. He supposed that suffocating was a better way to die than being burned alive.

John smiled wryly in the darkness. There was no good way to die when you were only twenty-seven. How old was Joanna? Certainly older than him, as she had an adult daughter training to be a doctor. He'd discovered this information by chance – he wasn't stupid enough to ask direct questions.

Lady Joanna Harcourt – the title and the name suited her to perfection. More than half a head shorter than him, with the most stunning corn-coloured hair, deep blue eyes and curves in all the right places. He thought she must be in her mid-thirties, but she could be older. Living the life of Riley with every imaginable luxury, and servants to do the menial tasks, could make her look younger than she was.

His mum was in her fifties but looked twenty years older – being short of a bob or two, having to work as a cleaner, as well as taking care of her family, had taken its toll. Another thing he'd do when he was out – he refused to contemplate the alternative – was write to his parents. He'd always been the odd one out, the oldest of five, and the only one to escape from the drudgery of his family's life.

He'd scarcely had any contact with his family since he'd got a full scholarship to university and then volunteered for the RAF. The only thing he had in common with his dad was that they were both staunch socialists.

A further hour drifted past and now he was becoming seriously concerned about the well-being of his men. Two of them were no longer responsive and he feared that they would all perish in the next couple of hours.

He too was becoming confused but was roused by a noise in the ceiling. He pushed himself upright, switched on his torch and pointed it at the place the sound had come from. Was this the rescue he'd been hoping for? Would it be too late for some of his men?

* * *

Joanna preferred to leave the shelter door ajar as she'd discovered, to her dismay, that she was more than a little claustrophobic when it was shut. They'd been chatting happily for an hour when, during a lull in the conversation, she heard the loud chink of glass against glass.

'My goodness, something large must have crashed nearby to make the wine bottles rattle like that,' she said nervously.

'I'll go and check, Ma, and I'll take Lazzy, as he probably needs to relieve himself,' Joe said, completely unbothered by the possible danger.

He'd vanished before she could stop him. She must remember not to think of the twins as children, they were both almost adults. Young people of nearly fifteen left school and went into full-time employment. This was what the twins would have been doing too if they'd not come to Goodwill House. She prayed that this beastly war would be over before either of them were old enough to be conscripted – especially Joe.

'I don't suppose there's any whisky or brandy lurking in the shadows out there?' Elizabeth asked hopefully.

Joanna hoped either Liza or Jean would volunteer to look but they both remained silent. With considerable reluctance, she stood up. 'I'll go. I'm pretty sure we've drunk all of it, but you never know, there might be one somewhere that I missed.'

At least it wasn't dark and she didn't need her torch as the electricity down here, and presumably everywhere else, was still functioning as normal. She took a deep breath, steadied her nerves, and then, shoulders back, marched bravely into the bowels of the house.

She smiled at her nonsense. There was plenty of red wine, not quite so much white, more than enough sherry and even a few bottles of Port and Madeira. She almost jumped out of her skin when the dog pushed his cold nose into her hand.

'Lazzy, I nearly had a heart attack. Joe, what did you see out there?'

'I nipped up to the attic after letting the dog out, as you can see for miles out of those windows. Something big's going on at Manston; I can see smoke and flames but the trees blocked my view. I think a German bomber crashed two fields away – smoke and flames there as well.'

It was a concern having the base so close, but she hoped half a mile would be enough to keep them all safe.

'Has the all-clear gone?'

'It hasn't, or if it has, we missed it, but I'm pretty sure it's safe to go up now. Are you looking for something in particular, Ma?'

She explained and he grinned. 'I'm sure I can find Grandma what she wants. I'll bring it to you in the drawing room, shall I?'

Liza rushed around opening all the doors and windows when

they emerged from the cellars – they needed plenty of fresh air to remove the residual smell of damp plaster and wood. They'd eaten a light luncheon downstairs, but it was late afternoon and she was sure Jean would be rustling up her own version of afternoon tea with Liza's help.

'Elizabeth, do you want to sit in the drawing room or go outside on the terrace?'

'Outside, we've been cooped up long enough. After tea, perhaps we could do a trial run on the new arrangements for daytime air raids?'

'I was going to suggest that myself. Joe thinks he can find us what you wanted. I'm not sure that strong spirits so early in the day is a good idea.'

'Fiddlesticks, my dear girl. We could all be dead tomorrow, so we must enjoy every moment we have.' Her mother-in-law laughed, not her usual cackle, but sounding more like a young woman, the woman she must have been when she was gallivanting around the south of France, enjoying herself. 'Well, I suppose that's more likely to refer to me than any of you, as I'm at my last prayers.'

'Elizabeth, I think you're fitter than you were when you arrived and apart from being a little forgetful now and again, I'm confident you'll be around and enjoying life to the full for another decade at least.'

Joe came out, carrying an armful of dusty bottles, and placed them triumphantly on the table. 'I'm not exactly sure what these are. I'll leave you to examine them. I'm going to check the horse and the other livestock. Also, I'm pretty sure the gardener might have been here during the raid, so I'd better find him too.'

'Thank you, I should have thought of that myself.' Joanna turned to her mother-in-law. 'I'll get a damp cloth for each of us and then we can have a look at these treasures. I'm sure that at least two of them are cognac because of the oddly shaped bottles.'

A delicious aroma of baking filled the kitchen when she went in. 'Scones will be ready in ten minutes, Joanna, and Liza's just making the sandwiches.'

'We're on the terrace, Jean. Joe's gone to check Star and the chickens.'

The acrid smell of the smoke drifting from the nearby base and the field half a mile away was an unpleasant reminder of the fire that could have been so much worse here. They'd been lucky this time, but would this continue as the fighting in the air got worse?

The bottles turned out to be brandy, Calvados and two that were anonymous as the labels had disintegrated.

'Shall we open one of these, Joanna?'

'Yes, but not now. It doesn't seem appropriate to be having some sort of celebration when we don't know how many people died in the air raid.' She was thinking about John when she said that but could hardly tell Elizabeth this.

The scones, sandwiches, and tea had been set out on a pretty floral tablecloth and still her son hadn't returned. She was becoming anxious and was about to go in search of him when he arrived from the far end of the terrace.

From his grave expression, she knew it was bad news. Her stomach clenched and her hands were clammy.

'It's not good, Ma, I went to have a closer look,' Joe said. 'A few bombs were dropped on the accommodation block, a couple on the runway, but one of the bombers crash-landed at the far end of the runway where the fire tenders and ambulances are. I think it's fallen on the shelter those men use.'

'Oh, my god, how absolutely dreadful. Do you think anyone in there would have survived?'

* * *

John watched and listened, pushing himself upright with some difficulty. Percy remained with his eyes shut, which was a bad sign. A few moments later, a metal pipe poked through the ceiling. It was rapidly followed by three more, each one wider than the last.

Fresh air wasn't exactly pouring in but there was a noticeable difference in the oxygen levels. This wouldn't be enough to save them unless somehow a hole large enough to let the foul atmosphere out was knocked through.

The pipes were now long enough for the men able to stand under and gulp in oxygen. As the pipes weren't flexible, there was no way he could administer the life-saving air for those who needed it most.

John cleared his head by breathing in what was coming down the tube and then heaved Percy to his feet. Soon his corporal was functioning more or less normally.

'Right, you lazy sods, on your feet. That's an order.' He injected as much authority into his command as he could and it seemed to do the trick. He and Percy half-carried, half-dragged all but three of them to the centre of the shelter, where the air was more or less breathable.

'They need to get this bloody door open, never mind putting pipes through the ceiling. Those three will be goners if we don't get them outside pronto,' Percy snarled.

'There's nothing anyone can do about the door, but from the racket on the roof, I don't think it'll be long before we can get out that way,' John said.

Those that were able to took a welcome drink. The three men who were barely alive were now lying directly beneath the metal pipes. There was nothing more anyone could do.

He'd shouted up one of the pipes that there were three critically ill men who needed to be got out immediately but wasn't sure anyone had heard him. He put his ear to the pipe but heard nothing but banging and drilling.

A continuous stream of concrete, dust and debris showered down, and he was forced to move the blokes from the floor; they were now being held upright on the benches. Suddenly a crack appeared just above his head and the ceiling fell in. There was a searing pain in his head, and his world went black.

* * *

When John next opened his eyes, he was lying in a hospital bed with a large bandage round his head. His chest was tight, he had a bloody awful headache, but apart from that, he wasn't too bad.

A vigilant nurse must have seen him wake and she was beside him instantly. 'Sergeant, you've got a nasty head wound and a possible concussion. I don't advise trying to sit up as you'll probably vomit.'

'Got it. What about my men? Did they all get out alive?'

She shook her head sadly. 'I'm sorry to tell you that two of them didn't survive. However, it's a miracle any of you did considering what happened. One of your men is in the adjacent bed, one in a critical care ward, but the others recovered sufficiently to remain at Manston in the care of your own doctor.'

Even so short a conversation exhausted him. He gratefully sipped a few mouthfuls of water and then drifted off into the welcome darkness. The next time he came round, he was able to shuffle up the bed without any ill effects.

'About bloody time, Sarge, you've been malingering there for three days,' Percy said from beside him.

'Christ, that long? Why are you still here? You look perfectly fit to me.'

'Twenty-five stitches in my belly. When the ceiling caved in, we got the worst of it. Silly buggers didn't think it through. Two of our blokes didn't make it.'

John was saddened. What a bloody stupid way to die.

'I remember the nurse telling me. What about damage and casualties elsewhere on the base?'

'We lost two tenders, but they've already been replaced. Our hangar has had it. Bloody thing collapsed on the shelter. We're being moved to an empty one halfway down the runway.'

'Casualties?'

'No fatalities, minor injuries being treated by the nurses and medic on the base.'

John risked moving his head a little from side to side. 'So, it's just the three of us in hospital? I need a leak. Where's the bog?'

'Outside the ward door and on the left. I'm not allowed to get out of bed so have the privilege of a bedpan.'

'I'm not using one of those. There's nothing wrong with my legs.'

There was no sign of any nurses and he thought it might be their afternoon break. Tentatively he put both feet on the floor. His head remained on his shoulders and the contents of his stomach remained where they should be.

He got a good grip of the metal head of the bed and gingerly pulled himself upright. Apart from his legs being a bit weak from lack of use, he was good to go. He found the WC without difficulty. He then washed his face and hands and felt considerably better. He ran his fingers over his shaved cheeks – some unfortunate student nurse had no doubt been given the task of shaving him every day, but she'd done a good job of it.

He made it to the ward door before being discovered out of

bed. You'd have thought he'd committed a capital offence, the fuss the ward sister made about it. Once he was safely between the sheets, she stopped scolding him.

'What if you'd fallen and nobody knew you were there?'

'Better that than I wet the bed, Sister. I don't suppose there's anything to eat? I'm absolutely starving.'

'If you promise to stay where you are, then I'll have something fetched from the kitchen for you.'

After a large bowl of vegetable soup and two corned beef sandwiches, he felt a lot better, but even this minimal amount of activity had exhausted him.

He was drifting off when he sensed there was somebody beside him. He opened his eyes. 'Joanna, I can't tell you how glad I am to see you.'

Her smile was warm. 'And I you, John. I shouldn't be here, but when I heard you might be grievously injured, I had to come and see for myself. I'm pretending to be visiting on behalf of the WVS in my capacity as chairwoman.'

'Fair enough. I thought of you when things were looking bad. I'm not imagining this connection between us, am I?'

'No, but it's remarkably inconvenient for both of us. I spoke to the doctor, he's a good friend of mine, and he said you won't be fit for duty for another week, at least, and neither will your corporal. I had an RAF pilot convalesce at my home and, of course, offered the same welcome to you both.'

She leaned down as if adjusting her skirt and touched his hand. 'I thought you might be dead or dying and had to come.' Her words were little more than a whisper.

'I'm glad you did.' His reply was equally quiet. A nurse was staring across at them, so he raised his voice when he spoke next.

This was the last thing he expected and, despite his thumping headache, he grinned. 'That's very kind of you, my lady. I don't think Percy will be discharged for a bit, but I should be out in a day or two. We'd both be happy to accept your offer of accommodation until we're able to return to duty.'

He'd used her title because the nurse had drifted towards his bed, obviously curious as to why he'd received such a prestigious visitor. Joanna understood immediately and, as she'd not actually sat down, things looked on the surface to be just the lady of the manor offering to help two injured RAF men.

They both knew it was a lot more than that. She smiled, nodded, and walked away, every inch a lady and possibly, in the not-too-distant future, *his* lady.

7

Sal enjoyed the second week of her training but was eager to start doing real work. During their two weeks of instruction, they'd got ten shillings a week, but after they'd taken out national health and unemployment insurance from it, she was left with only a couple of shillings. At least their board and lodging had been free.

She wasn't exactly sure how much they'd get now they were going to be working and not training, but she thought Charlie would know. They were busy packing, like the other girls, so they could catch the nine o'clock bus to the station in an hour's time.

'We get thirty-two shillings a week and have to pay for our board and lodging out of that,' Charlie said. 'We're supposed to work forty-eight hours and then get eight pence an hour for overtime, but I'm sure that doesn't always happen.'

'It said on the posters that it was like having a holiday in the country – don't reckon that's right,' Sal said. 'Do we get free travel and holidays and such?'

'We're not entitled to an actual holiday, but I believe time off can be arranged with our employers. The thing that really irks me is that we don't get free travel like the other services – in fact, we don't get any of the perks they get because we're not considered to be in the forces.'

Daphne joined in this conversation. 'That might be true, Charlie, but at least we can resign if we want to. Once you've signed on for the ATS, WAAF or WRENs you can't get out unless you get pregnant.'

'I don't intend to leave until the end of the war. And I certainly ain't going to get in the family way,' Sal said as she pushed the last of her belongings into the canvas kitbag someone had kindly found for her.

'Right, all tickety-boo. Let's get out and down to the bus stop. We've got a very long and boring journey ahead of us. It's a considerable distance from Devon to Kent.'

Charlie wasn't wrong about that because by the time the twelve of them tottered from the local bus near their destination at nine o'clock that evening, they were all worn out. They walked from the bus stop to the end of the drive and those in front stopped so suddenly those behind bumped into them.

'Would you look at that? I thought that college was posh, but this is even better,' Sal said in awe.

'Goodwill House – a right funny name if you ask me. Look at the right-hand end, I reckon there's been a fire recently,' Jill said sourly.

'That end is obviously unoccupied, so it doesn't affect us. Shall we proceed, ladies? I, for one, am seriously in need of a hot cup of tea and something to eat,' Charlie said.

'I need the bog, I'm that desperate I'm tempted to nip behind the hedge,' Sal replied with a laugh.

'Don't you dare. We want to make a good impression.'

That last few hundred yards seemed like a mile or more, but

somehow Sal managed to reach the front door without wetting her knickers. If anyone made her laugh, she'd burst.

A beautiful golden-haired woman appeared at the grand front porch. This one had columns, marble steps and everything.

'Welcome, girls, I'm Lady Harcourt. I'm sure you're tired after your long journey from Devon. My daughter, Liza, is waiting to show you to your rooms. Bathrooms and lavatories are on the same floor as you. Don't unpack now, your supper will be on the table in fifteen minutes.'

They bundled in and Daphne kindly took Sal's bag so she could make a mad dash for the nearest WC. After she'd washed her hands and her face, she went in search of her friends, hoping they could share a room.

'In here, Sal, we've got somewhere for just the three of us,' Daphne called from an open door just across the passageway.

'Blimey, this is a bit of all right. There's three chests of drawers, three bedside cabinets, but where do we put the things we have to hang up?'

Charlie pointed to a door in the wall by one of the big windows. 'That's a walk-in closet, Sal, loads of room for all our clothes as well as our other bits and pieces.'

She poked her head in and was suitably impressed. 'I reckon we've landed on our feet here. That Lady Harcourt looks like a princess. Her daughter's ever so nice too and not a bit stuck up. I think I'm going to love it here.'

The passageway where their rooms were led to a big gallery sort of place where you could look down into the huge hall below. The other side of the gallery led to the family rooms, Daphne told her.

Liza was waiting to take them to the dining room, which was ever so classy. The table was big enough to seat fifty, let alone the dozen of them. One end was laid up with a smart white cloth and all manner of knives and forks that she had no idea what to do with.

Supper was smashing – loads of vegetable soup, freshly baked bread and a large slice of apple pie and custard for afters. This was washed down with as much tea as they wanted.

Lady Harcourt came in to speak to them as they were finishing. 'I hope you enjoyed your first meal here. A bit of housekeeping first – I need your ration books and so on. I gather from Mrs Dougherty, your area organiser, that you'll be paid directly and then give me the sixteen shillings for your board and lodging at the end of every week.'

Charlie had already collected their ration books, insurance stuff and all that, and she handed it over to Lady Harcourt in a manila envelope.

'Do you have any maps of the area, or directions to the farms and market gardens where we're going to be working?'

'I'm sorry, no, I don't have any maps. You don't have to start until Monday, which gives you the weekend to become familiar with your new surroundings. I'm hoping that you'll attend church with us on Sunday. That will give you the opportunity to meet some of the locals.'

'Not all of us are C of E, my lady, so those of us that aren't will make our own arrangements with the Almighty. I was told that there's a horse and cart available for transport?' Charlie sounded the same as Lady Harcourt. Sal reckoned her friend must come from a family like this one.

'Yes, my oldest daughter's mare, Starlight – Star – is for your use. I was told that there was someone familiar with horses. I take it that's you.'

'It is. I'm Charlotte, usually called Charlie.'

'Good. There are also four bicycles permanently available,

and another three, those that belong to the family, that you can use when we don't need them.'

Lady Harcourt nodded and then continued. 'There are two RAF men presently recuperating at Goodwill House. They are accommodated on the family side of the house, so you'll have no contact with them. They were injured just over a week ago in an air raid at Manston and Goodwill House is occasionally used for the convalescence of officers and senior NCOs.'

Sal thought this was good of Lady Harcourt and then forgot about it. She was far more interested in the fact that they had two whole days off and were living in the lap of luxury.

Joanna didn't regret her invitation to host the two injured RAF firefighters. Surprisingly, not even her mother-in-law thought it odd of her to have extended a welcome a second time to members of the Air Force.

John – she no longer thought of him formally – hadn't in fact been released until several days after her visit. By this time, his corporal was also ready to leave hospital. An RAF driver had delivered both of them to Goodwill House yesterday. They'd settled into the room they were sharing and hadn't appeared downstairs so far.

She'd spoken to Dr Willoughby, and he'd said that neither of them would be fit for duty for at least another ten days. Therefore, there was no rush to further her acquaintance with John. It had been her suggestion that the men share a room – having John sleeping alone would have been an invitation she might have difficulty resisting. How could she be thinking about a man she hardly knew in such a way? What was it about this handsome and charismatic young man that made her heart race and made her contemplate doing something so outrageous as having an affair with him?

For some inexplicable reason, the moment he'd smiled at her on the night of the fire, she'd been drawn to him.

'Ma, Auntie Jean has given me a list of things we need from the village and she wants me to register the girls at all the shops so we can use their ration cards. Some of the land girls are going to catch the bus and I thought I might go with them. Is that all right?'

'Of course it is, Liza; they seem a jolly lot and as they're likely to be here for the duration, the sooner we get to know them, the better.'

'It's the three of them in the room that Di and Millie had that said they were going, The one called Charlie, and her friends Daphne and Sal, invited me along. That Sal comes from the East End like Joe and I did. She's a real corker, isn't she? I wish my hair was the same colour as hers and not mousy-brown.'

'Your hair's very pretty and so are you,' Joanna said. 'However, I do think the three of them make a striking group, especially in their smart green and brown uniform. I think Sal is the fair-haired one, Charlie the brunette and Daphne the redhead.'

'That's right. The others don't seem quite so friendly. How old do you reckon those three are?'

'I received a list of their names yesterday. Let me think – Charlotte, or Charlie as she wishes to be called – is twenty-three, Sal's the same age, and Daphne, I seem to remember, is twenty or twenty-one. One of the girls is seventeen, most of them are under twenty but there are two others the same age as Daphne. I expect we'll be able to identify them after a while.'

'Are those two RAF men going to join us for meals or are they going to eat with the land girls?'

'Good heavens, of course they'll eat with us. They are our

guests; having them here to recuperate is one way we can assist with the war effort. Somehow, looking after those injured in the line of duty seems a lot more useful than knitting balaclavas and mittens for the sailors.'

Liza giggled. 'I do my best, Ma, but I don't think any sailor would be happy to get anything I've knitted.'

Her daughter rushed off to fetch the necessary shopping baskets. No money was needed, as everything was put on account and then settled at the end of the month. There'd been a constant coming and going of aircraft at Manston, but no further bombing raids or crashes.

The three ladies from the village who took it in turns to work in the house were a godsend and were happy to turn their hand to whatever was needed. The new arrivals had to keep their own rooms tidy, were expected to do their own personal laundry, but this still meant a lot of extra cleaning and, of course, catering.

Liza left happily with the three girls and from the noise coming from the far end of the house, she thought the other nine must be making themselves at home. The room that had been used as a sitting room for the WAAFs wasn't large enough for twelve of them, so Joanna had opened up the ballroom for their use as a recreation space. Joe had found a set of table tennis bats and the necessary table for it to be played on. Jean had donated her record player and records and Dr Willoughby had kindly loaned a spare wireless.

The girls had been delighted with this large space, but she thought in the winter, when it wasn't heated, they would be less pleased to spend time in there. When they were working, Jean and Liza would have to provide them with a packed lunch of some sort, but whilst they were here, they would get a cooked meal at midday.

'Excuse me, would you mind if I sat on the terrace? Percy's

happy to lie on his bed reading the newspaper, but I need some fresh air.' The handsome sergeant had strolled casually up beside Joanna. Her cheeks coloured and she wished they hadn't.

'Good morning. I'm glad to see you up and about and looking so much better. Yes, of course you can sit wherever you like. You must treat Goodwill House as your own home whilst you're here.'

John smiled and his eyes crinkled at the corners. She'd never met anybody with different coloured eyes before and she knew she was staring.

'I know, one green and one brown's a bit odd. No one else in my family looks like me and I'm pretty sure most of the neighbours think my mum had an affair and I'm the result.'

Joanna wasn't used to such plain speaking and was a bit flustered. 'It's none of my business, of course, and I apologise for...' She couldn't think what she could apologise for, so she stammered to a halt.

'I'm used to people staring at me. I honestly don't mind. What are the land girls like?'

She was relieved that he'd changed the subject. 'They seem a pleasant enough bunch, a lot noisier than the girls we had before. I expect you could hear them enjoying themselves in the ballroom, as your bedroom's directly above it.'

'One of the reasons I came down. We don't need waiting on, Joanna, I'm quite capable of fetching our food from the kitchen.'

His use of her first name was a shock. He was looking at her speculatively, waiting to see her reaction, and instead of expressing displeasure at his lack of respect, she smiled.

'I've no intention of calling you Sergeant Sergeant, so in future I'll call you John. If you go through the drawing room, the French doors are open and there are chairs and so on out there.'

He nodded, his expression warm. 'Thank you. I think, with a few more coats of beeswax polish, your parquet floors will hardly show the water damage. The plaster's going to take a lot longer to dry and you might well need to have it replaced eventually.'

Talking about mundane things like polish and plaster gave her time to recover. He was a most disturbing young man and if just chatting to him about domestic issues made her unsettled, she must make very sure the conversation never turned to anything personal.

* * *

John thought he'd hidden his elation well. He'd deliberately used Joanna's name to see her reaction and it had been more than he'd dared hope. Instead of snapping at him for his impertinence, she'd used his in return.

He wasn't a womaniser by any means but had always been successful with the ladies. He was certain she reciprocated his interest – why, otherwise, would she have invited him to stay under her roof if it wasn't to initiate an affair? He'd been somewhat mystified by having been put in the same room as Percy, when there were at least four other empty bedrooms on that corridor, as this was a contradiction.

When he stepped onto the sun-drenched terrace, he almost retreated, as the old lady was out there. Unfortunately, she saw him and beckoned him over.

'Join me, young man, I'm becoming bored with my own company. All there is in the newspaper nowadays is talk of the war, rationing, deprivation, and disaster. I really don't wish to read about such things on a daily basis. Why can't they write about something jolly for a change?'

He hid his smile as he crossed the terrace but didn't take the adjacent chair. He wasn't going to push his luck by sitting next to her. 'Good morning, my lady, I hope it finds you well.'

'Better than you, which is a bonus at my age. You and your man are the second lot of RAF personnel we've taken care of. It seems to be a hobby of my daughter-in-law's. Don't loiter there, sit down and talk to me.'

He did as she suggested. 'I'm afraid I don't have anything jolly to talk about. I can tell you about how my men and I nearly suffocated, how two of them died...'

'I certainly don't want to hear that,' Elizabeth said 'What do you think of Goodwill House? As I observe that you're not an officer, but are very well spoken and obviously well educated, am I to presume that it's your choice to remain un-commissioned?'

He wasn't sure which question to answer first but decided it might be better to take them in order. 'I think Goodwill House is magnificent and will be even more so when the hideous Victorian wing is demolished. I think the grounds must have been splendid before they were ploughed up. I am a socialist and have no wish to be an officer.'

'I don't see that being socialist in your political views should prevent you from becoming an officer. Where did you go to university?'

'Oxford.'

She nodded and pursed her lips. God – what was coming next?

'Scholarship boy? I detect a slight flaw in your otherwise excellent diction. That would explain your political views.'

To his surprise, he was enjoying this extraordinary conversation. 'Exactly so, my lady. I'm a working-class lad with brains. Not always a good combination.'

'Are you well enough to fetch us tea? I believe there actually might be biscuits this morning.'

Now he laughed out loud. 'I certainly am. Would you not have asked me if I was an officer?'

Now she laughed herself. 'I asked you because you're young and I'm old. I might be going doolally, young man, but I'm not prejudiced against people of your class.'

He stood up, holding the edge of the table briefly to make sure he wasn't dizzy. Sudden movements still made his head spin.

'I'm so sorry, Sergeant, I'd no idea you were still so unwell. Please forget the tea – I'm sure my daughter-in-law will bring it out eventually.'

'It will be my absolute pleasure, ma'am, to find us both some tea and biscuits. I'm quite capable of carrying a tray without falling flat on my face.'

John found the kitchen with no difficulty, knocked on the door, then, receiving no response, he pushed it open. A middle-aged woman with grey hair spotted him hovering.

'Sergeant, has Lady Harcourt sent you to find her morning tea?'

'She has, ma'am, and has invited me to drink it with her.'

'Don't call me ma'am. I'm Jean, or Miss Baxter if you're uncomfortable using my first name. Joe has just taken tea through to the girls in the ballroom. There's no need for you to wait, Sergeant, he'll bring yours through next.'

'I'm John. Pleased to meet you, Jean.'

He hoped that Joanna would join them but rather thought she wouldn't. Probably better, as the sharp-eyed old lady might well spot the growing chemistry between them.

When he returned to the terrace, the older Lady Harcourt was on her feet. She pointed dramatically towards the hedge that bordered the remaining flower garden.

'We no longer intend to skulk in the cellar if there is an air raid. There's a summerhouse, you can't see it because of the foliage, at the end of the hedge, and we all think it's perfectly safe there.'

He wasn't quite sure what this had to do with him but smiled politely. 'As long as you don't go down there in the dark, because that would break the blackout regulations, I don't see why not.'

'Do you have a watch, young man?' He nodded and slipped back the cuff of his uniform jacket so she could see it. 'Then I wish to demonstrate to you that I'm perfectly capable of getting to the summerhouse before any sharp-eyed German can drop a bomb on us.'

She held out her arm for him to take and he had no option but to comply. They set off at a brisk walk in the shadow of the hedge. She moved remarkably gracefully for a lady of her age and didn't really need to hold onto his arm for support.

They emerged at the summerhouse and he was unsurprised to find it fully equipped. There was a Primus, cups and saucers, cushions, blankets, books, board games and two stone jugs with stoppers, which presumably contained water.

'Check the time, young man. How long did it take us to get here?'

'Five minutes exactly, ma'am. I think you'd all be safely inside long before the air raid siren stopped howling.'

She beamed. 'Excellent. My daughter-in-law is still not convinced that I can get there quickly enough, and you've just disproved her theory.'

They returned by a more direct route down the central path that divided the rose gardens and flower borders and, as they walked up the central steps to the terrace, the boy came out with a tray.

'I can do it in five minutes, Joe,' the old lady said triumphantly.

'That's good, Grandma, I never doubted it for a moment.' He nodded at John. 'When you've finished your tea, sir, I'll show you how to get down to the cellar if there is an air raid at night, as that's where we'll be going.'

John rather thought he was going to enjoy living at Goodwill House, despite the fact that on principle he disapproved of stately homes and aristocrats. The Harcourts weren't as he'd imagined they would be and were just like an ordinary family – albeit one living in a huge house and with more wealth than most.

8

On the bus, Sal was sitting next to the young Miss Harcourt, who seemed a bit shy and didn't make any effort to talk to her. This suited Sal, as she'd got things on her mind. Then it occurred to Sal that the girl could probably answer her most pressing question.

'Miss Harcourt, I've not seen any oast houses. Do the hop pickers come into the village in September?'

'I don't know. Oh, please don't call me Miss Harcourt, I'm just Liza. What's your name, if you don't mind me knowing?'

'Sal, ta for asking. I'd have thought that living so close to Stodham, you'd notice if a lot of folk like me turned up.'

'I'm sure I would, but my brother and I only arrived in Stodham at the beginning of the year,' Liza said. 'We came from the East End and Ma adopted us last month.'

The penny dropped. Sal had wondered why the twins didn't look nothing like their ma nor any of the brown pictures of dead relatives hanging on the walls. A slight quiver of fear ran through her as she wondered if they might come from Poplar too. Then she relaxed. They were too young to know about Den and her.

'It's ever so pretty round here. I hope I'm working in them fields over there, that one's full of red flowers.'

'They're poppies, Sal, and unless you're going to be doing dairy work, I shouldn't think you'll be in that one. All the farms around here belong to the Harcourt estate, which is why the Land Army was so keen to billet you with us.'

'I don't like cows, I ain't any good with them. I reckon I'm best with things what don't bite, kick nor run off.'

Liza giggled. 'Three miles in the other direction there are a couple of market gardens and I know some of you will be working there. Can you ride a bicycle?'

'Blimey, why would I be able to do that? Don't need no bicycle in London. Plenty of buses and the Underground if Shanks's pony ain't no good.'

'Then you'd better hope that wherever you're working, you can go in the cart pulled by Star. Charlie's good with horses, isn't she?'

'Ever so good, and I take back what I said earlier. I do like them big Shire horses, as long as they don't tread on your blooming feet. Feet as big as dinner plates they've got.'

'I've never seen one.'

'A dinner plate?'

Liza giggled again. 'No, silly, a carthorse. I *can* ride a bike and I'll ask my ma if I can visit if you're working on the farm that still uses horses. I think there's only one, as all the others have now got tractors.'

'I'd like to try – to ride a bike, that is – you reckon you could learn me when we get back?'

Daphne and Charlie were sitting behind them on the bus and overheard her question.

'I can't ride one either,' Daphne said cheerfully. 'Perhaps we could both have a go later? It's so much quicker than walking everywhere. In London, we caught a bus or the Underground or walked.'

'Some of the bikes aren't that good, my brother cobbled them together from bits he found in the barns. They work all right, though, but I wouldn't rely on the brakes on a steep hill.'

* * *

The village had loads of shops considering how small it was. There was even a café as well as three pubs and a village hall, where they had a bit of a knees-up once a month.

Everywhere they went, they were greeted with smiles and words of encouragement. They'd been warned that not all farmers were eager to have land girls working for them, but they'd fallen on their feet here, as their landlady owned all the places they'd be working on.

They had a wander around the place, but Sal didn't buy anything as she was skint. They returned in time for lunch, which was smashing. Bubble and squeak and fried eggs – now that was just the ticket.

Charlie retreated to their bedroom to write letters.

'Come on, Daphne, shall we give this bike riding lark a go? Joe says he'll learn us.'

'Right, let's see if we can master a bike. I can now drive a tractor, so this should be easy.'

'I never got a go on one of them tractors, but I can drive cart horses,' Sal said.

'Then we'll have no problems at all.'

Joe had two smart bikes waiting for them. 'Ma said you can learn on these. She doesn't want you on the old ones until you're confident. I might need to adjust the saddles to fit you.'

Sal was the same height as Daphne, about average, and

neither of the bikes needed changing. 'You go first, Daphne, I'll see how you get on before I have my turn.'

'I'll ride down the drive and you watch what I do. It's just a question of balance, really. Apart from the fact that you have to steer and pedal at the same time,' Joe said.

Joe had a man's bike – a woman's bike didn't have a crossbar like his – and swung his leg over the saddle in one smooth movement and was then cycling away, making it look ever so easy.

'I reckon I can do that. Don't look that difficult, do it?' Sal balanced on one leg. 'See, I don't fall over when I do this so I should be all right on a bicycle.'

'I'm not sure it works like that, but let's hope you're right,' Daphne said. 'He's coming back now. I don't think I'm going to try until he's here to hold me up.'

'Blimey, he's only a lad. He'll not be able to hold either of us upright. We need a big bloke to do that.'

Joe dismounted and propped his cycle against the wall. 'Don't look so worried. Neither my sister nor I could ride a bike when we came here, and it only took us half an hour to get the hang of it. We only fell off a couple of times.'

Sal laughed. 'That's all right then. I reckon if you and Liza did it easy like, then that's good enough for me.'

Daphne seemed to be having second thoughts. 'Then you have the first try. I'll cheer you on from the sidelines.'

Getting on wasn't too hard and once she was perched on the saddle, she could still put most of her feet on the ground. This made her feel safer.

'I'm going to hang on the back of the saddle and balance you. When I say go, start pedalling and remember to keep the handlebars straight.'

Sal's heart was thumping. She wasn't sure she could do this, but the twins came from the East End like what she did, and had mastered it easily, so it couldn't be that hard.

Joe pushed and she pedalled. At first, she was wobbly, but then she got the hang of it and started to press harder on the pedals.

'Not so fast, I can't keep up,' Joe yelled from behind.

She ignored his warning, loving the feeling of speed, and was sailing down the drive at a cracking pace. Only then did she realise she'd not asked about how to stop. She was heading for the end of the drive and there could be a bus or a car coming and she'd go straight out in front of it.

Even though she wasn't pedalling, she wasn't getting any slower. If she turned the handlebars a bit, maybe she could steer it away from the road. This was the first time she'd attempted to direct the bike and she pulled hard with her left hand. The front wheel turned sharply and she veered off the drive and straight into the spud field.

The fall knocked the wind from her, but she wasn't hurt, just a bit bruised and covered in dirt. At least the spuds had made a soft landing. She was lying there like a beached whale, gasping for breath, when Joe arrived at her side.

'That was spectacular, Sal, but you did the right thing. Next time, don't go so fast and apply the brakes when you want to stop. Going headfirst into a field isn't ideal.'

He was trying not to laugh and she didn't blame him. She was still clutching the handlebars of the bike and he leaned down and unpeeled her fingers.

'Let go, Sal, and I'll take this. Then Daphne will see if she can get you on your feet and give you a brush down.'

Her friend arrived, openly laughing. 'Joe said he fell off twice, so you've only got one more to do. Here, give me your hand, you can't lie about there all afternoon.'

* * *

Joanna wanted to eat her meals away from John but decided that might draw attention to the attraction between them, which was the last thing she wanted. He'd eaten outside on the terrace with Elizabeth, so that was luncheon solved. Meals were still being taken upstairs by the other RAF visitor and she thought things would be easier if he joined them as well.

Perhaps, if she spoke to the corporal, she could persuade him to come down tonight. If she emphasised the fact that they didn't have any live-in staff apart from the housekeeper, he'd not want to put them to more trouble than was necessary.

The door to the bedroom was open and she called out as she approached. 'Corporal, it's Lady Harcourt, could I possibly have a few words with you?'

To her surprise, he appeared fully clothed in the doorway. 'I was just coming down, my lady, and wanted to bring the tray with me but I find I can't carry anything comfortably.'

'Of course you can't. I'm sure it'll be easier when the stitches come out. Dr Willoughby said he was going to do that next week sometime.'

'I'm feeling much better today and thought I'd venture out onto the terrace with Sarge. I don't know who he's talking to, but they've been laughing non-stop, and I could do with cheering up.'

'Good heavens, he's out there with my mother-in-law, the older Lady Harcourt. She's not famous for having a sense of humour but I'm delighted to be proved wrong. I'll bring your tray...'

She smiled at his horrified expression. 'I might be Lady Harcourt, but I'm quite capable of carrying a tray. I'll have after-noon tea served on the terrace for everyone.'

There were full-length windows on either side of the front

door, and from the gallery it was possible to see the drive. She almost dropped the tray over the balustrade as she watched one of the land girls fall off a bicycle into the potato field.

'Oh dear, I do hope Sal hasn't been hurt by her crash.'

'She's on her feet, I reckon she's fine,' the corporal said. 'Funniest thing I've seen for a long time.'

'As she's obviously unharmed, let's hope the bicycle is too. Finding spare parts for cycles is all but impossible now.'

'Factories are making stuff for the war and civilians just have to make do and mend.'

'Good heavens, Corporal, I wouldn't have expected you to read the propaganda posters.' She smiled. 'The Government is aiming them at women and especially the ones about sewing and so on.'

They were now on their way downstairs and he chuckled. 'I like that one. The posters trying to recruit girls for the services make it look glamorous. I can tell you that the WAAF on the base have worse billets than we do. I don't envy them, living in those Nissen huts when the winter comes.'

'We had some girls here before they moved onto the base. I'm hoping the land girls will be a permanent fixture.'

'It's good of you to open your house to all and sundry, my lady, not many grand folks would do the same.'

'I feel a strong connection to Manston, it being so close to us. Also, my future son-in-law is a flight lieutenant at Hornchurch, flying Spitfires.'

'Poor bugger, we call the Brylcreem boys *dead men walking*.'

For a second time, the tray wobbled dangerously. He just strolled away as if he'd not said anything untoward at all. What an absolutely beastly thing to say about pilots. Was their life expectancy so very short? Small wonder they spent all their free time drinking or chasing young women.

The thought that Angus – her daughter Sarah's fiancé – could die at any moment was quite ghastly. Millie, a WAAF who'd billeted with them at Goodwill House, had married a fighter pilot called Ted, and Di, another WAAF, was now engaged, or possibly married, to a pilot called Freddie. Both of these young men she now considered friends of hers.

She'd no intention of going out to the terrace and was glad she could legitimately spend time in the study completing the pile of paperwork associated with registering the twelve new residents of Goodwill House. There were also the household accounts to bring up to date, wages to see to and some correspondence to deal with.

Liza brought her in some very welcome tea later that afternoon. 'That's the best fun I've had in ages, Ma. Sal and Daphne can now ride a bike, but they both fell off a few times before they got the hang of it.'

'I saw Sal go headfirst into the potatoes. I've got the list showing where the girls are going to be working from Monday. Would you be a darling and pin it up on the notice board that Joe put in the hall?'

'Sal doesn't like cows, so I hope she's not been sent where Bert Smith used to be.'

'No – Charlie, Daphne and Sal are going to Fiddler's Farm. It's mostly arable, they just keep a few pigs, a few cows and poultry for their own use. Syd Pickering is the only one of my tenants still using horses and all three of them enjoy working with them.'

'They can use the pony cart so won't even need to ride a bike.' Liza scanned the list. She was now a fluent reader. Her tutor, a retired schoolmaster, was delighted with the progress the twins had made with their education. When they'd come to Goodwill House, neither of them could read or write well and spoke poorly, but now one might believe they'd been born into the Harcourt family.

'There's three going to the market garden – isn't that the one owned by Mrs T's son-in-law? That's near enough to walk. That means there's enough bicycles if they use mine and yours for the others to get to work, Ma.'

'I prefer to catch the bus into the village or to Ramsgate, so I don't use mine very much. You and Jean can share the other one and then Joe has his own.'

'All the girls are coming to church tomorrow. There aren't any buses, so they'll have to walk the two miles. Good thing it's not going to rain.'

The house shook as fighters screamed overhead on their way to do battle somewhere in the Channel. Both Joanna and Liza were silent for a few moments, braced for the howl of the siren from Manston and the village. The sirens remained silent.

'Thank goodness for that. I don't think the Nazis are coming here today,' Liza said as she went in search of more interesting company.

When Joanna's husband, David, had been alive, they'd always changed their clothes for dinner. Thank goodness that archaic custom had been abandoned. Joanna did, however, pop upstairs to tidy her hair, wash her face and replenish her lipstick.

One always needed to look one's best in company. Her heart skipped a beat when she considered in whose company she would be at dinner tonight.

* * *

John had enjoyed his afternoon with the old lady. She was intelligent and had led an interesting life. Her politics were far away from his own, but she wisely kept her views to herself. Percy treated her like anybody else, no deference, and they got along just fine.

'We dine at seven o'clock, so you'd better get yourselves spruced up.'

He offered his arm to help her out of her chair but she shook her head. 'I'm quite capable of standing up without your assistance, Sergeant. We usually have wine with our dinner – are you familiar with this beverage?'

'I am, ma'am, but prefer beer. After all, I'm a working-class lad, so what would I know about such highfalutin drinks?'

She was laughing as she walked away.

'I don't know what she expects us to do. Spruced up? I've shaved, cleaned my teeth, but these are the only clothes I possess as my spare shirts and so on are still at the base,' John said to Percy.

'Give the mess a bell. They can get one of the drivers to bring our stuff over here.'

'I should have done it yesterday. I suppose I'd better ask permission to use the telephone.' This gave him an excuse to go in search of Joanna, who was quite obviously avoiding him.

He didn't have far to look as she was coming down the staircase as he walked out of the drawing room. 'Joanna, I need to call the base. Can I use the telephone?'

'Of course, you don't need to ask. I expect both of you need your kit brought here.'

He grinned. 'Got it in one. We don't even have a clean pair of socks between us.'

She was as jumpy as a kitten and dashed off without replying to his comment. He knew the number and was connected after a lot of whirring and clicking. He arranged for an orderly to pack their bags and the NCO he'd spoken to said they would be brought down first thing in the morning.

Did they bang on the gong when it was time to go through to the dining room? He didn't have long to wait before he found out. Joe thundered down the stairs and poked his head into the drawing room.

'It's seven o'clock and Grandma doesn't like to be kept waiting. Follow me, I don't suppose you know exactly where to go.'

The boy meant well, so John didn't point out he wasn't a blithering idiot and was quite capable of finding his own way around the house, especially as he'd seen most of the ground floor when fighting the fire a few weeks ago.

A reasonably sized room was being used for dinner. The table, which would still seat a dozen at least, had been spruced up, even if he and Percy hadn't. The officers had the same sort of setup – crisp white tablecloths, matching napkins (he'd learned the hard way not to call them serviettes) and a ridiculous amount of solid silver cutlery. There were also three glasses for each person. Ostentatious nonsense, in his opinion, and the food would have to be spectacular to match this table.

Joanna and her mother-in-law were already seated, one at each end of the table. The old lady gestured imperiously to her right. 'Those are your seats, gentlemen. The children and Jean sit opposite.'

He nodded politely to both of them before taking his place. Percy seemed to be struck dumb by all the splendour and John guessed his corporal was probably panicking about which piece of cutlery he should be using for which dish.

'I'd offer to help but am not well enough to do so at the moment.'

'You are my guests, Sergeant, and therefore are exempt from domestic duties. My children, however, are not.' Joanna actually smiled at him before continuing. 'Don't look so horrified. We have staff here during the day and there's always one of them on duty to help with dinner. Joe and Liza just act as waiters.'

There was a rattle of a trolley approaching and the house-keeper wheeled it in. The food was already plated and the twins handed the plates round.

There was a jug of water on the table, a bottle of white wine and a bottle of red. Joanna saw him looking.

'I wasn't sure which you'd prefer, if any. I gather from my mother-in-law that you prefer beer – Joe will try to buy some bottles of light ale when he goes into the village next.'

'We're uninvited guests and don't expect preferential treatment,' said John. 'I'm still a bit lightheaded so will be happy with water, as will my corporal.'

Percy got the message and looked relieved to have the decision taken from his hands. John wasn't exactly sure what he'd been presented with, but it smelled appetising enough.

'It's hare, in case you're wondering. Joe's an expert shot now and keeps the larder stocked with rabbits, pheasants and the occasional hare. As we also have chickens, ducks and geese, we don't go short of meat here, despite rationing.'

This was obviously the main course – meat wouldn't be served first – so he wondered why they'd got three sets of knives and forks.

Lady Harcourt must've seen him looking at the cutlery. 'I'm afraid we've got rather more than we need tonight, young man, as you've noticed. The ladies from the village have been taught to lay up this way regardless of what might be served. We often have an hors d'oeuvre or soup first, then a fish course, an entrée and dessert.'

Joanna shook her head. 'Elizabeth, I can't remember the last time we had four courses. I doubt we'll do so again until the war's over. I can assure you, Sergeant, that there's no extravagant eating here.'

He couldn't stop himself. 'If that's the case, why not tell the women who lay up for you to just put out what's needed?'

There was an awkward silence and John knew he'd put his foot in it but just kept his eyes on his food and carried on eating.

9

Joanna frowned. It wasn't a guest's place to criticise how things were done, but he had a point. 'It is a lot of unnecessary work and the three women who work here have more than enough to do. I'll get Jean to show them what to do in future.'

'I apologise, ma'am, how you run your household is none of my business.'

He must have sensed that she was cross with him, and she wasn't used to a man being so aware of her feelings. She smiled more warmly than she'd intended and something she didn't recognise flashed in his eyes.

He was waiting and she realised he thought they might say grace before they started. Immediately she picked up her cutlery and began to eat and he did the same. There was just the sound of people eating for a few minutes and then his corporal broke the silence.

'I've never had hare, I've had rabbit often enough, but this tastes nothing like it.'

'Are you enjoying it, Corporal?'

'I am, my lady, best dinner I've ever had.'

Jean beamed. 'I'm glad you like it, it's a strong taste and not to everybody's palate.'

John nodded. 'It's delicious. Did you put redcurrant jelly in the gravy?'

'Imagine you recognising that – I'm impressed. Fresh redcurrants from the garden this morning. We're almost self-sufficient here.'

The conversation moved on to the new arrangements for air raids. Elizabeth looked at John expectantly. He grinned at her.

'I think the summerhouse an acceptable alternative to your cellar. You're probably even safer there than you would be downstairs.'

'There, Joanna, didn't I tell you my suggestion is perfectly safe for all of us and certainly more pleasant?'

'You certainly did, Elizabeth, and I fear that we're going to have to spend a great deal of time there in the not-too-distant future. Manston is busier than ever with a constant stream of aircraft in and out all day.'

'They also fly at night now, Ma,' Liza said. 'Seems daft to me to be tearing through the sky when you can't see where you're going.'

John smiled warmly at the girl. 'They don't need to see, Miss Harcourt, they fly with instruments to guide them. They also have somebody on the radio giving them directions.'

Joe was listening attentively and asked several intelligent questions during the course of the meal.

'By the way, gentlemen, if you wish to smoke, you must do it outside. I don't like the smell of cigarettes,' Joanna said.

'We'll go for a stroll, shall we, Percy? I'll come with you in case you get lost.' He looked directly at Joanna. 'I don't smoke. I inhale more than enough of that with my job and don't want to put any more into my body.'

John and his corporal thanked Jean for the meal and wandered off in the direction of the terrace, chatting happily to each other. The twins had homework to complete for the next morning, so they excused themselves too.

'I'm going to retire, my dear, all the fresh air today has quite worn me out. No, I can manage quite well on my own.' Elizabeth had no difficulty ascending the stairs; it was coming down that she needed help.

'I'll come up in an hour. If you're still awake and need anything, I can fetch it for you then. Good night, Elizabeth.'

Her mother-in-law nodded vaguely and drifted off in a cloud of navy-blue chiffon and silk, leaving just her and Jean at the table.

'I'll help you clear, Jean, as Aggie will have gone home by now. Shall we wash up tonight or do it first thing?'

'I'll put it in the sink in the scullery to soak and whoever's working the early shift can do it as soon as they get in. There's no need for you to do anything, Joanna, I'm the housekeeper and it's my job.'

'Then I'll take Lazzy for a walk. For once, it's a quiet, perfect summer's evening.'

The path that led to the perimeter fence of the base that the WAAF girls had used for a while to get to Manston would be an ideal route. Angus, engaged to her daughter, had put in a gate for the girls to use whilst he'd briefly been CO there. This route was only half a mile, whereas going by road was over two.

Joe kept the path free of nettles as he knew that she enjoyed this particular walk. There were nightingales in the woods, but they didn't sing so late in the year. It was dusk when she decided to turn back, and she wished she'd brought her torch with her as it was much darker under the overhanging branches.

Suddenly Lazzy raced off, leaving her stranded. She'd been

walking with her hand on his collar as she was confident he wouldn't lead her astray. How was she going to find her way back without her torch and without falling headfirst into a patch of nettles?

She was dithering, deciding whether to call Lazzy back or move forward without his support, when she heard John talking to the dog somewhere along the path. Now she had a real dilemma – did she really want to meet him in such a secluded spot when there was already a tug of attraction between them?

* * *

Sal crept out of bed on Monday morning at dawn, intending to get dressed in the bathroom and not wake the other two. She'd heard the three working at the dairy farm cycle off half an hour ago. Another reason she didn't want to be anywhere near cows if it meant starting work at four in the morning.

'It's all right, Sal, we're both awake too. You can pull back the blackouts and then we can all get up.'

'Charlie, it ain't fair that those three have to start so early and don't get no breakfast neither.'

'They'll be finished by eleven and can then come back and eat a leisurely lunch. They don't have to be back on duty until four o'clock. They actually work fewer hours than we do.'

'Still, I'd rather do all the work in one go than be backwards and forwards like what they're going to be doing. Do we get breakfast before we go?'

'Yes, and a packed lunch to take with us. We get our main meal in the evening and are supposed to finish by six o'clock, but I expect we have to work until we've finished whatever we've been asked to do. Obviously, in the winter our working days will be much shorter.'

'If you go now, Sal, you should get the bathroom to yourself, as I can't hear anyone else moving about,' Daphne said as she yawned, stretched her arms but made no move to clamber out of bed.

'Right-o, I'm off. It's a smashing day, going to be a scorcher, so I'm going to wear me overalls and roll up the legs. It'll be cooler than breeches and long woolly socks.'

'I'll do the same,' Charlie said. 'I don't think Mr Pickering, the chap we'll be working for on Fiddler's Farm, will care what we wear as long as we do our work properly.'

By the time Sal finished in the bathroom, she could hear voices coming from the other rooms. Daphne was waiting outside and nipped in quick before anyone else could take her place.

Sal was stumped as to what to put on her feet. Charlie solved that problem for her.

'One of the instructors told me that it's possible to roll down the gumboots and the socks so that our legs can get the sun. I expect we'll be mucking out stables, cowsheds and pigsties so would have to wear our boots anyway.'

'What would the lady in charge say if she saw what we're doing with our new uniform? I don't want a black mark and to get sent packing.'

'I think if we travel to work in our jodhs, socks and shoes and change when we get there, I don't see that she'd make a fuss,' Charlie said. 'We won't be letting the side down in public, and that's all that matters to those sorts of people.'

'I stuffed newspaper into my boots and put them in the sun by the window and they're nice and dry and don't pong too bad.'

'Jolly good. I'll wait for Daphne; you go down and see if you can give a hand with setting up the table and so on.'

Sal didn't like to say that she'd be useless at table laying but was prepared to give it a go. Charlie was getting on her nerves a bit, bossing her about as if she was a skivvy, but she didn't want to upset her new friend, so wasn't going to rock any boats. She'd keep her head down and her mouth shut.

She poked her head around the kitchen door and saw Jean was there with another lady that she didn't know. 'I'm the first down, can I give you a hand with anything?'

'No, all tickety-boo in here, but thank you for offering. You could ask the others to be down here in five minutes. Porridge isn't very pleasant if it's overcooked.'

Sal thought porridge wasn't pleasant at any stage. She'd settle for a couple of bits of toast and give the porridge a miss. In her opinion, it was a slippery, lumpy mess which tasted horrible.

There was no need for her to go in search of her friends, as everybody was coming down. They were being ever so polite, not clumping about or talking loudly in case they woke up the family.

She walked into the dining room and saw that a bowl of steaming porridge had been put in every place. She prayed she could give it to somebody else, as good food was hard to come by and shouldn't be wasted.

Jean pointed to a bowl of sugar and a jug in the centre of the table. 'I know that looks like a lot, but could I ask you to limit yourselves to just one spoonful of sugar? The cream has got to do for all of you.'

This was a new one on her – sugar and cream on porridge? Sal sprinkled sugar on the top, added a dollop of cream and then took a tentative spoonful.

'Blimey, this is a bit of all right. Don't taste nothing like the porridge I've had at home. Blooming lovely, that's what it is.'

The housekeeper overheard her compliment. 'Here it's made with milk and served with sugar and cream, or sometimes with jam instead. I'm glad you like it, as you're going to get it most mornings.'

The other lady brought in three racks stuffed full of lovely hot toast. It was a choice of butter and jam or dripping and salt. This was right down Sal's street. It reminded her of a time when she'd been living at home and bread and dripping had been a real treat.

Although they didn't have to, they cleared their plates and put them on the trolley. Charlie had left a few minutes ago to see to harnessing the horse that was going to pull the cart. The market garden team had the bicycles and the rest of them were going to squeeze into the cart somehow.

The horse was grey, like a big rocking horse, and ever so sweet natured. The cart had seen better days but was big enough for them all to cram into.

'Hang on, girls, I don't want to lose any of you on the way.' Charlie snapped the whip above Star's ears and they were off. They travelled down a country road at a spanking trot and the cart rocked to a halt at the end of the drive that led to the farm where three of the other girls were working.

'If we don't turn up at six o'clock, then you can either walk back to Goodwill House or walk up to the farm and wait for us,' Charlie told them.

'That's all very well, but what if you finish first?' one of the girls asked.

'I'm not taking the cart up that narrow track, so if you're not there, I'm afraid you'll definitely have to make your own way back.'

Then she snapped the whip and they trundled off, leaving three very grumpy girls behind. Maybe Sal should say something to Charlie about being so bossy? When they arrived at the farm, it was five minutes to seven, perfect timing. However, the bloke who must be the farmer, or maybe the foreman, didn't agree.

'What time do you call this? By the time you've got that mare put away, you'll be late. Get here earlier tomorrow.'

Even Charlie didn't argue. This wasn't going to be the pleasant experience they'd all hoped for.

'I'll put Star away,' Charlie whispered as they clambered out of the cart. 'Do what you can to smooth things over.'

'Sorry, Mr Pickering, we thought we had to be here at seven o'clock. We'll be earlier tomorrow,' Daphne said hastily.

'See that you are. Now, you've got three cows, half a dozen pigs and dozens of chickens to see to first. You won't need me to show you how to do it as I'm told that you're all fully trained and experienced. Get the livestock fed, watered and cleaned out by nine o'clock.'

He stomped off and Sal looked at Daphne. 'I ain't doing no cows, I'll leave that to you and Charlie. I'll do the pigs.'

There was no need to ask where the porkers were housed as she could hear them snorting and crashing about in their sty. She didn't care if the miserable old git moaned but she was going to change into her dungarees and gumboots before she fed them. She wasn't going to get pig muck on her smart new uniform.

She found the pig swill and added some extra carrots in the hope it might improve the look of the stuff. It smelt rank – maybe she should boil it up before she served it to them?

The food they'd fed to pigs at the college had been pre-cooked and didn't look anything like this. She looked around but couldn't see anywhere to cook the disgusting swill so had no alternative but to give it to the pigs, who were going mad. They could hear her on the other side of the wall to their sty.

'All right, you noisy porkers, I'm coming.'

Sal dipped two buckets into the barrel and carried it through to the pigs. She almost choked at the stench. She reckoned they'd not been cleaned out for days. She tipped the food into the troughs and they were snout first, gobbling it up in seconds. Maybe they'd not been fed recently either.

She returned twice more with full buckets and gave them that as well. There were six of them and she thought they needed at least one bucketful each just to be going on with. She thought that Charlie had said all the farms they were working on belonged to Lady Harcourt – she reckoned her ladyship would be disgusted at the state of these poor animals.

She didn't know anything about farm management but at one of the lectures she'd sat through at the college, the man had said that a big estate had a bloke in charge who kept an eye on everything. He wasn't doing a good job here, that was for sure. She hoped the cows and the chickens hadn't been as badly neglected as the pigs.

It wouldn't be a good idea to go in until the pigs were fed and feeling better. Somebody had told her that if pigs were hungry enough, then they'd eat anyone who went into their sty. She hoped that wasn't true.

There was a decent field outside the pigsty. She checked carefully and it was properly fenced, no holes anywhere, and she reckoned she could open the gate and herd them into the field while she mucked out.

There was no water where they were living, and she couldn't even see somewhere to put it. Then she had a brainwave – if she put three buckets of water in the field, they might well be so thirsty they'd charge through the gate without her having to do anything to encourage them.

This proved to be the case and, confident the pigs would be happier in the field than in their stinking sty, she set about improving their living conditions. She was on her tenth wheelbarrow full of muck when Daphne and Charlie came out of the cowshed to join her.

'How could anybody leave animals in the state that these were in?' Charlie said, shaking her head. 'The cows needed a good wash, but they've been milked regularly and as they live out, they've not got in such a state.'

'Did you have to fetch them from the field?' Sal asked as she tottered past them to the massive pile of manure on the far side of the yard.

'They were standing at the gate waiting to be let in. It didn't take long to milk them, but we've spent the last two hours cleaning the dairy and the cowshed. It's almost eleven o'clock. I'm surprised that man hasn't been out to complain that we've not finished.'

'I reckon he knows what a dreadful state everything's in and is happy to let us get on with it. The chickens are obviously out because I've seen them wandering about the yard, but I expect they need feeding and the eggs collecting and so on,' Daphne said and Charlie nodded.

'There's straw in the barn over there for you to put down when you've finished cleaning. Then I think you'll want to get cleaned up before we find somewhere to eat our lunch,' Charlie told her.

The pigs were happily rootling around in the field. By the time she'd made their indoor living quarters ready for them, she was smelly and tired. They'd knocked the buckets over in the field, so she refilled them from the pump in the yard and put them back.

'There you are, I'll give you something else to eat later.' She wasn't sure if she should leave the gate to the sty open so they could go back. Better leave it closed, she didn't want to clean it out again today. It would be lovely and fresh for them when she put them back before she went home tonight.

10

John sent Percy back after he'd finished smoking a Woodbine. 'Don't overdo it, Percy, this is the first time you've been out for a walk since you were injured last week.'

'I don't feel too clever, so I'll do as you suggest, Sarge. You don't need to come back with me, finish your walk.'

'I'll do that. It's far too fine a night to be indoors. I'll try not to wake you when I come in.'

They'd been strolling around the flower garden, but he decided to venture further, as his head had cleared and he was no longer dizzy. He checked he had his torch in his pocket, as it would get dark when the sun set. Even with double summertime, it was still dark by ten thirty.

He wandered through the courtyard at the back of the house and realised he was now facing Manston. There seemed to be some sort of path leading in that direction, so he took it. After walking for ten minutes, he heard something approaching at speed and for a second his heart pounded, then he smiled.

'Good evening, Lazzy, I didn't know you were out here too. Are you on your own or is someone walking with you?' Daft to be asking the dog questions, but the animal bounced around as if it understood him.

It was quiet under the trees, not even any noise from the base tonight. Blackbirds were singing, there was the rustle of small animals coming from the undergrowth, but he couldn't hear anybody walking towards him. The dog must be by himself.

'I'm going to walk the perimeter fence – are you coming with me or going back?'

He continued on and the dog dashed off ahead of him. The path curved and he saw a shadowy figure standing on the path ahead. He recognised who it was immediately. The faint hint of the perfume she wore had drifted towards him on the night air.

'Good evening, Joanna, I didn't expect to meet you out here.'

She was now stationary. It was so quiet, he could hear her catch her breath at his comment. 'I live here, John, so it's hardly unexpected to find me on my own land.'

'True, but to be honest, I didn't take you for a night-time wanderer. Are you on your way out or coming back?'

She still hadn't moved and he was reluctant to continue forwards. Having to pass so close to her, to be in a position to reach out and touch her, might be disastrous for both of them. He'd never felt so drawn to a woman before and wasn't sure he wanted to get involved in something that wouldn't be good for either of them.

Eventually she spoke, her voice soft, almost inaudible. 'I haven't quite decided what I'm doing. Have you?'

This question was innocent enough but they both knew this was a pivotal moment. He didn't answer and without consciously deciding, he was striding towards her. He stopped, and the urge to take her in his arms and kiss her was so strong his hands were shaking.

She remained where she was and that was answer enough.

'Are you quite sure, Joanna? I don't want to put you in a difficult position and we both know this is going to end in tears.'

'At this moment, I really don't care how it ends. I just want it to begin.'

He needed no further encouragement, but something told him not to rush things. Gently he gathered her close and just held her. She was trembling – but then so was he, but for a different reason. She was nervous, he was having difficulty controlling his desire. It had been too long since he'd had a woman in his life.

There was no need to speak. He ran one hand tenderly down her back and this time, she shuddered – the trembling had stopped – she was as eager as he to continue.

He cupped her cheek, loving the feel of her skin beneath his fingertips. Everything about her was perfect. Having her breasts crushed against his chest was making it almost impossible not to move things on too swiftly.

'You're the most beautiful, desirable woman I've ever met and completely out of my reach. And yet all I want to do is make love to you.'

Her hands slowly moved up his chest, causing ripples of pleasure that were rapidly becoming unbearable. If he kissed her, he didn't know if he had the willpower to stop and, however much he wanted to, he wasn't going to tumble her onto the path and make love to her here.

'I didn't love my husband, had no interest in him physically, but for some reason, you've ignited something in me. Something wild and totally out of character. I know we shouldn't do this, I know it can't go anywhere, but I just can't resist you.'

It took every ounce of his rapidly evaporating willpower to step away. 'I feel the same, but I'm not going to start something we might both regret until you've had time to consider the repercussions.'

'I knew you were a gentleman. Thank you for having the strength to say no. I'll return, you continue with your walk.'

She was several yards away, the dog at her side, when she spoke again. 'I will give the matter of our affair some thought. My mother-in-law recently told me that she has had several lovers and I don't see why, if she did it, then I can't do the same.'

Then she was gone, and he wasn't sure which of her revelations surprised him more. The idea that the old lady had not only had one affair but several or the fact that Joanna had more or less said she wanted to sleep with him.

What he needed was a long, cold shower. He couldn't return to the shared bedroom until his ardour cooled. He desperately wanted to be able to hold her naked in his arms, to kiss every inch of her and then for them to make passionate love. What he didn't want was to fall in love with her.

Wasn't it inevitable that their emotions would become involved if they slept together? Nothing permanent could come from this relationship and he had absolutely no intention of becoming involved with someone who already meant a lot to him and then leaving her broken hearted.

No – better for both of them to resist the temptation and not start anything at all. He would see the local quack tomorrow and get himself declared fit for duty, then he could return to base and need never see Joanna again.

* * *

When she'd finished with the pigs Sal washed at the yard pump and then went in search of her friends. They were sitting well away from the farmhouse under a shady tree. She didn't know what sort it was and at the moment didn't care.

'There you two are. I'm knackered.' She flopped down beside

them and then remembered she'd not fetched her sandwich from the cart. She was about to heave herself up again when Daphne stopped her.

'We've got your lunch. You've been ages, were the pigs very difficult to get into the field?'

'No, they wasn't no trouble. It were like I told you earlier, it's the state they were in. No one had cleaned them or fed them for days. I'm blooming fuming at that farmer.'

'He's not been out since we arrived at seven. I'm not budging from here for an hour,' Charlie said.

'Does he live here with anyone? A wife or any kiddies?'

'I feel sorry for them, Sal, if he has.' Daphne chucked over the greaseproof-wrapped sandwiches. 'Although I think the children around here have been evacuated. Maybe the wife went with them. That could be why Pickering's so miserable and not doing his job.'

'This farm's too much for one man to manage. If his wife looked after the livestock, then he'd be struggling. The late potatoes need to come up soon and I expect that's what we'll be doing.'

'Were the horses all right, Charlie?' Sal asked as she bit into a spam and pickle buttie.

'They were a bit unkempt, not been properly groomed for a week at least, but there was hay in the stables and plenty of clean water. Pickering hasn't ignored everything.'

'Now we're here, we'll get everything shipshape,' Daphne said.

They were halfway through their break when the farmer stomped round. 'You can get off your arses and get back to work. I don't pay you to sit around.'

Charlie smiled sweetly. 'This is our entitled lunch break. We'll be back to work at twelve thirty.'

The man went beetroot, stepped forward with clenched fists and for a moment Sal thought he was going to lash out at Charlie. Her friend was on her feet and faced him without flinching.

'If you attempt to assault me or either of my teammates, I'll report you to the police, Lady Harcourt, and the Land Army. Is that what you want?'

The nasty bit of work backed down and moved back. 'You'll be picking taters. I want the field done before you leave.' Then, head down, he left as suddenly as he'd arrived.

'Blimey, that was a turn-up for the books. Thought he were going to clock you one, Charlie.' Den wouldn't have backed off so easily and Sal was relieved that she hadn't had to intervene.

'Bullies usually back down when confronted,' Charlie said. 'I have to pop behind a bush, I'll be back in a tick. Let's hope we can harness the horses and find the correct equipment.'

The gentle Shire horses were no trouble and Sal soon got the hang of driving them up and down the spud field. The other two did the picking up at first, as she'd had such a hard job that morning.

The spuds were picked up from the turned soil, dropped in a bucket and when this was full, it was emptied into one of the three trailers. Backbreaking work, Sal turned over three rows and then left Maisie and Bill, the horses, to graze whilst she went to help her friends.

'We need a rest, two hours is enough without a break or a drink,' Charlie told them.

Sal stood up, groaning, and rubbed her aching back. Her dungarees were filthy and her boots were full of mud. 'Good job it ain't raining. It would be murder doing this in the wet.'

'It's murder at any time. I suppose we're not as fit as we should be. Will this get any easier, Charlie?' Daphne asked.

'It'll be less painful after a few weeks.' She pointed at the horses. 'I'm going to take them some water and hay whilst you finish picking this last row.'

'Last row? You've got to be joking. We've only done half the blooming field so far, and I heard the clock strike three a while ago. We're never going to be done by six. Don't forget we've the animals and that to see to as well.'

'The trailers full of potatoes will have to be taken back to the yard. They'll then be put into sacks, I expect, so they can be sold,' Charlie told them.

'We'll be here till blooming midnight if we have to do that as well. Ain't there rules about being exploited?'

'I shouldn't think so. When I was working for my uncle, we just kept going until the job was done – that's what it's like on a farm.'

'Then we'd better get on with it,' Daphne said with a sigh. 'I hope there'll still be enough hot water for a long soak tonight.'

'The girls working at the market gardens will be back first, but I don't know about the others. If you turn up a few more rows, Sal, I'll go and speak to Pickering. He's the tenant farmer so should be doing his fair share, too.' Charlie rushed off as if she hadn't been slaving in a spud field for hours.

'I don't understand why there's no workers on the farm. Farming's a protected job and the men working here don't get their call-up papers,' Daphne said.

'I reckon the blokes jumped at the chance to get away from this nasty bit of work. 'I would've stayed, mind you, as it might be hard but at least you ain't going to be killed.'

'I expect Charlie will discover everything. I wonder why she left the family farm. Do you think she'll tell us one day?'

'Doubt it, we all have secrets better kept that way.' Sal had no intention of telling anyone of her life with Den for the moment.

Maybe later she'd let them know how bad things had been for her.

Daphne nodded. 'I certainly do, and I might tell you when I get to know you better.'

The horses made no objection to working again. Sal was proud of how she was doing with them and reckoned she was a dab hand at this horse lark. The Shires were plodding down a third row by the time Charlie was back.

Daphne stood up and carried her full bucket to the nearest trailer and Charlie joined her. Sal would have to wait until she'd completed the row before she discovered the reason her friend had been gone for so long.

She pulled gently on the reins and called for the horses to stop. 'Good horses, fine fellows, you can have a breather for a bit.'

They couldn't run off attached to the spinner so would be all right for a few minutes. 'Here, Charlie, tell us what's going on.'

'Pickering has agreed to feed the animals if we finish the field. We can bag the potatoes tomorrow. We were right in our speculation. He had two labourers as well as himself and his wife running the farm, but the men joined up a few months ago and his wife and children are now living in Norfolk somewhere.'

'I almost feel sorry for the old misery. Did you go inside?'

'I didn't, that would have been presumptuous and possibly dangerous.'

'Dangerous? How?' Daphne asked.

'He was looking at me in a way I didn't like.'

Sal understood at once. 'You reckon he might try it on? He ain't a big bloke, I'd flatten him if he tried with me. Dirty old bugger.'

'Please don't use bad language, Sal, I don't like it.'

'None of your business how I speak. Are you picking or

driving?' Sal hadn't meant to snap at her, but she was tired, and fed up with being told what to do.

She didn't wait for a reaction from either of them. Daphne was all right, not stuck up and bossy like Charlie. Should she go back and apologise? No – the sooner this job was done, the sooner they could go home and get something to eat. A couple of sandwiches and a drink of water wasn't enough when you were working so hard.

When the field was done, she drove the team to the barn and unhitched the spinner. 'Sorry, we've got to bring the trailers back before you can stop for the night.'

She wasn't sure how to attach the horses to the trailer so would have to ask for help. 'Here, Charlie, I'll finish that row and you can take the trailers back.'

This was the first time she'd been the one to make any suggestions and she enjoyed not being on the receiving end of orders.

'Right, that makes sense, Sal. I'll take this trailer so you can still put your potatoes in the other one. It only needs one horse between the shafts, so I'll get Maisie ready and use Bill first.'

There seemed to be no bad feeling between her and the girls and this surprised Sal. Where she came from, people bore a grudge for months. She was smiling as she grovelled in the dirt, picking up the last of the spuds.

'There, we're done, Daphne. Just right as Charlie's coming back to collect the last trailer.' Sal ached all over but had a sense of satisfaction at a job well done. She tipped the very last bucket from the field into the cart and looked back over the empty field with pride.

'I reckon I'll be good at being a land girl, Daphne. We've picked up tons of potatoes today as well as looked after the animals and such.'

'I agree, seeing that huge field cleared of taters and knowing that we did it on our own is really gratifying. We make a good team, don't you think?'

'I reckon we do. Oy, Charlie, are the other lot waiting for us?'

'I'm not clairvoyant, Sal, and can't see around corners. They certainly haven't come here and it's well past six o'clock. I wonder if we get fed in turn or as we get back, or if supper's served at a set time and those that aren't there just have to eat it cold.'

Talking about food reminded Sal just how hungry she was. 'My belly thinks me throat's been cut. I ain't bothered if it's hot or cold as long as there's lots of it.'

Star was trotting briskly towards Goodwill House, as eager to get home as they were. Daphne was sitting facing forwards and she spotted the three girls they'd dropped that morning.

'Look at that, Charlie, they must have finished late as well,' Daphne said.

The three girls piled in, and they were swapping horror stories all the way back. Sal was enjoying being part of the group – she'd not had any close friends of her own when growing up and in the last year she'd been cut off from her roots living with Den. Being a land girl had been the best decision she'd made. Now she was free to live like the others and forget her past.

The next morning, getting out of bed was horrible. Sal felt like an old lady and didn't know how she was going to do another day of backbreaking work. She was last up and both Daphne and Charlie were already dressed.

As she was cleaning her teeth, the house shook, the windows rattled, and she almost wet her drawers. Blooming heck, she was a bag of nerves. These were just the planes taking off from the base next door and she'd have to get used to them.

Breakfast was the same tasty porridge and as much toast and tea as you wanted. She wasn't so nervous this morning, as she knew what to expect on the farm.

The cows were mooing – Pickering hadn't milked them yet. 'Same as yesterday, Charlie, you and Daphne do the cows and that. I'll do the pigs and chickens. Won't take so long today.'

'Then it's unloading the trailers, but I don't know what we'll be doing this afternoon. Probably hoeing, unless there's another field of potatoes to get up.'

Sal was pleased that she was able to make suggestions and didn't always hang back, waiting for someone else to tell her what to do.

11

Joanna hadn't seen John alone since their exciting encounter two days ago. She hadn't meant to eavesdrop but she'd heard him talking to Dr Willoughby and asking to be signed off. From the end of the conversation that she could hear, his request had been denied.

'I don't agree, Doc, I'm perfectly well apart from a few stitches in my head. I'm not dizzy, and my team are two men short. I need to get back to the base today. I tried to get hold of you yesterday but failed.'

He put the phone down and muttered something she couldn't quite hear but guessed it was probably very rude. This time, he wasn't going to vanish before she could speak to him. Elizabeth was on the terrace with the dog, reading a book, the twins were in the study with their tutor and Jean, of course, was busy in the kitchen. Nobody around to overhear what might be said.

'Don't rush off, John, we need to talk. Come to my sitting room, where we can be undisturbed.'

She thought he might refuse but then he nodded. 'All right,

but I don't think we've got anything to say to each other that needs to be said in private.'

'I disagree.' She left it at that and walked briskly towards the small room she used during the winter, not sure if he would actually follow her.

He walked remarkably quietly for a tall man in heavy RAF boots. Strange that the pilots could wear normal lace-up shoes to fly a fighter – boots seemed so much safer and more sensible. Why was she thinking about footwear when John was walking behind her and just having him so close made her giddy?

She'd envied her daughter, Sarah, and Millie and Di for feeling so passionately about their fiancés, as it was something that she'd no experience of. Now she understood that physical desire was overwhelming, all-consuming, and made one forget the rules.

John pointedly left the door open and remained standing, despite the fact that she'd sat in the nearest chair. His expression wasn't encouraging and for a moment she thought she'd misjudged the situation and made the most catastrophic and embarrassing error. Then she saw his hands were clenched into fists, his whole body was tense. He wasn't as disinterested as he was pretending to be.

'John, I know what the repercussions would be for me and am prepared to take that risk. If it became public knowledge, it is I who would be socially disgraced, nothing untoward would happen to you.'

'I don't think you've thought this through, Joanna. I'm not an expert on the subject of women's emotions, but I don't think you could sleep with a man without becoming emotionally involved.' His voice was gruff and he swallowed noisily before continuing.

'We both know that whatever we might wish, we can never be together. Someone like you can't marry someone like me.

However careful we are, you could become pregnant – do you really want to bring a bastard into the world?'

'Sit down, John, please. Don't stand looming over me.'

With some reluctance, he complied, and this gave her a few minutes to compose herself and think how she could best explain how she felt.

'Let me deal with each of your points in turn. I've no wish to offend you, but it never occurred to me that marriage was a possibility. Apart from the difference in status – which I can assure you wouldn't stop me marrying you if that's what I wanted – I'm ten years older than you.

'My mother-in-law had, so she tells me, several enjoyable affairs whilst she lived in the south of France. Like me, she had no wish to give up her financial independence by marrying a second time. I'm never going to marry again and I can't have any more children. When Sarah was born, something went wrong and that has left me infertile. Does that make your decision easier?'

He smiled at her and if she hadn't been sitting, then she thought her knees might have given way. 'What about me? Have you considered how I'd feel if I fell in love with you and was left heartbroken?'

For a second, she thought his question serious and then saw his lips twitch. 'I'm sure you'd soon get over it. We both know this can only be a fleeting relationship but I've no reason to think it can't be a wonderful experience for both of us.'

He leaned forward, his eyes blazing. Surely he wasn't thinking of beginning the affair right now? She couldn't look away. She was pinned to her chair like a butterfly to a board. The clock ticked loudly. The tension in the room was unbearable.

Then he sat back with a sigh. 'Not now, not here. But soon, Joanna, very soon.' He was now far more relaxed than she was. 'I can guarantee our affair will be something memorable and something neither of us will ever regret.'

When her breathing had returned to normal, she was ready to ask some questions and reveal more about herself to him than she'd ever done to anyone else. She knew instinctively that he'd never betray a secret.

'I've little experience in bedroom matters, as you might imagine. My husband was a lot older than me and regarded me as his possession, not a woman he was in love with. When he visited my room, I don't believe he enjoyed it any more than I did. After Sarah was born and there was no possibility I could give him the much-wanted heir, he ceased to come altogether.'

His eyes widened and he leant forward for a second time. 'Bloody hell, are you telling me you've lived like a nun these past two decades?'

'I am. Now perhaps you can see why I'm so eager to understand what all the fuss is about.'

'Well, I'm honoured and delighted that you've decided I'm to be your first lover.' He said this with a straight face, but she knew he was teasing.

'You might well be my last. It could be that I don't find the physical side of a relationship at all enjoyable. In fact, I'm rather hoping that's the case, then I won't have to take a second lover when this relationship ends.' This too wasn't intended to be taken seriously but unfortunately, he misunderstood.

It was as if her words were an affront to his masculinity. He launched himself from his chair. Before she could react, she was in his arms, crushed against his chest, and he tilted her head back so he could kiss her.

At first, his lips were gentle, the pressure firm but not demanding. Then everything changed. Eventually he allowed her to catch her breath but instead of apologising, he gently pushed her back into her chair and resumed his own seat.

John made every effort to appear calm and sophisticated after kissing her, but he was having a hard job doing so. He'd wanted to show her that making love with him was going to be extraordinary.

She recovered first. He was still uncomfortable and was glad he was wearing his uniform jacket, which was long enough to cover his embarrassment.

'I was intending the comment to be humorous, John, I wasn't criticising your prowess as a lover. However, if I needed any convincing to take this further, you've just provided the evidence I needed. I can't wait to enjoy the full experience. How are we going to organise this?'

'It can't be here…'

'It can't be anywhere else. I'm not meeting you in a seedy hotel, even if you could get leave to do so, which is unlikely, and I'm certainly not entranced by the idea of a rug in the bushes somewhere.'

This was an extraordinary conversation to be having, but he was rather enjoying it. 'I share a room with Percy and can hardly vanish without him knowing about it. He's a light sleeper.'

'There are a dozen empty bedrooms in the Victorian wing. I'm sure one of them would be suitable – as long as we don't fall through the ceiling.'

He thought for a moment that she was referring to the vigour with which they might make love but then realised she meant it might not be safe after the fire.

'The upstairs was barely touched, so apart from smoke damage, it's perfectly safe.'

'Then I'll leave you to arrange things. I can hardly poke about the Victorian wing, as everybody knows I've only set foot in it once since I was married and that was to rescue my dog.'

'And then?'

She smiled. She was unaware just how beautiful she was and to have someone like her look at him the way she was doing made him feel like a film star.

'I leave that to your ingenuity, John. It would be a shame if Dr Willoughby now decides that you're fit to go back just when things are getting interesting.'

'He said I can't even think of returning until the stitches are out. Being an RAF fireman is a physical job, not something that can be done as a semi-invalid. If I don't pester him, I should have a few days at least because he said he'd take out my stitches at the same time as Percy's.'

'You work twelve-hour shifts, so you could always come here when you're not on duty. We'll work out the details later. My schedule's flexible apart from the monthly WI and WVS meetings.'

'I'm not sure how that would work. Your mother-in-law sits on the terrace most days and would hardly miss me arriving on my motorbike.'

'Good heavens, I wasn't suggesting you arrived so publicly. I don't think there's any need to think about that at the moment. I'll join you next door in an hour.' When she reached the door, she turned back for a moment. 'There are servants' stairs in the passageway by the side door. We'll use those.'

Things were moving far quicker than he'd anticipated. The last thing he'd expected from someone like Joanna was for her to be so matter-of-fact about something so daring. She was a member of the upper classes, and yet here she was, arranging a clandestine affair as efficiently and calmly as if she was arranging a Whist drive for the ladies of the village.

He needed a shave and a bath – he had no intention of being anything but fragrant for his first encounter between the sheets with this lovely woman.

He left her in the sitting room and was tempted to go up the stairs at a run but thought that would draw unwanted attention from anyone nearby. Percy, thank god, had caught the bus into the village as he needed some more smokes and wouldn't be back until lunchtime. It might have been difficult to explain his sudden need for personal hygiene if his friend had been in the room.

He stripped and washed and then ferreted out some clean underwear – fortunately his kit had been brought down yesterday, or he'd have nothing to change into. The twins were busy with their lessons until midday and the old lady slept most of the morning on the chaise longue on the terrace.

This meant they had two hours – hardly ideal and not nearly long enough. This wasn't the best way to conduct a romance. He'd had three relationships, only one of them serious, and none had been arranged like this. Making love should be spontaneous, a mutual feeling of desire moving the people involved gradually from one step to the next.

He wasn't sure how things would work when they were both going to this room with the express purpose of having sex. He wanted to make love to her – of course he did – but he wasn't sure he could perform to order.

He now knew the house well enough to be able to slip out through the side door without being seen by anybody sitting on the terrace. He'd forgotten about the dog. Lazzy, ever alert, had heard him and jumped off the terrace and rushed up as he was heading for the side door to the Victorian wing.

'Good morning, Lazzy. What do you want? I can't take you for a walk, I'm busy, and you can't come into this building as it's not safe for a dog.' What the hell would he do if the dog insisted on accompanying him?

He needn't have worried as when the animal realised where he was going, he whimpered, his ears drooped, his tail went between his legs and then he galloped off. No doubt the place had unhappy memories for him.

The idea of making love to Joanna anywhere but on clean sheets just wasn't acceptable. When he'd explored up here the other day, he'd looked into most of the rooms. There was one on the far side, furthest away from the main stairs, that would be ideal if it was clean enough.

There was a matching set of bedroom furniture consisting of a dressing table, wardrobe, chest of drawers and a large double bed. This bed was covered by a gold satin counterpane which, although faded and dusty, appeared to have no smoke damage.

He pulled it off and saw there was no bedlinen or pillows. The mattress was pristine, didn't look as if it had ever been slept on. He leaned down and sniffed the surface – it smelled all right – and it wasn't damp and there was no sign of mice living inside it. He grinned at the thought of Joanna's reaction if, whilst they were in bed, they were joined by a family of mice.

He remembered peering into a linen cupboard on his previous visit and thought there might still be sheets and so on in there that were usable. He was lucky and at the back, underneath several piles of not so fresh linen, he discovered exactly what he wanted.

He checked his watch and saw he only had twenty minutes before Joanna arrived, expecting their love nest to be ready. He put two blankets on the mattress first and followed this up with a sheet. Did they need a top sheet and a blanket? What about pillows? Would these be necessary?

He was quite happy to strip naked in front of anyone – you got used to it in the forces – but it wouldn't be the same for her. Hastily, he closed the shutters, and this made the room look slightly less clinical.

Joanna called his name softly and he answered. When she walked in, he was still deliberating about what else was needed to make this room more romantic.

'Oh dear, I really didn't think this through, did I?' She smiled apologetically. 'You've done your best, John, but this looks like an examination room at a hospital. Rather off-putting, don't you agree?'

* * *

Sal had finished her chores before the others – cows took longer to look after than pigs and chickens. She washed the eggs and arranged them on the trays, carefully putting any that were cracked in a bowl for the farmer to use. These didn't have to be handed in, but all the rest were part of the rationing.

The horses were happily grazing in the field, and their water trough was full, so she headed for the barn. The three trailers piled high with the spuds they'd picked up yesterday were waiting to be put into sacks. She might as well get on with that, as it was something she didn't need showing how to do.

She reckoned that if she filled them to the point where she could still lift them, that would do. No point in making them so heavy it would take two to do it. What she didn't know was where all this produce went and how it got there. Maybe Charlie would be able to tell her, as she was the expert.

'I say, well done, Sal,' Charlie said when she and Daphne

arrived an hour later. 'You've made a good start on the potatoes. We should get these trailers emptied by lunchtime.'

'Have you seen Pickering this morning? He needs to tell us what we're doing after this.'

'I don't want to be the one to find him,' Charlie said. 'We'll get on with this, Sal, if you go and ask him. I noticed that the barley, wheat and oats are ready to harvest, too. I expect that might be on the cards next.'

'That sounds a bit of all right and not as backbreaking as spud picking.'

'It's more fun, certainly. The horses cut the wheat and we have to collect it. Then it has to be put into stooks...'

'Hang on a tick, I ain't got the faintest idea what you're talking about.'

Charlie laughed. 'Never mind, Sal, it'll become clear when harvesting starts. The only drawback is that we have to work from dawn till dusk in case it rains and ruins the crops before they can be threshed and so on.'

'I get the bit about working blooming hard, but I'll not bother about the rest until it happens.'

'I've heard about haymaking,' Daphne said. 'Do we have to do that too?'

'That's already been done. You must have noticed the haystacks in the fields.'

'Can't say that I have. I'll get off and speak to that old misery, then.'

Sal wasn't afraid to confront this nasty geezer. She'd been living with someone much worse than him for a year and survived it. She marched around to the back door and hammered on it.

A few moments later, she heard shuffling footsteps. She stepped back and waited. The farmer seemed less belligerent this morning. 'The lorry'll be coming for the spuds later. Will they be ready?'

'Yes, Mr Pickering, we'll be done by midday. Charlie wants to know what you want us to do with the spare butter and cream. Will somebody come for that and the eggs today?'

He looked puzzled, as if he didn't understand the question, then he shook his head. 'You've got to take it to the village. It should have gone first thing, but I never told you.'

'Where do we take it?'

'Raven's, the general stores, first, but what he doesn't want, take to the others.' He closed his eyes and swayed, having to clutch at the door frame to stay upright.

'Are you poorly?'

He shook his head. 'I'll do. You girls get on with it and leave me be.'

He was drunk and it was only ten o'clock in the morning. Sal didn't understand what he had to be miserable about and had no sympathy for him. She explained to the other two what they had to do and the state the bloke had been in.

'He needs to get a grip or he'll lose his tenancy. We have to report this – there must be an estate manager we can talk to. I'd rather not bother Lady Harcourt, but I'll do so if we can't find this other chap.' As usual, Charlie knew what to do.

'It won't take all three of us to make the deliveries. If you and Sal go to the village, then I'll cut across the fields to the farm next door and see if I can get the information we need from the farmer there,' Daphne suggested.

'Okay, that makes sense,' Charlie said, but she didn't seem too pleased to be told what to do. She was the sort of girl who liked to be in charge.

12

Joanna didn't know quite how to extricate herself from this humiliating situation of her own making. What had she been thinking to ask him to prepare somewhere for them in such a matter-of-fact way?

She was about to retreat when she risked a glance in his direction and saw that he was as uncomfortable as she. 'This isn't your fault, John, as I just said, I really didn't consider what I'd asked you to do.'

He shrugged and sat on the edge of the bed. 'You said this looks like something in a hospital – I think it looks like a room in a brothel.' He sounded so despondent that for a moment, the words didn't register.

'Are you suggesting that I'm... I'm...' She couldn't bring herself to say the words.

He surged to his feet and in two steps was in front of her. 'Don't be daft, Joanna, you know very well I'm not suggesting that.' He gestured towards the white draped bed. 'But desire can't be turned on like a tap – it has to be something spontaneous, something exciting, and this is as far from that as you could possibly get.'

Her head was spinning. She was no longer sure why she was angry with him, but it was easier than being embarrassed. 'That's all very well, but our circumstances are such that doing anything spontaneous, as you so casually suggest, will be impossible. Unless we meet at predetermined times, we'll not be able to meet at all.'

'I told you this wasn't a good idea and we've just proved that I'm right. The fact that you find me physically attractive isn't enough to risk your reputation and overcome the obstacles.'

For some reason, she ignored most of his comment and focused on the two words about physical attraction. 'Are you suggesting that you don't find me attractive enough to find a solution?'

He made a strange noise, more like a groan than anything else, and the next thing she knew, she was being kissed with a passion and determination that would have scared her if she hadn't been so stirred by it. He left her in no doubt that he was as eager to make love as she was.

Her hands were entangled in the thick curly hair at the base of his neck, she was pulling his head down, encouraging him to deepen the kiss, wanting to feel every inch of his body against hers.

Then he was holding her at arm's length. 'Are you quite sure? There's still time to say no, but if we go any further, I can't promise to stop.'

Her heart was hammering. She'd never been surer of anything in her life. She was a woman and wanted to know what it felt like to really make love with a man, and not just to have what David had called 'marital relations'.

Her mouth was dry. She wasn't sure she'd be able to find the words to tell him. Instead, she nodded and with shaking hands began to unbutton her frock. His smile rocked her back on her heels. She'd never felt more desirable, more feminine, or more eager to tumble onto the sheets.

While she fumbled with her buttons, he removed his clothes in seconds. She'd never seen a man naked – everything in her marriage had been conducted in darkness and nightclothes. Carefully avoiding looking at his arousal, she stared instead at his magnificent torso. His shoulders were broad, muscled, and there was sprinkling of black hair on his chest.

'Here, sweetheart, let me help you.'

His deft fingers completed the unbuttoning and slipped her frock over her shoulders so it puddled around her feet. Then she was in just her camiknickers. He waited, hands poised, for her permission to continue undressing her.

Again, no words would come, so for a second time Joanna nodded her assent. The silk slithered down her overheated limbs and she was as naked as he. There was now no embarrassment. They were just two adults enjoying something that up until now had been a mystery to her.

He moved closer and every inch of his body was pressed against hers. The feel of his flesh sent such spirals of heat, of desire, rocketing around her body that she had to clutch his shoulders just to remain upright.

He swept her from her feet but didn't toss her onto the bed, he put her down gently, as if she was a precious object. When David had visited her, there been no preliminaries, he'd pushed up her nightgown and plunged into her and it had been a painful and unpleasant experience.

John held back, he caressed and kissed every inch of her until she was on fire and desperate to consummate the union. She was as wild as he was, calling his name, arching her back in ecstasy, and finally understood why this act was called making love, why men and women fell into bed with people they weren't married to.

He kissed her tenderly afterwards. 'Do you think it was worth the risk?'

She laughed, and even to her own ears, she sounded abandoned, different, a woman of experience now. 'Absolutely. I'm afraid you've opened Pandora's box, my love, and let out the demons within me. I'm a different woman, and it's because of you.'

He pushed her tangled, damp hair from her cheek and kissed each of her eyes in turn. 'Not demons, never that. What we did was the most natural thing in the world – it's how things should be between a man and a woman, and I'm honoured to have been the one to show you.'

She loved the feel of his hip and thigh against hers and wanted to remain in his arms, but common sense prevailed. 'I'd better get dressed. I'd love to stay here all afternoon and do it again, more than once, if possible, but duty calls.'

He nibbled her ear and her breath caught in her throat. 'You said you had two hours, we've only been here half that time. Just give me fifteen minutes.'

She pushed herself up on one elbow and looked at him. 'Why do you need fifteen minutes?'

His smile was wicked. 'I'd forgotten how innocent you are, or dare I say ignorant? A man needs time to recover before being able to make love again. It's different for a woman.'

Her cheeks turned pink at his teasing. 'Good heavens, I'd no idea that's how things worked for you. Thank you for explaining.'

She'd intended to lie quietly against his shoulder until he was ready but instead her fingers started to explore his body of their own volition. His skin was rougher than hers, he tasted of salt, of masculinity and love.

He lay still for a few minutes, allowing her free access, but then gripped her wrists and raised them above her head.

The second time they made love was even more spectacular than the first. If he hadn't muffled her cries with his mouth, she was sure Elizabeth might have heard her on the terrace.

* * *

John had known the moment he'd set eyes on Joanna that getting involved with her would be stupid and mean heartbreak for both of them. As he held her in his arms, feeling her heart beating against his, he knew all the talk about a casual affair was crap.

He'd had his fair share of excitement with women, but nothing like this. He was pretty damn sure a bloke didn't get this sort of feeling if it was casual sex. Too late for both of them. She might not realise it, but this was more than a fling – they were in love.

His fingers were buried in her thick, glorious golden hair and were caressing the base of her neck. Her skin was damp, as was his, and he didn't want to let her go, to go back to harsh reality, where someone like him could never marry someone like her.

She was totally relaxed and the touch of her bare skin was something he'd never forget. He'd not been in love before and to fall for her had been inevitable but the worst thing he'd ever done in his life. This wasn't going to end well, but he was certain it was going to end.

'Darling, this time I really must get dressed. I'm sure we've been here almost two hours.'

'We have.' Reluctantly he rolled away and swung his legs to the floor. Better to keep his back to her, as he didn't want her to see his expression when he told her this couldn't happen again. There was only one way to end things and that was for him to behave like a bastard – make her hate him – pretend that it had just been sex and nothing else.

'This was a one-off, Joanna, it won't happen again. I can't risk my career. Not only will I be gone in a couple of days, but the builders will be here to start knocking this place down.'

He waited for her to react, to be justifiably angry at his callous reaction to what had happened between them. Then, to his surprise, she was close and her arms were around him.

'You don't have to pretend, my love, I know this meant as much to you as it did to me. I'm also well aware that it will be impossible to keep this a secret for very long but, please, let's not abandon this before we have to.'

'It's not me that will suffer, sweetheart, it's you. We should never have started this...'

'Don't say that. I'll never regret this afternoon, never. It was the most wonderful two hours of my life. I didn't intend to fall in love with you, but I have. I know it's hopeless, but let's snatch what little pleasure we can before it crashes down around our ears.'

Gently he removed her hands and stood up, keeping his back to her. Long practice meant he could dress fast and today was no exception. When he was secure in his uniform, he turned.

She had her silky undergarment on her and was holding her dress in her hands. With her hair tumbling onto her shoulders, she was unbearably beautiful. Her expression was as wretched as his. He couldn't watch her distress without offering comfort.

'Don't cry, love, I can't bear to see you so upset. We've got to have lunch with the others and you can't go down with red eyes.'

He held her, stroking her back, knowing he didn't have the strength of will to break things off as he should.

'I'm sorry, you warned me what would happen. I don't care about the repercussions. I love you and am going to enjoy whatever time we have together.' She recovered her composure and stepped away and was soon respectable again. He found her shoes and handed them to her.

'Do you need help putting up your hair?'

She shook her head. 'I do need help with finding the pins to hold it. Can you see if you can locate them on the floor?'

Ten minutes later, she was Lady Joanna Harcourt again. He looked at her critically. 'I don't think anyone but me will know what's happened. That said, I think it better that I don't join you for lunch. However careful we are, it will be impossible not to react differently to each other.'

'You can miss luncheon, but you have to come to dinner, as your absence then would create more speculation. On another subject entirely, I heard from the builders yesterday that they can't start until the twentieth.'

'That means we've got a week, but I doubt I'll be able to stay here that long,' John said. 'My stitches are coming out in three days – I'll have to return to active duty then.'

Her smile was sad. 'In which case, we'll meet here after everybody's asleep. Will your corporal gossip? Do you trust him to keep our secret?'

'Percy's a good mate as well as my second-in-command. I've covered for him more than once over the past couple of years and we can trust him if we have to.'

'Then we'll meet at eleven o'clock.'

Then she was gone, leaving behind a trail of the floral perfume she wore. He hoped to god nobody came up here, as even one of the twins would have to be blind not to know what had been going on. Before he left, he ripped off the soiled sheet and replaced it with a clean one. Doing something practical always calmed him down.

The *what ifs* crowded into his head, but he pushed them aside. If Joanna was prepared to take the risk, and it was far greater for her than for him, then who was he to cavil? He wanted to spend every moment he could with her, not just to make love, but to get to know her better.

What a bloody awful mess this was – falling in love was supposed to be the best time of your life, a time when you made plans for the future together, talked about what you'd do when the war was over. Instead, they had three days and then they must part, carry on with their lives as if they'd never met.

Sal knew how to harness Star, but Charlie told her it would be quicker if she did it. 'You fetch the milk churns from the dairy whilst I get the cart ready. Our cart is better than the one Pickering owns, so we'll use that.'

'Didn't Pickering say there's a lorry coming for the spuds today?'

'He did, but he's also told us to take the fresh food down to the village. We haven't finished putting the spuds in the sacks. I tell you what, I'll go to the village, you and Daphne do the potatoes...'

'No. We're a team so we do things together. One job at a time, regardless of what the farmer said. Ain't that right, Daphne?'

'Actually, Sal, I agree. If the lorry turns up and the potatoes aren't here, there could be endless repercussions for all of us. As long as the fresh food gets down to the grocers by lunchtime, I'm sure that'll be satisfactory.'

Sal thought Charlie might kick up a fuss at being overruled, but she smiled and nodded. 'All right. Potatoes first, village and the other farm after that.'

Bagging the potatoes they'd picked up yesterday was far easier. They found a rhythm for the task. One of them held open the sack, one of them filled a bucket and passed it to the person in the middle. They took it in turns and had just got the last sack filled when they heard the rumble of the lorry approaching.

'There's two men in the cab,' Sal called out happily. 'That means we can leave it to them to load and get on with the next jobs.'

Daphne supervised the men loading the lorry, counting the sacks as they went on, and when she was sure they'd entered the correct number on their chart, she signed it. Meanwhile, Sal fetched the stuff from the dairy that was going to the village and Charlie, after harnessing the mare, added half a dozen trays of eggs.

The lorry left first and at no time did the farmer come out to see things were being done as they should. Daphne disappeared down the path that led to the next farm and Sal sat in the back of the cart, hoping to keep the four half-size churns and trays of eggs from toppling over on the journey to Stodham.

Each churn had a tap on it so folks could fill their jugs when they came in to buy their milk. Seemed a lot of fuss when it could just come in a bottle like it did in the East End.

Sal wasn't too impressed with Raven's, the largest of the general stores that served the village. She thought that having cats sleeping on top of the bags of rice and so on wasn't hygienic.

'I've given you up, ladies, I expected the delivery earlier,' Mr Raven said sourly.

'I'm sorry, sir, but we had to get the potatoes into bags ready for the lorry before we could come. Mr Pickering said if you don't want anything, we can take it to the other two shops.' Charlie was polite and Sal reckoned her posh voice did the trick.

'Go on then, I'll take my usual order.'

This consisted of two trays of eggs and a churn of milk. Charlie took care of the paperwork and Sal was grateful she did, as she wasn't too clever with writing and such.

They were able to sell everything on the cart and were told to pick up the empty churns when they brought down a fresh supply.

'I can smell fish and chips, Charlie,' Sal said, sniffing eagerly. 'Let's get some for lunch. I reckon I've got enough coppers to pay for all of us. It can be my treat this time.'

'What a spiffing idea. Look, I can't turn the cart here and will have to go out of the village to do it. That will give you ample time to buy our lunch. If you walk down to the village hall, then I can collect you there without holding up the traffic.'

* * *

Sal sat clutching the large newspaper-wrapped, delicious, vinegary parcel on her lap. Daphne was waiting for them and was thrilled to have a hot lunch. Charlie took care of the horse and cart and she and Daphne took the rug and bottles of water around to their chosen lunch spot.

'Have you seen any sign of the farmer all morning?'

'I haven't, but I've got the name of the estate manager. It was better at that farm, but I don't think I'd like to work where there's no livestock.'

'Did you see the other girls there?' Sal asked as she licked the last of the vinegar from her fingers.

'I didn't, they're working on the far side of the farm. They're harvesting and it's this farm next. The farmer's wife told me that thresher machine goes to each farm in turn. There were folk from the village helping out and then she makes them tea and cake. We don't get anything like that here.'

They hadn't waited to eat as there was no point in letting the fish and chips get cold, Charlie wouldn't expect them to anyway.

'What's happened to her? We've finished and she's still not here and it doesn't take that long to put a horse in the field,' Daphne said.

'I was thinking that meself. We better go and see what's what. We'll take her lunch with us, it's kept lovely and warm tucked up in all this paper and with me jumper over it.'

The yard was empty, the horse contentedly grazing in the field alongside the two massive cart horses. They shouted but got no response.

'This ain't like her, I don't like it. Do you think somethink's happened to her?'

'We've looked everywhere apart from the farmhouse itself. I can't see her going back there, especially after what she told us, but we've got to tell Pickering she's missing. He's our employer, even if he's useless.'

Sal left the parcel in the cart, safe from the chickens. They'd love a bit of fish and chips if they could get their beaks on it.

'Blimey, the back door's open. That ain't good. Do we just walk in or bang on the door?' Sal took the lead and stepped into the passageway. The floor was thick with mud and hadn't been washed for weeks.

'Charlie, Mr Pickering, are you there?' Sal called out but didn't expect a response so almost jumped out of her skin when the farmer yelled back.

'In here, girls, there's been a bit of an accident and I'm taking care of it. I need one of you to fetch the doctor here smartish.'

They burst into the front room to find Charlie, white as a

sheet, stretched out on the sofa. For a horrible moment, Sal thought her friend was dead.

'I fetched her in here. I found her unconscious in the barn. She must have tripped and hit her head on something. There's no blood and I can't see any injury neither.'

Sal reacted first. 'Where's this doctor bloke live? I'll go, I reckon I'm a fast runner. None of me brothers or sisters could ever hold a candle to me in a race.'

'Dr Willoughby is this side of the village, he's in the big house set back from the road,' Pickering said. 'It'll be quicker across the fields. You can see the chimneys of his house from here.'

'Righty ho. Daphne, you stop here and look after Charlie. I'll be as quick as I can.'

Sal hurdled two fences and scrambled over a ditch and arrived at the doctor's door in record time. She hammered on it and a lady opened it.

'We need Dr Willoughby urgently. Accident at Fiddler's Farm. Land girl unconscious,' she managed to gasp.

'Come in, my dear, I'll get you a drink of water whilst I fetch the doctor from the garden.'

Sal gulped the water down gratefully and wiped her sweaty face on her handkerchief – if you could call a square of scruffy rag a hanky. A nice bloke, a lot younger than she'd expected and not bad looking, dashed past her with a smile.

'Just getting my bag, then I'll give you a lift back and you can tell me what happened.'

13

Joanna took the back stairs of Goodwill House and slipped into her bedroom. She stripped and washed from top to toe and then put on fresh undergarments, as only then could she be sure that no lingering traces of her encounter would be noticeable.

She looked into all the rooms on the family side and was pleasantly surprised at how tidy those belonging to the twins were. She then did the same with the five rooms being used by the land girls – these too were commendably well-ordered. The ladies from the village only cleaned the passageways and bathrooms, everything else had to be done by the girls themselves.

She was halfway down the main staircase when her mother-in-law called out to her. 'There you are, Joanna, Liza just came to say that luncheon is ready. It would seem that our RAF visitors have gone into the village. If they are well enough to do that, then I think they are quite well enough to return to Manston and resume their duties.'

'I was just doing an inspection of all the bedrooms and am delighted at how tidy they all are,' Joanna said. 'I think it likely our two guests need some masculine company, as here they're surrounded by women.'

Elizabeth chuckled. 'I believe you might be correct, my dear.'

The house shook as yet another squadron of planes screamed overhead. Things were definitely busier at Manston and there was the constant thump thump of anti-aircraft guns and the chatter of machine guns from the fighters overhead.

'We've only had to use the summerhouse once, but I fear that might be about to change.'

'I've no wish to think about what might or might not be going to happen in the future. Today everybody is well and safe, the weather is fine and I'm looking forward to my meal,' Elizabeth said.

'I think your positive attitude does you credit. You're right not to dwell on what might be going to happen and just to enjoy the moment. I intend to follow your advice.' Joanna turned away to hide her smile. Her affair with John had to be brief, they both knew that, but every stolen minute was precious, and she was going to make the most of it.

Joanna agreed to sit in the shade with Elizabeth, as she enjoyed the old lady's company. Today was one of her good days and Joanna feared these might be numbered so intended to enjoy these whilst she could.

Sitting out of the sun was pleasant and she closed her eyes and let her mind drift. It didn't matter how often she and John were able to meet. She was determined to snatch what happiness she could before the affair had to stop – which it inevitably would.

'Joanna, I believe that's Dr Willoughby's car approaching. Were you sleeping?'

'Almost, but I'm awake now. I'd better go in so I can be there to greet him.' Her heart was thudding uncomfortably; she could think of only one reason the doctor would be arriving when he hadn't been summoned by anyone in the house. Had Percy or John collapsed in the village? Or was it one of the land girls who needed medical attention?

The unpleasant smell of drying plaster was still a nuisance in the grand hall, so the front door was left open all day. She waited under the portico for the car to pull up. The doctor jumped out of the driver's seat, opened the rear passenger door and helped, not an RAF man as she'd expected, but one of the land girls to climb out.

She shouldn't have been relieved it wasn't John, but she was. She rushed forward. 'Oh dear, let me help you. Have you been taken unwell?'

Charlie didn't answer and was barely able to stand, even with the doctor's arm around her waist.

'I don't think she can make it under her own volition, my lady, I'm going to carry her in. If you would be kind enough to direct me to her bedroom.'

Joanna went ahead and he followed with the almost unconscious girl in his arms. She wondered why Charlie hadn't been taken to hospital.

The doctor carried the girl with no difficulty and wasn't even out of breath when she opened the correct bedroom door and pointed to the bed under the window. 'I believe that's where she sleeps. Is she ill or has she had an accident? Shouldn't she be in hospital?'

'She fell and hit her head. I've done exactly the same examination as I'd do if she was taken to hospital and decided she's concussed, but not seriously. She'll do better here.'

He put her down and then stepped back. Joanna wasn't at all happy about having someone so obviously unwell literally dumped on the household.

'I'm so sorry, Dr Willoughby, but I really don't have the staff to take care of her and I'm not happy at the thought of her being alone up here. I'd love to help but I don't think I can.'

He looked genuinely surprised at her comment. 'Good god, I've not thought this through, have I? Obviously, she can't remain here.' He stared down at the deathly pale girl.

'What are you going to do? If you wish to call an ambulance, then please feel free to use my telephone.'

He shook his head. 'No, I'll take her to my house. I have a residential housekeeper as well as a maid and really don't require the services of both. Miss Somiton will do very well being nursed at home with me.'

Not waiting for her to argue, or even agree, the unfortunate girl was picked up a second time and the doctor retraced his steps. Without saying another word, he strode back to the car and put Charlie in the back again. Then the car roared off down the drive.

'How extraordinary! Whatever is going on, Joanna?'

Elizabeth had walked to the end of the terrace and was peering over the balustrade, shaking her head.

Joanna quickly explained. 'I believe there's a telephone number for Mrs Dougherty. I have to ring her if any of the girls are unwell or injured. I'll do that now.'

The woman who was in charge of billeting the land girls in Kent wasn't home, which was hardly surprising, so Joanna left a message with her housekeeper. The entire episode had taken up less than half an hour, but she was still mystified by the usually sensible doctor's behaviour.

* * *

'Nice of Lady Harcourt to have the land girls and for you RAF boys to convalesce at Goodwill House. Folks around here say Lady Harcourt should hand it over to the authorities to be used as a hospital or something like that.'

'I believe the house has been in the family for hundreds of years. I can't see them giving it up, can you?' John said. 'Nobody can say they're not doing their bit for the war.' He didn't wait to hear the reply but returned to his lunch. This turned out to be even more delicious than he'd expected, and it went down just right with the beer.

'Do you want to walk back or shall we catch the bus, Percy?'

'Walk, it's too blooming hot to be in a bus. That old codger's right, we should be back at work. It doesn't seem right lounging about in the sunshine when our mates are working.'

'I feel the same. I tried to persuade the doc to take out our stitches before Friday, but he refused. I have to be careful not to stand up or turn my head too fast. Any sudden movement makes me dizzy but apart from that I'm fine. What about you? Your injury was far worse than mine.'

'I reckon you got the worst of it. Let's enjoy these extra three days, as I doubt we'll get any more leave now things are kicking off.'

When they turned into the drive, he decided to take Percy into his confidence. 'Don't worry if I'm not in my bed tonight, I'll be meeting someone.'

'Good for you. I won't ask which one of those girls it is, none of my business.'

'Thank you. I'd do the same for you.'

'Ugly bugger like me? None of them's likely to give me a second glance, but the ladies fall over to attract your attention.'

As they approached Goodwill House, the dog raced up to greet them and further conversation was impossible. He waved

John met Percy when he reached the village. 'Let's go for a bevy, Sarge. I'm parched. The chippy's doing a roaring trade get the beer if you get the fish and chips.'

'We'd better check the landlady won't object to us eating the garden,' John said. 'After the incident at the village hall while ago, we've been given strict instructions not to upset the folk here.'

'Fair enough. If we can't have beer, then we'll get a bottle of pop from the general stores. There's a couple of benches outside the village hall we can use. Plenty of salt and vinegar on mine, please, Sarge.'

John joined the queue and by the time he reached the front, his mouth was watering. He handed over the coins and walked out with the newspaper parcel under his arm. As he approached the pub, he saw Percy standing outside, clutching two halves of bitter triumphantly.

There were a few locals in the scruffy garden at the rear of the pub, but nobody in uniform. They were getting a few odd looks. He supposed they both looked like skivers.

'I'm going to talk to that old bloke, put him straight before he starts. He's got a belligerent look about him.' John strolled across and explained the reason he and Percy were able to sit about eating fish and chips and drinking beer when their comrades were working on the base.

'We have to be 100 per cent fit. Your doctor bloke's taking out our stitches at the end of the week. We'll be back on shift pronto after that.'

'Do you think there's going to be bombs dropped on us?' asked the man.

'I think it's quite likely. Stodham's so close to Manston that the odd one or two might go astray. I think Ramsgate might be deliberately targeted as it's a coastal port.'

casually to Joanna and the old lady, and they waved back. He couldn't believe his luck – it hadn't occurred to him that Percy would think he'd hooked up with one of the land girls, but it made a lot more sense than that he was having an affair with Joanna.

The talk at dinner was about the girl who had been injured at work and he was able to behave as if there was nothing untoward going on. The girl had tripped and fallen and now had a serious concussion. Head injuries, as he knew only too well, were potentially very serious. Joanna was equally relaxed and he was certain not even the old lady would have suspected anything.

John had a bath and then stretched out on his bed. The minutes dragged by. Percy was snoring quietly but still the hands on his watch appeared to be stuck in one place. Eventually it was time for him to sneak through the house and meet Joanna.

He carried his boots – socks were so much quieter. It occurred to him, as he paused in the darkness to restore his footwear, that he might well have met Joanna doing the same. Everything about this affair was extraordinary and, even if they only had three days together, he was going to make the most of it. He'd never understood when one bloke or another had said he was *madly in love* with a girl, but now he did.

He kept the reduced beam of his torch pointed towards the ground. It was doubtful there would be an ARP lurking in the shrubbery, but it would be sod's law for one to be there tonight and yell at him to put the light out.

The door they'd used earlier was ajar. He slipped through and was about to push it closed behind him, but he couldn't do this if Joanna hadn't arrived. He could hardly yell up the stairs so would have to wait until he got to the room.

When he emerged from the servants' staircase, he saw a faint flicker of light coming from under the door of the bedroom.

Should he return and close the door? It was possible Lazzy was out and if he saw an open door, he'd immediately come in to investigate and that wouldn't be ideal.

After returning and pulling the door closed, he hurried up the stairs.

'I thought you'd changed your mind, darling, when I heard you go back down.' Joanna spoke from the passageway and he dropped the torch on his toe.

'Bloody hell, you scared the wits out of me, woman. Of course I haven't changed my mind; I was just closing the door to stop the dog coming in after us.'

Her laugh echoed around the empty space. He thought it might be the first time he'd heard her laugh and he hoped it wouldn't be the last. 'Woman? I believe that will be the first time I've been addressed as such. I quite like it – very egalitarian.'

'I'm sorry if I'm late, sweetheart.'

'You're not. I came early to arrange things a little better for us.'

He shone the torch directly on her. She was wearing a floating garment, he thought it was called a negligée, but as he'd never seen one before he couldn't be sure. The girls he'd slept with didn't own such things. She looked breathtakingly beautiful.

In two strides, he was beside her and she came willingly into his arms.

* * *

Sal had warmed a little towards Pickering after his kindness to Charlie. The doctor hadn't been too concerned, but he had said it was a serious concussion. He drove Charlie away and it didn't seem right there being only the two of them.

Their boss had told them to sort out the animals before they left that evening as he had to go into Ramsgate. There was still a trailer full of spuds to bag and things to do in the dairy, so they'd got plenty to get on with.

'I hope he's going to have a wash and shave before he goes,' Daphne said as they returned to the barn.

'He ain't as bad as I thought. He did the right thing by Charlie – I'm surprised that in his state he managed to carry her into the house.'

'Do you think Dr Willoughby has taken Charlie to hospital?'

'I reckon so. He can't expect Lady Harcourt to look after her.' Sal looked around the barn, puzzled by the accident. 'I can't see how Charlie fell and hit her head so hard. There's nothing here to trip over, is there?'

'We'll have to wait until she's better and then she can tell us what happened.'

They'd filled three sacks with spuds when Sal heard the creak of an old bicycle. She straightened, rubbing her back and looked around. 'Cor, would you look at that? He scrubs up lovely, don't he?'

The farmer pedalled past them without looking in their direction; they both stared at him with interest. 'He ain't half as old as I thought and ain't that bad looking neither. Maybe it took the shock of Charlie's accident for him to pull himself together.'

'Not good news for our friend, but possibly excellent news for the farm. We need someone to tell us what to do and how to do it now Charlie's not here – two weeks' training doesn't make us experts in anything. Do you think you'll be able to harness Star and drive us home?'

'I know I can. I like horses, porkers, and hens – it's just them blooming cows I'm not too fond of.'

'You just had a bad experience the first time. If you like pigs, I don't see how you can dislike cows, as they're much nicer and don't smell as bad. Have another go this afternoon. The six here have names. The only one who's a bit feisty is Buttercup, but the others are sweethearts.'

'I'll give it a go. Let's get these blooming spuds done as the lorry's coming to collect them sometime this afternoon.'

As Sal was going to help in the dairy, Daphne suggested that she do the chickens, Sal do the pigs and they do the cows together.

'Seems sensible to me. I want to get off on time tonight. I'm worried about Charlie.'

'So am I, but if that Dr Willoughby said it wasn't too serious then we have to believe he knows what he's talking about,' Daphne said.

Sal was now fond of the pigs and they were happy with their new routine. First thing, she fed them and turned them into the field while she mucked out their sty. She just had to open the gate in the afternoon and they galloped in, always ready to eat, no matter that the swill was blooming horrible.

She washed her boots, her hands and face and then, for the first time since she'd arrived, she put on her clean brown coat – the one they used in the dairy. Daphne pointed to a cow in the end stall.

'That's Daisy. She's easy to milk and won't kick you. Do you need to be shown how to do it or can you remember?'

'Squeeze and pull the teats at the same time.' Sal peered underneath the nearest cow. The udders looked clean already. 'Have you washed them?'

'I did all of them to save time. The milking doesn't take as long as everything else. We have to cool the milk, fill the churn when it's cold enough and then skim off the cream to make butter.'

'That Daisy looks quiet enough. I ended up covered in muck last time.'

Daphne laughed. 'I remember, but it won't happen today, I promise you.'

Her friend was right. Daisy stood patiently whilst she fumbled about and then, once she got the hang of it, the milk streamed into the bucket. Sal couldn't believe how easy it was with a cow who didn't try to murder you.

'Good girl, I reckon you've got a bit more in there. I'll just put this bucket somewhere safe and see what's what.'

The other two cows she milked were just as nice as Daisy and by the end, she'd changed her mind about dairy work. When she eventually hung her coat on the peg, she was happy.

'I reckon I can do the cows all right now, as long as I don't get that Primrose. The girls that work at Brook Farm leave at dawn – shouldn't we be coming earlier to do these six?'

'We should, but Pickering hasn't asked us to,' Daphne said. 'Why volunteer to do extra hours if we don't have to? We only get thirty bob a week and have to give Lady Harcourt sixteen shillings of that.'

'Don't seem fair to leave the girls suffering. They should be milked at five or thereabouts and I'm going to use one of those old bikes and come early and do it meself.' Sal wasn't sure what had prompted her to volunteer like this. She'd been brought up to avoid extra work, do as little as possible, yet now she was going to do hours of extra for no extra money. She reckoned she was turning into a country girl if she was putting the welfare of the animals before her own.

'If you do, then you'll have to do Primrose. You can't leave her and just do the other five.'

'Then why don't you come with me? There's going to be lots more to do with Charlie out of the picture.'

Daphne shook her head. 'No, you're on your own if you decide to do this. I don't think Charlie will like it either when she's better. Don't you think she'd have suggested it if it was necessary? After all, isn't she the expert amongst us? You're a girl from London – what do you know about farming?'

This was said with a smile, or Sal might have been offended. 'Fair enough, but I'm a quick learner. I joined the Land Army to get away from London, from some bloke that was threatening to kill me, but I reckon I'll be happy to do farm work until the end of this blooming war. Better than being bossed about by toffee-nosed officers, that's for sure.'

Now Daphne laughed. What had she said that was so funny?

'I think, on balance, I'd prefer to be given orders than have to work for someone like Mr Pickering. The services have rules to protect the people who enlist. I'm thinking seriously of transferring to the WAAF.'

'Don't do that, I thought we were mates. I couldn't do this without you and Charlie.'

'Well, Sal, you might just have to.'

Just as things were working out for her, Daphne might be leaving. There was a blooming war on, so she'd better get used to how things were and stop complaining.

14

Joanna had spent an hour preparing their love nest – she'd brought a bottle of red wine and two glasses, as well as several candles to make the room look more romantic. She'd found the same linen cupboard as John but had rummaged deeper and discovered pillows and pillow slips. The bed was now complete with both top and bottom sheets and a pretty satin counterpane.

It was a considerable time later before she was able to point out these improvements to him. She lay blissfully happy and relaxed in his arms, both unwilling and unable to hold a coherent conversation.

He recovered first. 'Is that wine on the table over there?'

As his question was rhetorical, she didn't bother to answer. He strolled across, completely unabashed by his lack of clothes, allowing her to admire his form from the rear for the first time. She decided that a man looked more attractive from the back as the apparatus needed for making love didn't have the same appeal as his well-muscled shoulders, narrow waist and long, strong legs.

In the flickering candlelight, the room looked a hundred

times better than it had this afternoon. She doubted that he'd even noticed, but she was wrong.

He returned with a full glass of wine for them both and handed her one before slipping between the sheets beside her. 'This is perfect now, so much better than my attempts this afternoon. I didn't even think about candles.' He smiled ruefully. 'To be honest, I didn't think about anything but you and what we were about to do together.'

She held up her glass so he could clink his against it. 'To us. I'll never regret this and will never forget you.'

'My head tells me that we've made a serious mistake, but my heart says the opposite. I know we weren't supposed to be having more than a fling, but I've fallen in love with you. I'm going to enjoy every single moment of this brief affair and hope you do too.'

She could see tears glinting in his extraordinary eyes and she wished she could reassure him, tell him that somehow they'd make it work, that they'd be able to overcome the obstacles, but she couldn't.

'I've fallen in love with you as well. Madness, but sometimes you just have to follow your heart and snatch what joy you can before it's too late.'

She drank a few mouthfuls, as did he, and then they put down the wine. They made love again and she fell asleep in his arms as if she belonged there. She was woken by him kissing her. 'Time to go, my love, whilst it's still dark. I love you.' Then he was gone.

She remade the bed, wondering if they'd have the opportunity to use it again and praying that they would. It was dark, not even a glimmer of dawn, so it wasn't as late as she'd thought.

She snuffed the candles and then, using the light of her torch to stop her stumbling into anything, was ready to return to her own bed. It would have been awkward, to say the least, if the air raid siren had gone off in her absence. Perhaps fate was shining on them, at least for the moment.

She tiptoed through the sleeping house, pausing only to speak to Lazzy, who was in his usual position at the bottom of the stairs. The wine had made her thirsty.

'I'm going to make a cup of tea. Do you want me to let you out for a bit whilst I'm doing it?'

He thumped his long tail on the floor but didn't move. This was odd, as John must have walked past him a few minutes ago and disturbed him. The dog was behaving as if having two of his family wandering around the house in the middle of the night was perfectly normal.

She was sitting at the kitchen table, enjoying a mug of tea, when the door opened. 'Ma, there you are. I woke up and thought I heard someone walking about. I came to investigate.'

'Joe, how brave of you. I couldn't sleep. But if Lazzy's quiet then I don't think you need to worry. Would you like to join me and have a cup of tea now you're here?'

'No, thank you. I'm going back to bed. Good night.'

Her son yawned loudly, making his jaw crack, and then was gone, leaving her alone with her thoughts. If only things were different, she wasn't Lady Harcourt, then maybe there'd be a future for her and John.

Suddenly the dog started to howl. The next moment, the sirens in the village and at the base began to join in.

Joe would make sure everybody was up safely and escort Elizabeth downstairs. She found the three Thermos flasks and had filled all of them by the time the family, John and Percy, and the eleven land girls trooped into the kitchen.

The windows had rattled several times as the fighters on the base took off and went in search of the approaching bombers.

'I don't like it in the cellar, Joanna, why can't we use the summerhouse?'

'Elizabeth, you know why. Come on, everybody, we need to get into the shelter before any bombs are dropped.'

She carefully avoided doing more than nod at John and his corporal. Jean picked up the basket with the three flasks – this was her task – and she and Liza collected the pillows and blankets.

The siren was still wailing but as soon as Joe closed the door that led down to the cellars, they could no longer hear it. This was the one disadvantage of having an underground shelter, but Joanna was well aware they were the lucky ones.

Hiding under a Morrison shelter – little more than a rein-forced table – in one's front room wouldn't be comfortable. The Anderson shelters that people had built in their back gardens were damp, smelly and cold.

'I know it's a bit cramped, girls, but there are enough seats for everybody. The armchair is for Lady Harcourt, but you can sit where you want.'

With eighteen of them, plus a large hairy dog, in the shelter it was decidedly cramped, but at least it was warm. Elizabeth continued to grumble until she fell asleep, which was a relief to all of them.

Jean made tea using the boiling water from the flasks, and Liza and Joe handed it round. No one was fully dressed apart from the two RAF men.

Sal, the blonde land girl from the East End, asked the question they were all thinking. 'How come you two are dressed and the rest of us are in a nighties and that?'

'We can be fully clothed in less than a minute,' John said with a smile. 'It's a necessity in our line of work.'

'I reckon you'd have to sleep in your drawers to be able to do that.'

Percy laughed and nodded. 'Course we do – and everything else is laid out ready.'

* * *

John had only just flopped into bed when the siren went off. He was dressed and ready to leave more quickly than Percy. The gods – or God – were definitely smiling on them tonight. He could just imagine how everyone would have reacted if he and Joanna had turned up together from the other wing.

The door was left open and the dog got out of everybody's way by settling down outside in the dark passageway. A few of the girls took a cushion and blanket and curled up wherever they could and tried to get some sleep. The others chose to sit around the long central table and either chatted or played cards.

'Percy, they didn't plan to have us here. Shall we sit out there with the dog?'

Joe grinned and snatched up a couple of blankets and some cushions. 'I'll join you, if you don't mind, I feel a bit of an odd one out in here with all these women.'

The three of them made themselves comfortable on the stone floor and John was just preparing to go to sleep when the boy asked him a question – the same one that Joanna had asked him the night of the fire.

'Shouldn't you be an officer? I thought all well-educated blokes were commissioned and most of them are pilots or aircrew too.'

'My choice, Joe. I'm a socialist and don't mix well with the chinless wonders who make up most of the officer class. I prefer to be with down-to-earth blokes, men like me who work for their living.'

'Were you a scholarship boy?'

'I was, and I studied maths at Oxford. I volunteered last September and, after basic training, settled for the firefighters.'

'I'm going to be a flyer,' Joe said. 'I hope the war's still going on when I'm old enough to join the RAF.'

'How old are you?' He thought the boy to be about sixteen.

'I'm fifteen in September.'

'Bloody hell! Another three years? I hope we've won it by then.'

Percy answered from the darkness. 'Unless the bleeding Yanks get off their arses and come to help us, it will be jackboots marching through England before you're old enough to sign up.'

'Talking treason, Corporal, not helpful,' John said firmly, and his friend grunted and fell asleep.

After sitting on the floor for a couple of hours, he decided he'd go and see if the raid was over. He and Percy should be at the base doing their duty and not malingering here enjoying themselves.

He had his head in the clouds, had been swept away in a tide of lust and romance, and it had to end. There was a war on, for god's sake, nothing was more important than that – even Joanna.

The light reflected from the shelter was sufficient for him to find his way safely up the stairs without putting on his torch and drawing attention to himself. He glanced over his shoulder and saw that both Percy and the boy were fast asleep.

If the all-clear had gone whilst they were downstairs, then they wouldn't have heard it, so it made sense for somebody to come up and investigate. Probably, when the Germans started bombing cities as they inevitably would, people would just stay down in the shelter all night, regardless of the all-clear having sounded.

The nearest door, the one adjacent to the boot room, was locked. He slid back the bolts and turned the key. He stood in the early morning gloom, listening, sniffing like the dog that had decided to accompany him.

No fires on the base, no sound of activity either. He thought the squadrons must have returned. The birds in the nearby trees were singing – they didn't care if there was a war as long as they had trees to live in and enough to eat.

The dog loped off and he let him go. John returned to the kitchen and riddled the range, added more fuel from the hod, and put two kettles on to boil. The blackouts could go up as soon as the sun came up. The clock on the dresser was ticking loudly and drew his attention. It was almost four o'clock – those working at the dairy would need to get off soon.

Everybody else could go back to bed for a few hours of kip, including himself. He thought putting on the water would be appreciated, but poking about in the pantry wouldn't.

He left the door ajar for the dog, confident there were no burglars about. The chatter from the shelter had stopped some time ago. He kicked Percy's foot gently. 'Wake up, sleeping beauty, raid's over and you can go back to bed.'

Percy mumbled, yawned, got himself to his feet and then wandered off without saying anything. Joe was instantly awake.

'Sergeant, you go back to bed. I'll get everybody else up.'

'I've put the kettles on and the range is going fine.'

'Thank you, that's a great help.'

John left him to it, as he really didn't want to interact with Joanna. He hoped he had the strength of character and willpower to stick to his decision and not spend any more time with her.

It hardly seemed worthwhile getting undressed, so he unlaced his boots, pulled them off and flopped back on the covers. He'd expected to fall instantly asleep as he always did but remained alert, listening as the others returned to bed.

He was still awake when he heard the three girls pedal off down the drive on the way to the dairy. If he wasn't going to sleep, he might as well be up making himself useful. However, the house was still quiet, even the housekeeper apparently not around.

The kettle was still hot and it didn't take long to bring it back to the boil and make himself a cuppa. There was the smell of bread baking, Jean must have put it on before she went up.

It was a little after six and he decided to walk down to the doctor's and insist that his stitches were removed so he could return to the base today, and remove himself from temptation, as he was damn sure that was the only way he could end this passionate affair.

* * *

Sal didn't go back to bed like Daphne but got dressed and headed for the kitchen as soon as she was ready.

'Golly, what are you doing up so early?' Edith asked. She was one of the dairy girls.

'I've decided to get to the farm and milk the cows at the time they should be done. It ain't fair they get left until seven because Pickering's too lazy to do it.'

'Good for you. Isn't Daphne coming with you?'

Sal grinned. 'Not likely, she's snoring away upstairs. There's going to be a lot more work with only the two of us at the farm for the next couple of weeks, so it makes sense to get started early, don't it?'

Edith was at the range, stirring a pot of what smelled like that lovely porridge they had every morning. Sal had been wondering what the three girls had or if they got any breakfast at all.

She could hear the other two banging about in the pantry and went to investigate. They were making themselves sandwiches for lunch.

'Morning, ladies, I need to make me own butties like what you're doing. Budge up and give us some room.'

The two girls nodded and did as she asked without making any snarky comments. As she scraped on a thin layer of the margarine they had to use, she thought of all the butter that was at the farm.

'Don't Lady Harcourt own all the farms what we work on?'

'She does, that's why we're billeted here,' Rose said as she finished wrapping her sandwiches in the greaseproof paper.

'Then why don't we have butter and not this? You'd think being the posh lady of the district and owning everything, she'd get plenty of butter and that.'

Rose's eyebrows vanished under her fringe of mousy-brown hair. 'That would be illegal, Sal, and I'm sure she'd never do that. Nobody decent buys on the black market or under the counter.'

'I reckon all the farms get as much cream, butter, cheese and so on as they want. Pickering certainly does. Can't see it's illegal if you're eating stuff you've produced yourself.'

The other girl, Polly, nodded. 'They've got chickens here and I know Jean uses all the cracked eggs. I bet a lot of those have been cracked deliberately.'

'There you go then. Where I'm working, there's only six cows, so there ain't that much of anything really. We have to take some of them churn things of milk, eggs and any butter and cheese we've got to the three shops in the village. Ever so much paper-work involved – I ain't too clever with that sort of thing, so I hope Daphne will be doing it now as Charlie ain't here.'

'Breakfast's ready, girls, come and get it whilst it's hot,' Edith called from the kitchen.

Sal offered to clear up as she didn't have to be at the farm at any particular time like they did. She scrubbed the porridge pot clean and left it to drain and then washed up the dishes and put them in the rack.

The dog had watched all this activity with interest. 'I ain't got nothing for you, Lazzy, but this old crust from yesterday.' She wasn't sure if she could drop it on the ground as handing it to him might mean being bitten. She wasn't that comfortable with dogs.

He took it from her fingers, gentle as you like, and she rubbed his head. 'Good dog, better manners than a lot of blokes I know.'

Her next task was to find one of the old bikes and then hope she could ride it safely without falling in the ditch. She'd only learned to ride a bike the other day and had never ridden more than a hundred yards or so without a tumble.

Today she was dressed in overalls, far too hot for breeches and woolly socks, although gumboots weren't exactly comfortable in the heat either.

She selected the cycle she'd used before as the saddle was at the right height for her. She had her bottled water and her sandwiches in the haversack slung over her shoulder so had both hands free.

The dog was sitting watching her. 'I'm off then, Lazzy, mind you don't follow me.'

The first few yards, Sal wobbled dangerously, but then she got the hang of it again and was more confident by the time she reached the end of the drive. At least there were no hills to speak of, as she didn't reckon she could pedal up one of those.

She was going along nicely when she heard a large vehicle approaching from behind. She wasn't stable enough to look over her shoulder and there wasn't room for her to pull over. It might have been all right if the driver hadn't hooted loudly as he approached.

She lost control of the bicycle, veered wildly across the road and went headfirst over the handlebars, over the hedge and into the field. She lay there winded, expecting the blighter who'd caused the accident to stop and see if she was injured, but he just carried on.

When she got her breath back, Sal flexed her arms and legs in turn and was glad she hadn't broken anything – especially the bottle of water – as her butties would have been ruined if she had. She stood up and looked at the hedge, astonished that she'd gone over the top and not headfirst into it.

She needed to find a gate to climb over and began to jog along beside the hedge. She'd not gone far when she heard the sound of an animal galloping across the field. She spun around in horror. The biggest cow she'd ever seen was thundering towards her and there was no way she could get out of its way.

15

Joanna slept fitfully when she returned to bed. Her dreams were nightmares, as in them she was constantly running from some unseen danger, and the more she ran, the more obstacles were in her path. Eventually she woke, her heart pounding, with a feeling of dread.

She remained where she was, trying to gather her thoughts, make sense of her dreams. Was it the fear of being killed by a bomb or the danger of being in love with John?

Now wide awake, she was about to get up when she heard heavy footsteps approaching along the passageway. She recognised that tread – it was John. Somehow it gave her comfort that he too was having difficulty sleeping and probably for the same reason.

The girls would be getting up, so now wasn't the time to follow him. She stretched out, tried to relax, and ran through every possible outcome. The most likely one was that their affair would be discovered, there would be the most horrendous scandal, her good name would be gone forever and she'd bring disgrace on her family.

Tears trickled unchecked down her cheeks. But if she hadn't met John, she would never have known what a joyous thing love between a man and woman could be. She doubted that she'd ever fall in love again, but that didn't matter. No one could take away the memory of this brief affair. It was her secret and, despite the heartbreak, she didn't regret for one moment becoming involved with John.

He would be leaving at the weekend and the builders would be coming on the following Monday to start demolishing the Victorian wing, therefore the affair would end naturally. There was really no need to do anything dramatic.

As she drifted off to sleep, her head was filled with images of him, and this time her dreams were pleasant.

The alarm clock went off at the usual time and after helping Elizabeth dress, the two of them made their way down for breakfast. The house was quiet and even the dog was missing. The girls would all have left for work an hour or two ago, the twins would be busy in the study doing their schoolwork and Jean would be in the kitchen.

However, two of the three ladies from the village ought to be working and she couldn't hear any activity coming from the wing in which the land girls lived.

'Elizabeth, I'll join you in the breakfast room in a few minutes. I just want to check something upstairs.'

'I'll tell Jean to wait until you arrive. Nothing worse than cold toast, in my opinion. Quite ruins my day.'

Joanna turned into the passageway and called. Immediately the bathroom door opened.

'Did you want something, my lady? I couldn't hear you with the door shut and the water running,' Aggie said cheerfully. She was, as always, enveloped in a floral wraparound apron and had her hair tied up in a scarf.

'No, sorry for disturbing you. After the excitement of last night, I just wanted to check you, Doris and Enid are fine.'

'The all-clear went after an hour and there were no blooming bombers at all – at least not over us,' Aggie said. 'The boys at Manston were busy – I pray they all returned safely. Must be so hard for the wives, girlfriends and mothers of the pilots.'

'As you know, my daughter's engaged to a fighter pilot and two of the girls who lodged with me are married to pilots. I try not to think about it. I won't disturb you, as I know you have a lot to do.'

She now had a man of her own to worry about, but John must be safer on the ground than the brave boys who did their fighting in the sky.

The telephone rang as she walked past it. It was Mrs Dougherty, the area organiser for the land girls.

'I've just spoken to Dr Willoughby, my lady, and Miss Somiton will be out of action for two weeks at least. A very nasty head injury, it seems.'

'Are you sending a girl to replace her temporarily?'

'Good heavens, no. The other two working at Fiddler's Farm will just have to pick up the slack. Miss Somiton won't be paid, obviously, and you'll need to arrange for her ration book to be taken to the doctor's house.'

'I'll ask my son to cycle down with it later. What an absolutely dreadful thing to happen and so soon after arriving too. Do you know how the accident happened?'

'It seems she tripped over a chicken and lost her balance. These things happen, but fortunately not too often.'

There was a click and the line went dead. No pleasantries, no goodbyes, and Joanna thought that rather rude. She could only suppose the woman was run off her feet trying to find homes for all the newly recruited girls but, in her opinion, that didn't excuse ignoring the common courtesies.

They had scrambled eggs with toast for breakfast, which she much preferred to porridge. This was one thing she and Elizabeth agreed upon.

'Where are our two guests this morning, Joanna?'

'I've no idea. As they are guests, not boarders, it's really none of our business what they do.'

'That's balderdash, my dear, and you know it,' said Elizabeth. 'Boarders pay for their keep, guests don't, so they should be more punctilious in their behaviour, don't you think?'

She smiled. 'You're right, I suppose. Are you suggesting that I go in search of them and read them the riot act for not coming down to breakfast?'

'There's no need. Good morning, gentlemen, did you sleep well after the alarms and excursions of last night?'

Joanna swivelled in her chair to speak to them. 'Neither of you look particularly well-rested. I thought all service people were able to sleep anywhere and at any time.'

They took their places before either of them answered. John seemed subdued, sad even, and her stomach plummeted. She could think of only one reason for his expression and that was that he'd come to the same conclusion as her – that their affair would soon be over, almost before it had begun.

'Sorry that we've kept you waiting,' said John. 'I tried to persuade the doc to take out our stitches, but he refused. We want to get back to work but have to wait until Saturday. I'm sure you both want to see the back of us too.'

'Not at all, young man, we enjoy your company. My daughter-in-law and I have decided that our home will be available for any from Manston who need somewhere to recuperate and don't have homes nearby to go to.'

This was the first time this had been mentioned and there certainly hadn't been any discussion between Joanna and her mother-in-law. Joanna could hardly say so, but she'd make sure Elizabeth understood these decisions couldn't be made by her – they were the responsibility of the head of the household, which Elizabeth was not.

'We've certainly appreciated your hospitality, ma'am, and thank you for it.' John didn't even glance in her direction as he spoke but kept his eyes firmly on Elizabeth.

* * *

John had met Percy on his way back from the doctor's house and given him the bad news. His corporal had been happy to have his sick leave extended but John was disappointed, knowing he wouldn't have the willpower to stay away from Joanna tonight.

The old lady seemed to be on top form and not showing any signs of the senility Joanna had told him about. He'd not expected there to be any breakfast this late and he wished he didn't have to sit at a table – no more than an arm's length from the woman he was in love with – and have to hide his feelings.

'You're not eating, Sergeant, are the eggs not done to your liking?' Lady Harcourt was looking at him speculatively and his guilt made him sweat. Was she about to accuse him of seducing her daughter-in-law?

'A lot on my mind, ma'am, but I promise I won't leave a crumb. *Waste not, want not* is etched on my memory.'

'I should think so too. If you were at the doctor's, do you have up-to-date news about the injured girl?'

'Obviously I didn't ask about the patient as it's none of my business. That said, I could hear voices coming from a bedroom and I think I recognised one of them as being the girl you mentioned. She certainly sounded wide awake and *compos mentis*.'

Joanna now joined in the conversation and even Percy had a word or two to add. The poor bloke was in awe of the ladies – after all, it wasn't every day that people like them got to live in a stately home and share the same table as two aristocrats.

It was easier for John, having spent three years at Oxford mixing with the sons, and occasional daughters, of the upper classes. He thought he'd been one of only a handful of working-class young men attending the university. He'd always been left-leaning in his beliefs, and this was confirmed by the behaviour and attitude of many of those he'd studied with.

Things were easier because both Joanna and her mother-in-law weren't like other toffs he'd met. They spoke in the same clipped, crystal-clear way, but what they said wasn't so class-conscious.

He excused himself, saying that he had letters to write, and returned to his shared bedroom. Percy had wandered off for a smoke so he had the room to himself. It had been some time since he'd corresponded with his mother and it wouldn't do any harm to bring her up to date.

He smiled wryly. She would be horrified if she knew he'd been injured, almost killed, but not as horrified as she'd be if she discovered he was sleeping with Joanna. She thought sex was just for procreation within the sanctity of marriage and not meant to be enjoyed by either party.

Small wonder his dad spent most of his time in the pigeon loft or at the working men's club if he'd not been welcome in his wife's bed for the past decade or so. Perhaps it would be better not to write to his mother at all. Well – perhaps a postcard with a pretty picture of Goodwill House. He'd bought some when he'd walked into the village earlier. This was something she'd enjoy hearing about and would brag to her friends that her son was staying somewhere grand.

He'd just finished the third card to another member of his family when there was a polite tap on the door.

'Sergeant, I'm going down to the village and Ma said you might have some letters that need posting.'

John blotted the card and opened the door. 'Thank you, that will save me a second walk to Stodham.'

'Do you think your corporal's right about the Germans being able to invade if the Americans don't join in the war?' Joe asked.

'I don't. Remember, we've got twenty-two miles of water between us and France; we've got a better navy, as well as the RAF boys patrolling. Think about it, Joe, the barges they'd have to use to transport the tanks and soldiers would be sitting ducks.'

'Blooming heck, course you're right. As long as the RAF's still flying and the navy's still sailing, we're safe from the jackboots.'

Joe dashed off and John thought he'd go and remove any evidence from the room that might reveal what had been going on in there. Certainly, it had to be done before the builders started work. Percy still thought he was having it off with one of the land girls and he'd no intention of putting him right.

He walked out through the boot room door, across the courtyard and down to the gate that led into the separate yard for the Victorian end of the house. He saw an old bloke working in the walled kitchen garden and gave him a wave. The gardener was unlikely to have any contact with the house but, if he did, John thought nobody would think twice about him going for an exploratory walk.

It was far easier to make his way to the first floor in daylight. Before he tidied up, he wanted to see exactly what Joanna had done to make the room more romantic. He hadn't really stopped to look last night – all he'd thought about was her.

He pushed open the door and stopped so suddenly that his

toes were crushed in the end of his boots. Joanna was picking up the candles. She'd obviously come for the same reason as him.

She froze. Then she dropped the candles and was across the room and into his arms. What happened next was inevitable. The power of their passion, their love, made them forget everything in their desperation to make love.

They continued kissing as they removed each other's clothes, but he still had his socks on when they fell onto the bed.

* * *

Sal pressed herself into the prickly hedge and prayed that the giant cow wouldn't kill her. Despite her terror, she wondered where the other cows were and why they weren't joining in. As the monster approached, she closed her eyes and waited to be impaled on the massive horns.

Now she could hear its hooves pounding the grass, hear it snorting. She was pressing her back so hard into the thorns that the pain made her whimper. Her head was spinning, her heart pounding. She could scarcely breathe.

Why wasn't she dead? The cow was so close she could smell it. It was breathing heavily and must be near enough to reach out and touch. Slowly, she opened one eye.

The massive head was barely a foot away from hers – the first thing she saw was a thick brass ring through its nose.

'Blimey, you ain't no cow, you're a bleeding great bull.' She'd spoken out loud and the bull grunted as if replying. Then he nudged her in the chest, pushing the prickles deeper into her back and arms.

'Here, mister, none of that. Back off a bit; I'm being torn to pieces by these blooming thorns.' Some instinct made her reach out and tentatively stroke the huge head. The animal sighed but instead of moving away, he came closer.

'Look here, bull, I like you too. But I ain't going to be impaled no more. I'll give you a lovely stroke and you can have me sandwiches too once I'm out of this hedge.'

She kept her hand firmly on the bull's nose and pushed. He didn't budge. She didn't like to pull on the ring in case she hurt him but decided she'd no option. She slipped her shaking fingers into it and gently turned his head.

To her surprise and astonishment, the huge beast seemed to understand and moved a few steps sideways, allowing her to emerge from the hedge. She continued to stroke the bull with her other hand.

'What a fine fellow you are. I thought you were going to kill me, but you just came over to say hello. I thought you were a cow, how stupid is that? Shows I come from the East End and ain't a country girl.'

Once she was free, she released her hold on his ring. When she stopped, so did he. He was as gentle and docile as one of the big Shire horses on the farm.

She dipped into her haversack and pulled out one of her marmalade sandwiches – there'd been nothing else to put in them unless she'd had spam and piccalilli, and she was fed up with that.

When feeding an animal, you held your hand flat and put the food on the palm, she'd learned this at the college. She did this and, after sniffing the offering, he took it and was soon munching away. Sal reckoned he was smiling as he ate it but she was probably imagining that.

She was a bit stiff and sore, but nothing too bad. All she needed now was a gate to climb over and she could find her bicycle and get on her way. She walked along the hedge and the bull followed her, giving her the occasional nudge as if asking if she had any more treats for him.

'Greedy bugger, I'll give you the other half when I find the gate. I reckon the girls will laugh when they hear what happened. Fancy me thinking you were a cow when you've got horns and a ring through your nose.'

They'd been walking side by side for a bit when she spotted what she needed. She gave him a final pat and then scrambled over the gate with more haste than dignity. Once safely on the other side, she gave the animal the other half of her sandwich.

She left him to eat it and ran back, far further than she'd thought it would be, to find her bicycle. It wasn't too badly damaged and seemed to go all right. She pedalled away, wincing every now and again as the damage from the hedge made itself known.

* * *

After her encounter in the field, Sal wasn't having any nonsense from Primrose and decided she'd milk her first. The cows were in the lower field, which meant she had to fetch them. This was easy enough, as all you had to do was open the gate and call and they rushed down the field, eager to be milked and fed.

She stood back, standing with the gate between her and them, and let them find their own way to the shed where they were milked. There was no point in closing the gate as the cows would go back in the field as soon as they'd been done.

The cows knew which stall they had to go in and were all waiting, munching on the cut-up mangelwurzels and swedes that had been put ready for them in the manger. Sal had already put on her brown coat, washed her hands, and had a bucket of clean water and several rags ready to deal with the udders.

As she was finishing the last cow, she realised that Daphne and the other girls wouldn't be able to get to work because none of them knew how to harness and drive the mare. Despite the delay caused by her unexpected visit to the bull, she still managed to finish and get the cows safely back by seven. Being a land girl suited her and she was happier and fitter than she'd ever been in her life. A few weeks back, she'd have been ready to drop after all the work.

She jumped on the bicycle and, head down, pedalled furiously and skidded to a halt in the stable yard of Goodwill House before any of the girls came out. She was still sticky with sweat, uncomfortably hot, when they arrived, but Star was safely between the shafts, and she was in the box seat waiting to take them to work as usual.

16

Joanna didn't want to move, wanted to lie in John's arms and relish the moment, knowing it would be the last time she would feel his hot skin against hers, taste his kisses, make love to a man she loved. Eventually, it was he who broke the connection.

'Darling, we have to go. Someone will come looking for you if you stay with me any longer.'

'I can't bear it, my love, to have found you and have to give you up so soon. It's just not fair.'

'War's not fair, sweetheart, we both know that. Better to part wanting more, your reputation intact, than to continue and for it to end badly. I'll always love you, doubt I'll ever feel the same way again, but there's nothing we can do about it.'

She kissed him for the last time. Without another word, she dressed and walked out. If he'd called her back, she would have gone, but he didn't. Her throat was clogged, her eyes stung; she couldn't return to the house as she was.

She headed for the woods at the far end of the grounds, skirting the lawn, which was now a field of potatoes, and making sure Elizabeth wouldn't spot her from her perch on the terrace.

Every step that took her away from him was agony. Why couldn't they brave the horror of the family, the disgust of her neighbours, and be together? She weighed up the pros and cons as she stumbled on.

He was ten years her junior, the son of a cleaner and a miner, perhaps no prospects and no pedigree. But he was intelligent, had won a scholarship to Oxford, had a first-class maths degree and with her help he could achieve great things.

She'd not shed a tear for David, the man she'd been married to for over eighteen years, and yet was distraught at parting from a man she'd only known for days. She reached the shelter of the trees and found a quiet spot to sit. She wasn't going to cry, didn't want to return to the house with red eyes and puffy cheeks, she had to be strong.

She knew her pain would lessen in time and she would have the memory of their passionate love affair to fill her dreams for the rest of her life.

After sitting for a while in the cool shade from the green canopy above her, she was ready to return. John wouldn't be going for another two days and it was going to be impossible to sit at the same table as him and not show her feelings.

She took her time walking back and was met halfway by the dog. 'Hello, Lazzy, did someone send you to look for me?'

He pressed his cold nose into her hand as if he understood her sadness. Having him walking beside her, being able to talk to him, made the remainder of the journey bearable. As she approached the terrace, Elizabeth's head bobbed up from behind the balustrade.

'Our guests have gone. The sergeant rang the base and the medics there agreed to take out their stitches. A driver collected them about twenty minutes ago. What a shame you weren't here to say goodbye.'

'It is, but it can't be helped. I walked to the woods but didn't realise I'd been gone so long. It must be almost time for luncheon.' Joanna was relieved she'd not had to say goodbye in person as it would have been hard for her to hide her feelings, and others were bound to have been there too.

'Another half an hour,' Jean said. 'It's going to be egg salad with berries from the garden for dessert.'

'Sounds delicious. I'm going to pop upstairs and tidy up and then I'll join you.'

* * *

John stayed in the bed for a while longer, wanting to savour the last few precious minutes before he too left the room. He stripped the bed, folded the sheets and pillowcases and put them to the very back of the linen cupboard. He then replaced the faded bedspread and made sure the room looked exactly as it had three days ago.

He put the candles in a cupboard in the kitchen and then walked briskly around to the house. His first job was to ring the base and tell them he and Percy needed a driver to collect them as they were returning to duty today.

The WAAF who answered the telephone said the car would be there in half an hour. This didn't give him long to find his corporal, pack his kit and say his goodbyes. Percy, fortunately, didn't argue or ask why the sudden change of plan.

He interrupted the twins at their studies, found Jean collecting eggs, and then went to the terrace and said goodbye to the old lady.

'I thought Dr Willoughby refused to take out your stitches, young man.'

'He did, but there's a medic on the base who can do it. We're fit enough to work and it's just not right we stay here any longer. I'm sorry I can't say goodbye to your daughter-in-law, please convey my thanks to her for her kindness and hospitality.'

'Take care of yourself, Sergeant, try not to get blown up or incinerated.'

He grinned. 'I'll do my best, ma'am. Goodbye, and thank you for making us feel so welcome.'

The car turned onto the drive whilst he was on the terrace, which made leaving easier. He'd seen Joanna in the distance as he'd left the Victorian wing and guessed she'd be gone more than an hour so had planned his departure carefully. This separation was going to be easier for him, as he could immerse himself in his duties, but her life was relatively quiet. This would give her far too much time to dwell on what might have been.

The medic was happy to take out his stitches and passed him fit for duty, but Percy was told he could only do light duties for another week.

'What does that mean, Sarge?'

'You can answer the telephone, potter about getting in everybody's way, read a paper – I'm sure you'll find something to occupy your time. You could hardly stay at Goodwill House on your own.'

'Fair enough. To be honest, it was all a bit la-di-dah for me. I'm surprised you fitted in so well with your socialist views and all that.'

'I avoided talking about politics or religion and so did they. We were lucky to get to stay at Goodwill House. I'm sure that in future they don't want RAF wounded at the house – they've got more than enough to do with a dozen land girls to look after.'

'To be honest, not everything the old lady said made sense, so when she told me they were planning an open house for RAF wounded, I ignored it.'

John wasn't on duty until midnight, which gave him more than enough time to stow his gear and then get over to the hangar and find out what had been happening in his absence.

The base showed no sign of any further damage and as far as he could see, all the kites were present and correct. The bell rang on the far side of the strip and immediately the flyers scrambled. He slung his kit bag over his shoulder and walked into his billet. As a sergeant, he didn't have to sleep in a Nissen hut along with the men. He shared his accommodation with the other sergeant who worked the second shift. They rarely saw each other, so it was the same as being on his own.

He'd kept an ear out for the siren, but it didn't sound, so this must be a party happening further away. His motorbike was where he'd left it and he kicked it into life and headed to the far end of the base.

All evidence of the crashed German plane had been removed and there was an empty space where the shelter had once been. Another one hadn't been constructed, so they would all have to hide in the nearest safety ditch, which was probably just as safe. The base had several underground shelters and some tunnels but none at this end. He smiled as he realised how he'd almost gone for a Burton but instead had fallen for Joanna and she for him. He'd never regret meeting her, however hard it was going to be to move on.

'What are you doing here, Sarge? Thought you were off until the weekend,' Sergeant Billy Fisher said.

'Couldn't stay away. Did I miss much?'

He followed Billy into the office and flicked through the logbook. Two near misses, but nothing else. The team were sitting about in the sunshine chatting, dozing, relaxed, but if they were needed, then they'd be on the tenders instantly and ready to go.

'I see they haven't replaced the shelter.'

'No, I told them we'd be better off in a ditch and our blokes offered to dig it. Want a dekko?'

The ditch was far enough away from the hangar where the tenders were kept to be safe, and not so far the men couldn't get there before a bomber arrived. Fine when it was sunny, but it would be bloody horrible in the rain.

'Right, Billy, I'll let you get on. I'm going to get a few hours' kip if I can. I'll see you at midnight.'

Sleep evaded him, but that was hardly surprising, as he'd not been working nights since his accident. It was going to take him a few days to adjust. What he wanted to do was get paralytic – drown his sorrows and push all thoughts of Joanna from his head. He wasn't a heavy drinker but was tempted to go to the mess. He'd never go on duty anything but sober, so he remained where he was.

John wasn't a romantic sort of bloke, hadn't expected to fall in love, but his misery was like a physical pain – as if he was actually grieving for someone who'd died. He should have stayed and said goodbye and not run away like a coward. He bitterly regretted the brief relationship, as now both of them were miserable. If they'd just showed a bit of restraint, then there wouldn't be this heartbreak.

It was his fault – it was always the man's fault in these circumstances. He should have said no, and part of him wished that he had. If it hadn't happened, neither of them would be feeling so miserable. Then he straightened his shoulders and nodded. No, he was wrong, he didn't regret one wonderful, amazing moment of it, and he hoped that Joanna felt the same.

* * *

Sal thought she'd save her story about the bull until the evening when they had their meal together. Nobody commented on the fact that she was red-faced and a bit untidy.

Daphne was sitting behind her. 'How did you get on with the milking?'

'All done, but I never had time to do more than put the milk in the cooler and the cows in the field. I'd have been late picking you up otherwise.'

'Can I have a go at driving? It looks easy enough. Then, if you show me how to harness and unharness Star, you won't have to come back in a rush to get us like you did this morning.'

Sal beamed. 'You can have the reins on the way back. Be a bit tricky swapping over here.'

She dropped the three girls at the end of the lane that led to their farm. They still had another two days of harvesting and then Pickering would have to start cutting his corn so it was ready for the threshing machine when it came. The hay was already made, and she was sad she'd missed that.

Daphne volunteered to do the pigs, but Sal refused. 'No, I like them porkers. They know me now and it won't take me long.'

She was just putting Star back between the shafts of the cart in preparation for taking the milk and eggs to the village when the farmer came out. She scarcely recognised him – his eyes were clear, he was spruced up and was actually smiling.

'Good morning, Sal, you and Daphne are doing me proud. I've let you down since you were here but I've pulled myself together now. The farm's looking more how it should be and I'll do my bit in future.'

'That'll be grand, Mr Pickering. There's a lot to do with just the two of us. Me friends what work at Admiral's farm next door said we've got to start cutting the corn. Is that right?'

'That's what I came to talk to you about,' Pickering said. 'We need more than the three of us to get the wheat and barley harvested. A friend of mine's agreed to loan me four of his men – but I'll be in charge. I promise you'll not be treated badly by the temporary workers.'

Daphne had heard them talking and come out from the shed where she was cleaning and stacking the eggs. 'Is one team of horses enough, or do you borrow a tractor to help out?'

'My two Shires can work all day, they just need a bit of water and a breather every couple of hours. We'll need to use your little mare and your cart.'

'I'll be able to do that as Sal's going to teach me…'

'I'll get a couple of nippers to take care of the cart. You'll be needed to stack the sheaves into stooks. You'll need to be here earlier and work 'til dusk. You done any harvesting?'

If Charlie was here, she would have put him straight, and Sal decided she'd be the one to speak up this time. 'Blimey, mister, we only signed up a few weeks ago. Give us a chance, why don't you?'

'Fair enough. I'll show you what you need to do. It's hard work but better than picking brussels sprouts in the winter.'

He smiled, it looked a bit forced, but was better than the usual scowl. 'Mrs Finbarr from the village is helping out in the house until my missus is back. She's making you lunch in future and she'll give you a bit of tea in the afternoon too. You deserve it – I reckon you work harder than the blokes who used to be here.'

He didn't walk away as he'd done on previous occasions but started to pile the things onto the cart. He rolled the milk churns easily with one hand and then hefted them into the back, easy as you like.

'Get this down to the village and then come to the house for lunch.'

'Yes, sir,' Daphne said and exchanged a smile with Sal. When he'd gone, they were able to talk freely about this happy change.

'This is a bit of all right, ain't it? It'll be lovely working here if we get a proper meal at midday and don't have Pickering swearing at us and that.'

'It seems he pulled himself together after the accident,' Daphne said. 'He's not the nasty, lazy man we thought he was after all.'

* * *

They sold everything on the cart, collected the empty churns and returned to the farm well pleased with the morning's work. 'Here, Daphne, what's sheaves and stooks when they're at home?'

'Sheaves are bundles of wheat that come from the machine and stooks are the piles you make of them afterwards. They look like little pyramids. When the field's cut, we go along with that huge cart you saw in the barn and have to pitchfork the sheaves onto the cart.'

'Sounds like hard work, but if old Pickering stays in a good mood, it won't be too bad here.'

They spent the afternoon hoeing and Sal had a few blisters by the time they'd finished. 'Here, Daphne, is there anything in that book what we were given when we joined to help with these?' She showed her hands and Daphne's were just as bad.

'I don't think so – I think we should have worn gloves. I expect our hands will get tougher after a bit. I seem to remember there's something for cracked hands and it said we should put castor oil or oil of wintergreen, but I don't think that would work for these. Just put a bit of glycerine on them and keep them dry.'

Daphne was a dab hand with the harness and drove the mare home with no trouble. When they got back to the yard, Joe was waiting. Sal hopped out of the cart and decided to leave her friend to put the horse away.

'You can take it all off without me helping, Daphne. I reckon you've got the hang of it already.'

'It's easier than it looks. Would you show me how to drive the cart horses?'

'I will ask old Pickering tomorrow – I reckon it'll be good if both of us can do it and then we can take turns at making them stooks. We'd better ask Lady Harcourt if we can use Star in the fields. She's not a workhorse, belongs to Miss Harcourt, I think she's a bit too posh to do fieldwork.'

'You seem to know more about horses than I do, so I'll leave you to sort that out.'

Sal walked over to Joe, leaving the other girls to dash off for a quick wash before supper. 'Was you waiting to speak to me?'

'It's the bike – I've spent an hour mending it. Are you all right? You must have had a spectacular crash for it to be so bashed up like that.'

'Some idiots in a lorry hooted right behind me and I lost my balance and went over a hedge. It pedalled all right after.'

'The brakes had gone AWOL and the front wheel was bent. All sorted now and I'm glad you're not hurt.'

'Ta, sorry about the extra work. Daphne will be driving the cart in future as I'm going early to do the milking.'

Over supper, she told everyone about her meeting with the bull and got the reaction she'd hoped for. She reckoned it would be talked about for weeks. Charlie was going to be away for some time and the girls agreed with her suggestion that they club together and buy her something – if something could be found in one of the village shops that would do.

For the first time, she was part of the group, not an outsider, and went to bed feeling safer and happier than she had for years.

17

Joanna kept herself busy and had two meetings to attend in the village hall. She was confident nobody would be aware of how unhappy she was. On Friday morning, the builder who was to start demolishing the other end of the house the following Monday turned up. He asked if he could have a look at what needed to be done before his men started knocking things down.

He returned a short time later looking bothered. 'Lady Harcourt, you've not cleared the furniture and so on. You need to get it done before Monday.'

'Oh, I thought the contents were part of the deal. I didn't realise it was up to me to remove everything.'

His eyes gleamed. 'I've got a mate who deals with second-hand stuff, my lady, and I'm sure he'll be happy to take it off your hands. You need to have a look round and make sure there's no family heirlooms. I don't want to be accused of stealing them.'

'I'll get onto that immediately,' Joanna said. 'How long do you think it will take you to demolish the building and remove the debris?'

'About a month, maybe a bit longer. Then it'll take another

couple of weeks to repair the wall that will be left exposed. It'll be done by the middle of October.'

'Thank you, I'm not looking forward to the noise and my mother-in-law won't be able to sit on the terrace whilst you're doing it. I can assure you she's most displeased about that.'

His answer was drowned out by yet another squadron of aircraft tearing across the sky. This was rapidly followed by the siren on the base and the one in the village. The builder ignored the warning and, with a happy smile, went back to his lorry whistling to himself. He was obviously pleased he was going to get an unexpected bonus in the way of second-hand furniture and so on.

They now had it down to a well-rehearsed routine and before the siren stopped, all of them were safely in the summerhouse. Two of the village ladies were there, the ancient gardener, the twins, their tutor, Jean, Elizabeth and Joanna.

'Goodness, why didn't the builder take cover? He'll be visible from the air,' Jean said as she watched the lorry tearing down the drive.

'What do the land girls do, Ma?' Liza asked.

'I expect they hide under a tree or a hedge. I think it's very unlikely anyone working on a farm will be in serious danger.'

Elizabeth had been on top form lately and Joanna was beginning to wonder if she'd imagined the mental deterioration in her mother-in-law.

'Sitting outside, even though the weather is wonderful, is becoming untenable, my dear. The noise is just frightful and once those builders start, it will be even worse.'

'You're right. We're going to have to keep all the windows and doors shut at the front of the house until it's done. It seems I was supposed to clear any items that we wanted and that's got to be done before Monday.'

'I never set foot in the place, so I can't tell you if there is anything valuable in there, but I doubt it.'

'We've already removed several trunks from the attics, and all the usable items from the kitchens,' Joanna said. 'At the WVS meeting the other day, one of the things we discussed was the necessity to have as many spare items of furniture stored in case houses are damaged by bombs. You can't buy such things, as all the factories are doing war work.'

'I'd be happy to go around with you,' Jean said. 'I've worked in grand places like this and think I'd recognise anything worth keeping.'

'Everything that's usable is worth keeping. Nothing will be destroyed, as what we leave behind the builder will take as part of his remuneration.'

The ominous sound of bombers approaching made her look anxiously in the direction of the coast. High in the sky, there seemed to be dozens of little aircraft fighting each other.

'Look at that, Ma, our boys have shot down two of those Nazi planes,' Joe shouted excitedly. He was on his feet and standing at the open door, gazing into the sky.

She watched him and a weight settled on her heart. Three years from now, if this beastly war was still going on, her beloved son could well be one of those risking their lives so bravely above them.

She sent up a fervent prayer that the young men she knew would return safely to their bases. Today the RAF triumphed and none of the bombers appeared to get past and drop their deadly cargo on Manston, the village, or Ramsgate. They might well have been more successful in their attacks at the other airfields in Kent, but here that wasn't the case.

When the all-clear sounded, it was time for lunch. Mr Kent, the tutor, politely refused the offer to join them, as did the ladies from the village and the gardener. There was smoke drifting from the base. The fire could only be from a crashed aircraft and Joanna refused to think about who might get injured fighting these fires.

* * *

Elizabeth went for a rest after luncheon, saying that the excitement of the morning had been too much for her. Joe had work to do somewhere in the vegetable garden, so Joanna, Jean and Liza made their way around to the Victorian end.

The thought of going into this place where she'd had a brief moment of perfect happiness was almost too much for Joanna, but she squared her shoulders and blinked away her tears, determined to do what was necessary.

Jean touched Joanna's arm. 'We took everything that we wanted from this place and there are still half a dozen trunks waiting to be investigated. I don't think there's anything else of value in there.'

'I think you're right. This is a bad idea. I'll let Mr Kent and his men have the furniture and linens.' Joanna smiled her thanks. 'Liza, we're not going in after all. I'm going to give everything left to the builders. I'm sure anything usable will eventually be recycled to people who need it.'

'That's good,' Liza said with a grin. 'Joe and I have got an invitation to go to Radcliffe Manor to play tennis.'

'Then go and enjoy yourselves. I did wonder why you've been batting a ball back and forth with those old rackets these past few days.'

'I'm quite good at returning the ball,' Liza said, 'but can't work out how to serve.'

'I'm sure you'll enjoy yourselves. Will you be back for supper?'

'We haven't been invited to stay, but would it be all right if we did? We'd definitely be back before the blackout.'

'There aren't any bicycles free, but it's only a mile to Radcliffe Manor, so that's fine with me.'

Liza hurried off without a backward glance. 'The two of them will be adults soon, Joanna, but you'll not lose them just yet,' Jean said.

'My biggest fear is that Joe will join the RAF and become a pilot, or at least aircrew, and then...' She couldn't continue. She'd already lost too much already, her throat constricted and tears trickled down her cheeks. Fortunately, Jean thought her distress was a combination of Betty's recent death and the worry about losing the people she loved to this ghastly war. She couldn't possibly know it was because her heart was breaking.

* * *

John was kept busy over the next few days and only when he was trying to sleep did the emptiness caused by Joanna's loss cause problems. Three wounded kites crash-landed, but he and his team were able to pull all the pilots out before they were seriously hurt. Easier to replace a kite than a pilot was what the bigwigs said.

The airfield was peppered with bomb craters, so squadrons had to be parked close together. This meant that when the next wave of Bf 109s arrived, they were able to destroy two Spitfires and seriously damage six others before they could be airborne.

There had been horrendous losses and at the last count, eight flyers had died and several more had been put out of action. The talk in the mess was grim. Replacing these men was becoming more difficult and it was clear training would have to be shortened if the squadrons were going to be kept at full strength.

On the Tuesday, there was another major attack by Bf 110s and E 210s. The siren wailed, the squadrons were scrambled and he and his men ran for the safety ditch. The ground shook and the noise was deafening as the Luftwaffe divebombed and strafed the base.

Eventually, they were driven back and John was delighted to see at least two of them go down in flames in the Channel. Now it was his job to put out the fires, rescue anybody trapped and prove that he and his men were good at their jobs.

A number of buildings had been badly damaged, as well as two hangars at the east of the base.

'Bloody hell, Sarge, the roof's collapsed over the temporary armoury. There's a lot of valuable weapons and ammunition stored in there,' Percy said.

'We can't handle all this on our own,' John said. 'Get back to the office and make sure the Margate and Ramsgate Fire Brigades are on their way.'

His corporal was still on light duties but the rest of the men were eager to pile out of the ditch and do their bit. 'We'll deal with the armoury. The civilian firefighters can take care of everything else.'

The four tenders raced towards the building, which at any moment could catch fire and explode, killing all of them. His blokes didn't hesitate and they had the collapsed roof removed in record time and then doused the area with water.

The munitions expert declared the place safe; John thanked his men and they returned, wet, filthy, and exhausted – but satisfied with a job well done – to their hangar.

The tenders were cleaned, the water tanks refilled and only then were they able to take a well-earned break. The civilian firefighters had arrived promptly and John was pleased with their response.

The NAAFI van was on its way but before it came, he decided to grab his motorbike and ride around the base to see just how bad the damage had been and how many casualties there were. He was pleased nobody had been seriously hurt and although the destruction was significant, there were enough blokes on the base to get everything repaired and back to working order in a day or two.

There was a constant arrival and departure of kites from Hornchurch and Debden, but they just landed to refuel and rearm and then took off again to continue what seemed to be a constant battle to protect the coast of Britain.

At midnight, when he finished his shift, he fell onto his bed fully clothed, not even bothering to take off his boots. For the first time since he'd left Goodwill House, he slept soundly.

Sal now took it in turns with Daphne to look after the horses. Daphne was a dab hand with the reins and Pickering had taught her friend how to manage the big Shires, so they could now share the driving.

'It's so much easier now our boss is doing his share,' Daphne said as she guided the mare into the lane that led to the farm.

'He's a decent bloke, not what I thought, I'm enjoying meself here. Not looking forward to meeting the four new farmworkers. I reckon they'll want to treat us like skivvies but I ain't having none of that.'

'Neither am I; we've done an excellent job without Charlie and when they move on, we'll still be here.'

They both flinched as planes took off from Manston again. They'd had to scuttle into a hedge a couple of times when the sirens went, but Sal thought they were safer in the open than in one of them shelters.

The farmer was now getting up and milking the cows, so she didn't have to come on her own on the bicycle, and she preferred to travel with the other girls.

'Blimey, them blokes are already here and it's not even seven yet. I reckon they're trying to show us up.'

'I think that they're men trying to avoid being conscripted,' Daphne said. 'All of them are the right age to be in the forces and yet here they are, large as life, working on a farm.'

'I think farm work is a reserved occupation, or they could be them conscientious objectors, I heard someone in the village say some of them are working on farms.' Sal didn't care why they were there as long as they could do a good day's work.

Pickering was talking to the men and the Shire horses were already harnessed and ready to go. He walked across to them, smiling as if he meant it.

'Morning, girls, early as usual. We need to get started. We don't need your little mare till later. The cart can be used to bring refreshments at lunchtime. The first field we're doing is over the back – Daphne, you take my wife's bicycle and then you can get back quicker.'

'Right, Mr Pickering, I'll do that. What about the horses? Will I bring something for them to eat?'

He pointed to the two nose bags attached to the side of the reaper. 'I've taken water up there – for the horses and for us. It's going to be a scorcher. You should have worn a hat.'

'Golly, he's cheerful today,' Daphne said. 'Quick, the men are leaving and you need to follow them. I'll put Star in the barn so she'll be easy to catch at lunchtime.'

Daphne was right and Sal ran across to unwind the reins and set the Shires in motion behind the men. The contraption they were pulling had rotating blades on the side which would cut the wheat. Pickering had explained that the sheaves tumbled out the side already tied and then the harvesters just had to pile them into stooks and leave them ready to be collected when the field was finished.

It didn't sound too complicated and she was sure she could do her part. Well – the horses would do most of the work, she just had to walk up and down behind them, making sure they were going straight.

* * *

After three hours' walking, Sal was ready for a rest and so were the horses. She guided them to an area shaded by the large hedge. 'Now then, you two, time for a drink and a bit of scoff.'

When she touched their noses, they lowered their heads and allowed her to slip off their bridles so the bit could drop out of their mouth. She then slipped it back over their ears so they could drink and eat without the nasty bit of metal in their gobs.

After making sure the horses were watered and fed, she got herself a much-needed drink of water. She was working more or less on her own, as the other six were busy collecting the sheaves and stacking them and this was the first time she'd got a good dekko at the travelling farm labourers.

They seemed all right, not too pushy, not really interested in either her or Daphne, which was good. She ladled herself a tin mug of water, hooked out the bits of chaff, and collapsed beside her friend.

'Not too bad doing this, do you want to change over, or do I keep going until lunchtime?'

'No, you finish the morning and I'll do the afternoon. It's going well and these new men seem to know what they're doing.'

Daphne paused and looked across at the group who were sitting together at a distance away. 'One of them was asking questions about you. He thought he recognised you.'

Sal's stomach clenched and for a second her head spun. These men were from London – did this mean her life was about to be ruined by the man she'd run away from? 'Tell me exactly what he said.'

'Not a lot, just that he came from London and thought he'd seen you somewhere.'

'I don't think I've met him before. I'm not going to panic. He might not even know the bastard I'm hiding from.' Sal was glad she'd decided to tell her secret to Daphne.

Daphne reached out and squeezed her hand. 'It doesn't matter if he does. You're safe with us. I wasn't sure if I should tell you but thought it better that you knew.'

'Thanks, Daphne. I'm going to stay away from all of them and keep me head down. If you don't mind, I'll stick to the reaping. Safer that way.'

They had half an hour to eat the tasty sandwiches and tea sent up from the house. A cuppa was always welcome, whatever the weather. By eight o'clock, the horses were done and, without asking permission, at the end of the row she turned their heads towards home. There were still a couple of hours of daylight but they wouldn't be fit to work the next day if she carried on.

It took a while to brush the horses, check their hooves for stones and then lead them both to the home paddock. They'd had oats in their nose bags so didn't need anything extra apart from water and their trough was full.

The men and Daphne hadn't returned from the field by the time she'd finished so she harnessed Star and went down to collect them. They were just about to leave the field and were happy to see her.

'That was hard work, but enjoyable,' Daphne said as she squeezed beside her on the box.

'I was a bit worried Pickering would be after me for leaving early, but I've only just finished sorting out the horses. They were done in and couldn't work any longer today.'

'He'd been about to send me across to tell you to go and was impressed that you made the decision yourself. The other girls will have walked home.'

Sal halted the cart to allow the men to jump out, clicked her tongue and the willing mare leaned into the harness. As soon as her head turned towards home, she broke into a lively trot without being asked.

Sal had a lot to think about. Of all the rotten luck, to find a perfect place to live, to make good friends and then for Den to maybe find her and take it all away.

18

Joanna was relieved that Monday and Tuesday had been relatively peaceful, as removing the contents, furniture, linens and so on from the deserted wing had caused no disruption or noise.

'That's the fourth lorryload they've taken, Joanna, and they are still loading up the ones that have returned. I rather think you made a serious error of judgement letting them keep the contents, as there is far more than either of us realised,' Elizabeth said gleefully. Sometimes she seemed to enjoy other people's discomfort.

'Perhaps, but I'd no use for any of it and I'd rather it was in circulation in Stodham and Ramsgate than sitting, unloved and unwanted, in an empty barn here.'

Elizabeth didn't take offence but merely nodded and smiled.

'It's getting very busy at Manston. The aircraft are taking off and landing constantly and you can hear the gunfire coming from the coast as well as overhead. How many times have we had to go down into the cellar since the air raids started?'

'Four, and five times to the summerhouse. We all know it's

going to get worse, but none of us are likely to be shot down and killed like the brave men you're complaining about,' Joanna snapped.

Since she and John had terminated their brief relationship, Joanna knew she had been bad-tempered, prone to tears, and this just wasn't fair on everybody else. She would do better in future, she decided, but it was going to be hard.

Having never been in love before, never having enjoyed the supreme pleasure of a satisfactory love life, she was finding it increasingly difficult to accept that three days were going to be her only taste of true happiness.

They were now being forced to keep not just the French doors and windows at the front of the house closed, but also those at the rear. The dust from the demolition was invasive, unpleasant and seemed to creep into any crack or crevice that it could.

It was a relief to all of them when the men went home at six o'clock and they were no longer deafened by the banging, the dust, and the debris.

The house was hot, unpleasantly stuffy, and the thought that this was how things were going to be for the next four or five weeks was unbearable. She shook her head at her nonsense. Being bombed, being shot at, fighting for one's life was unbearable – what they were putting up with was a mere inconvenience in comparison.

'Ma, did you know that Star's being used on the farm? She's not a workhorse and she's losing condition. I don't think it's right,' Joe told her that evening.

'Good heavens, I'd no idea. Daphne or Sal should have asked permission to do that. Are the girls still in the ballroom, or have they gone up?'

'From the racket coming out of there, they're having a right old time,' Liza said from the chair where she was curled up reading a book.

'Then I'll go and tell them that in future they'll have to walk to work and Mr Pickering will have to make his own arrangements. I know there's a war on, but I won't have Sarah's horse used in this way.'

Being angry about this was better than being angry about her life and about not being able to see John ever again. She marched to the ballroom and recoiled at the noise and the smell of cheap cigarettes.

She headed for the windup gramophone and picked up the arm with the needle from the record. The girls who'd been dancing with each other froze. If she wasn't so cross, she'd have smiled, as they looked like children at a party, playing the game of statues.

'Girls, I told you when you came here that smoking isn't allowed inside. There will be no more of it, or I'll have those concerned moved elsewhere.'

A ripple of unease ran around the large room. And the girls looked at her nervously as if she was a person to be feared and not just the timid widow of Lord Harcourt.

Emboldened by this, she pointed at Daphne and Sal, who were sitting at the far end of the ballroom. 'You two, come here, I'm most displeased with both of you.'

They jumped to their feet and rushed across to stand, hands behind their backs, heads lowered, like penitent schoolchildren being ticked off by an angry principal.

She was aware that the other nine girls were listening avidly to what was going on and she wished she'd not been quite so forceful, had asked the girls to step outside so she could talk to them privately, but it was too late to repine.

'Starlight was loaned to you for the purpose of transport only.

She will not be available to you in future, as you have abused that privilege. My daughter's mare is not a workhorse. Pickering must make his own arrangements and you and the other girls will have to make your own way to your place of employment in future.'

She didn't wait for them to answer but stalked away, nose in the air, every inch an arrogant aristocrat – something she wasn't and had never wished to be. She was tempted to go back and apologise but decided that wouldn't help the situation.

She paused in the hall and listened to see if the noise would start again. It remained quiet and her heart sank. What must they think of her? The poor girls would now have to walk two miles in either direction after they'd been working for hours, doing back-breaking work.

The fact that all but three of them – those on the market gardens – were working on her own farms made her feel even guiltier. She hoped that no one else in the household had heard her behaving so badly.

'You certainly made yourself very clear, my dear,' Elizabeth said with a smile of approval. 'About time you stood up for yourself. This is your house, they work on your farms, and they are lucky to be billeted here in such luxury.'

'Hear, hear,' Jean said admiringly.

'I could have handled it much better. I was behaving like David, and that's something I never want to do again.'

Joe dropped down beside her on the sofa. 'Serves them right, Ma, they should have asked. Neither of them know enough about horses to make that sort of decision. Wouldn't have happened if Charlie had been here.'

'I was going to ask about that girl, Joanna. Is she still living in the doctor's house?'

'I've no idea, Elizabeth, and it's none of our business. Mrs

Dougherty said she'll inform me if or when the girl will be returning.'

Again, Elizabeth appeared not to have heard, or perhaps understood, the previous comments.

'All the excitement has made me thirsty. I've got a surprise for you, my dear. Jean found two further tins of coffee at the bottom of one of my trunks when she was kindly helping me search through them. What we need is a large cognac and several cups of coffee.'

* * *

Sal knew this was her fault – she should have asked Joe about using the horse but had forgotten all about it. She didn't blame Lady Harcourt, as no one likes people to take liberties with their possessions.

'Now we've got to walk to work,' Gladys said. She worked on the other farm and always had something to moan about. 'We're taking the two bicycles, as that's only fair.'

'Hang on a minute,' Daphne said. 'Those bicycles are for all of us to use. You can have them tomorrow, but we have them the next day – now that *is* only fair.'

There was soon a bit of an argy-bargy, with everyone having an opinion. 'Maybe Lady Harcourt will change her mind after a week or two and, until then, Sal and I will share the bicycles.'

Gladys, the outspoken girl from the next farm, was still complaining. 'We had to walk home in the dark three times whilst you two travelled in comfort.'

Sal didn't want to argue any more and was prepared to give up the bicycles altogether, but Daphne was having none of it. 'The cycles belong to the Harcourts. I'll ask Lady Harcourt what she thinks, shall I?'

Sal had had enough of the grumbling and stood up. 'I'm going to make the cocoa.'

She headed for the kitchen and put a large saucepan of milk on to heat up. The kettle was already hot enough. She mixed cocoa powder and a teaspoon of sugar in the bottom of each mug and then added the almost boiling water.

Liza must've heard her banging about in the kitchen and joined her. 'I expect you and Daphne aren't very popular. Don't worry, Ma isn't usually so stern, and I think she might change her mind in a day or two. Let me help you with those mugs – you can't carry eleven of them on your own.'

'Ta ever so. I ain't very popular with them girls what work on the next farm as they were the ones what we gave a lift to every day,' said Sal. 'I'm hoping a nice hot cup of cocoa will smooth things over.'

'I know what will make things better. There's a tin of biscuits in the pantry. I was able to buy two packets of custard creams and some rich tea when I went to the village this morning. They're for you girls, as they were bought with your points. I don't suppose it really matters if you eat them all at once or eke them out over the next week.'

'I'll put one of each on a plate. No need to be greedy.'

Nobody had put the music on again and Daphne was sitting on her own. There was a bit of an atmosphere but nothing nice, sweet cocoa and biscuits couldn't put right, Sal thought.

She was right, and by the time they turned in, it was all smiles. She tumbled into bed in her knickers and bra, too tired to even put on her nightie. Daphne woke her the next morning and she reckoned if her friend hadn't done so, she'd have slept all day. She'd never been so tired, every bone ached; this must be what being an old woman would be like.

They had to leave half an hour earlier in order to be at work just before seven. The girls with the bicycles would probably get there quicker than travelling in the cart.

'It's not so bad now, it ain't hot, but it'll be different coming home.'

'It'll be dark, for a start, Sal,' said Daphne. 'We'll also be exhausted. This wouldn't have happened if Charlie had been here.'

'Blooming heck, don't you start. It were as much your fault as mine as we both drive the mare nowadays.'

They walked briskly and were going past the doctor's house much earlier than expected. 'I'm going to nip in and see how Charlie's doing, Daphne. We've got ten minutes in hand.'

'Good idea, I don't understand why she's not back. And to be honest, I don't know why she's living with the doctor at all.'

They were halfway up the path when they heard Charlie's voice coming from an open bedroom window. Sal didn't hesitate.

'Here, Charlie, what you doing lazing about in bed when we've got to work twelve hours on the fields?' She hadn't intended to yell so loudly and reckoned most of the village would have heard her.

There was the sound of someone moving and then the window was pushed wide open and Charlie leaned out.

'Hello, you two, I've been pronounced fit as a fiddle and will be back at work tomorrow. Why are you on foot?'

'We ain't got time to explain it all now,' said Sal. 'Are you going to be home this evening?'

'I certainly am. Dr Willoughby's kindly driving me back when he's finished his morning surgery.'

'We've missed you, Charlie, and it'll make things a bit easier at the farm having the three of us again,' Daphne said.

They waved, dashed back to the road and jogged until they

were only a couple of hundred yards from the lane that led to the farm. Sal wasn't even out of breath and neither was Daphne.

'I reckon we're a lot fitter and stronger than we were a few weeks ago. Working on the land is just the ticket.'

'It certainly is, Sal. Listen, I can hear a lorry coming. There's a gate just ahead; we can get out of the way there.'

This was the gate that Sal had climbed over after her encounter with the bull. She removed a jam sandwich from her haversack, hoping the massive animal might come and get it.

She'd forgotten to warn Daphne. Her friend reached the gate and the next moment, the bull shoved his head into the small of her back, knocking her onto her knees. She was just helping Daphne to her feet when the lorry went past.

There were several catcalls and rude remarks shouted at them by the soldiers sitting in the back. The bull hurled himself at the gate and snorted loudly. He didn't like the lorry one bit.

'Hang on, you big bruiser, I've got your buttie here.' Sal broke it in half and held out the first bit. She liked the pressure of his lips on the palm of her hand. She scratched him between his horns and he didn't object. The second half of the sandwich vanished just as quickly, and Daphne was watching open-mouthed.

'I didn't know you had it in you, Sal. I'm not sure I'd want to get so close to that animal, but he seems to like you.'

Daphne handed over one of her sandwiches and once that had gone, they had to jog all the way to the farm in order to avoid being late.

'It'll be a bit different having Charlie back, won't it? Will she want to work with the horses instead of me?' asked Sal.

'It doesn't matter what she wants, she'll just have to fit in with how things are now.'

* * *

The day was just as hard as the previous one. Pickering had taken the loss of the horse and cart well and hadn't made a fuss at all.

'Not to worry, I shouldn't have asked you to use her. It doesn't matter, as I'm borrowing a couple of work horses from a neighbouring farm. The weather's good and seems set for the next few days. I want to get the harvest in before it changes.'

'Mr Pickering, Charlie will be back tomorrow,' said Sal. 'Will you want her to drive the other team?'

'No, they come with a driver. A mate of mine's got a cob that can pull a bigger cart and he's going to lend him to me for a couple of weeks. Daphne, you'll have to get lunch. Bring it back in a wheelbarrow – be easier that way.'

Sal was seeing to the horses in the shade when she sensed someone was behind her. She looked round and saw the bloke who'd been asking questions about her.

'I've got a message for you from Den. He says he knows where you are and he's coming for you.'

Sal clutched the head collar. She'd known the moment that man had asked about her that she was in danger. Daphne had said she was safe at Goodwill House, that Den couldn't get to her, but she was wrong.

He could wait behind a tree, a hedge, anywhere on the farm until she was on her own. It might take him a week or more, but one thing she was sure of, he'd get her in the end. He wasn't looking to drag her back this time but to finish her off – murder her for leaving him. He'd threatened to do that often enough, and bloody nearly done it a couple of times.

She needed to think, decide what to do. She'd been wrong to think that being in the land girls was safe. If she'd been sent to anywhere else in the country, then she'd have been all right. But

Kent was where the hop pickers came, where East End folk spent what they thought of as a holiday working on the farms. And someone was eventually bound to recognise her.

John couldn't do more than ride his motorbike around the perimeter of the base, as all leave had been indefinitely cancelled. Hardly surprising with the number of attacks, dive bombers and general mayhem that was being thrown at the RAF.

The flyers were on permanent readiness, sleeping in their kit when they got a chance. Ground crew were equally stretched as they had to be on duty if the squadrons were active. His team had put out three fires but been unable to save one poor sod who'd nosedived into the deck.

The loss of pilots was horrendous and the loss of kites even worse. John held a pilot's licence, had learned to fly in a Tiger Moth a few years ago when lessons had been subsidised by the government. He wouldn't have bothered to learn but several of his friends at Oxford had joined a local flying club, so he'd tagged along.

But he'd not volunteered to be a pilot, as when he'd joined up, all of them were officers, public schoolboys, and he'd really not wanted to mix with those sorts of people. Now there were sergeant pilots, ordinary blokes like him, and he came to a decision.

When he finished that day, John headed for the admin building. The adjutant was the bloke to talk to about changing direction.

His request was listened to politely and then the adjutant nodded. 'How many hours in your logbook, Sergeant?'

'About a hundred, but all of them in old-fashioned kites – nothing like the Spitfires or Hurricanes.'

'Look here, I know there's a desperate shortage of flyers. I'm sure they'll be only too happy to have you transfer. I doubt you'll need more than a few weeks to be fully trained. You want me to set things in motion for you?'

'Yes, sir, I do. Thank you.' He walked out, knowing he'd made the right decision, the only one that made any sense. Some wag in the village had called a flyer 'the walking dead', but that didn't deter him, and the thought of spending the next few years putting out fires no longer appealed.

Better to die doing something extraordinary than live a miserable existence, regretting what he'd lost. He smiled wryly at his morbid thoughts. Nobody died from a broken heart, but they certainly died flying a fighter.

If he got the order to join a training unit – one of the blokes had said the flyers were trained in Scotland now, as it was safer – he'd get in touch with Joanna and say goodbye properly. He'd never forget her, and if he survived the war, then bugger the consequences, he'd come back and try to persuade her to marry him.

19

Joanna was reading in the small sitting room – the family and Jean had already retired but, as she wasn't sleeping well, she'd decided to stay up until she was so tired that she had no option but to go to bed.

She was surprised to be disturbed by a polite tap on the door. 'I'm sorry to intrude, Lady Harcourt, but could you possibly come to the kitchen? There's something we want to talk to you about.'

The speaker was the girl who had just returned from being concussed – Charlie – and Joanna didn't hesitate. She followed her to the kitchen and found nine of the girls gathered there. The ones missing were those that had to be up at four o'clock in order to go to Brook Farm for the milking. She thought they were probably going to ask her if they could have Star back.

'Good evening, girls, how can I be of help?' She listened with growing concern as Sal explained why she'd been summoned. 'I would suggest that you contact the local constable, but he'd be of no use whatsoever.' Joanna was horrified to discover that the girl was in genuine danger.

'It's my word against that man's,' Sal said. 'Who do you think they're going to believe?'

'As long as she's with two of us, then Sal will be safe,' Charlie said. 'However, we're often working on our own.'

'You must use the horse again, you're safer in the cart than walking in the dark along the road. As long as I have your word that she'll only be used to transport you back and forth, of course.'

'Thank you, my lady, that will certainly be a help, but it's not why we asked you here.' Charlie pointed to Lazzy, who was flopped under the table. 'We were wondering if we could borrow him. I think that if he stayed with Sal, then this man would think twice about trying to attack her.'

Joanna was about to agree when Sal interrupted. 'I didn't know you was going to ask that, Charlie. I'd have said no if you'd told me. Den will have a gun – he don't need to be close to use that. I ain't having that dog put in any danger or any of you for that matter.'

'In which case, Sal, we must have you moved from here,' Joanna said. 'There are land girls all over the country and I'm sure Mrs Dougherty, when she knows the reason, would be happy to transfer you.'

'Won't do no good, my lady, now he knows I'm in the Land Army, he'll soon find me. I thought I might see if I can get taken on as one of them WAAF girls. On a base like Manston, he'd never get near me.'

There was a general murmur of agreement. 'That makes sense,' Charlie said, 'but I'm not sure you can leave the Land Army and pop across to another service without a lot of fuss.'

'Well, I ain't hanging around here to be murdered and I ain't going to let any of you get hurt neither. I reckon if Lady Harcourt was to speak to the local lady what arranges everything and explained like, then there wouldn't be no trouble.'

Joanna agreed. There had to be some advantages to being an aristocrat and this, she believed, was one of them. 'I'll do that first thing tomorrow. But until we can have you safely away from Goodwill House, I insist that you take Lazzy. He will certainly deter the man who approached you today.'

'Ta ever so,' said Sal. 'I'll be glad to have him. I never meant to be a nuisance, I thought I'd be safe here.'

'I'm glad to be of help. I suggest that all of you get to bed, you've got a long day tomorrow.'

She left them to finish their cocoa and wash the mugs and returned to her private sanctuary. When her dog got up, intending to follow her, she told him to stay; he cocked his head, wagged his tail and then did as she asked.

It might be tricky getting the dog to go with Sal and the others tomorrow, but she'd make sure she got up early and make it clear to Lazzy that she wanted him to go with them.

* * *

Sal could do with a bath after being out in the sun and sweating like a pig all day, but with everybody else going to bed, she couldn't have the bathroom to herself. She made do with a lick and a promise in the bedroom.

'Before you fall asleep, ladies, I want to explain to you why I was away so long,' Charlie said.

Sal didn't care, she needed her sleep more than she needed to hear this story, but she remained sitting up in bed, trying to keep her eyes open, and waited.

'It's a bit embarrassing, but Andrew – Dr Willoughby – and I find that we get on very well. It's early days yet, but one might say that we're walking out together. I've a feeling that in a few months' time, you might not be the only one who's leaving the Land Army.'

'Blimey, that's a turn-up for the books,' Sal said, now wide awake.

'It is, but there's something else I want to tell you. I left my uncle's farm because... because my cousin, Giles, attempted to rape me. I gave him no encouragement at all, but I was blamed for it and sent packing.'

'That's absolutely ghastly, Charlie, and thank you for telling us,' Daphne said. 'As we are sharing secrets, I'll tell you mine. I was engaged to my childhood sweetheart, but he vanished a week before our wedding. I found out later that he'd joined the RAF.'

'You don't say! I ain't sure what that's got to do with anything,' Sal said.

'It took me six months but eventually one of his friends told me he was based at Manston. He's ground crew. I intend to find him and try to put things right between us.'

Now Sal was puzzled. 'I don't see why joining the Land Army has helped you find him. You could have been sent anywhere in the country.'

Daphne beamed. 'I joined because I wanted to do my bit for the war effort. I believe it was God's hand that brought me here. He obviously intends us to be together or would have sent me to Norfolk or even Scotland.'

Charlie nodded as if she believed this. 'I think you're absolutely right, Daphne. My accident was the Lord's way of putting Andrew and me under the same roof.'

Sal had had enough of this rubbish. 'So, this god of yours has put me here so I can be murdered? No wonder I don't believe in him.'

She slithered down in the bed and the moment her head

touched the pillow, she was asleep. If they'd tried to talk to her, she didn't hear them and didn't wake until the alarm went off as it always did at six o'clock.

Charlie assumed she would be in charge of the horse, but Sal soon put her straight. 'Daphne and I do the driving. You've been sitting on your arse for the past ten days flirting with the doctor. Things have changed and you ain't the boss no more.'

She hadn't meant to sound so sharp but was still smarting from what they'd said last night. Coming to Kent had been tickety-boo for them but could be signing her death warrant.

Lady Harcourt had got up with them and made sure the dog trotted along beside the cart. He was too big to get in but seemed happy enough on the road. He was on the inside of the vehicle, where he couldn't be knocked down if a car went past.

Daphne and Charlie chatted together but Sal kept her eyes firmly ahead and made no attempt to join in their conversation, even though they didn't actually exclude her. As they approached the farm, her stomach was churning, she'd been looking left and right continuously in case Den was already lurking in the undergrowth.

'Lazzy will take care of you, Sal,' Charlie said. 'We're both really sorry we upset you last night, it was stupid of us. You're quite right, God has far better things to do than manoeuvre anybody into a romantic relationship. Daphne's here by pure coincidence.'

'Ta, I were a bit upset. But I'm scared too. Do you think he's going to be coming today?'

'We were thinking that maybe he doesn't intend to come at all but just asked his friend to frighten you.'

She thought about this for a minute and then nodded. 'I reckon you're right. He were always a sneaky bastard. He'd enjoy knowing I was scared.'

'Then you don't have to worry, as between Daphne, me, and the dog, you'll be just fine. Daphne has been telling me how Mr Pickering has changed. I must say the farm looks as it should and obviously the animals have already been fed – presumably by him.'

'We don't have to do anything apart from the mucking out and cleaning the milk parlour. I don't know who's taking the milk and eggs to the village, but we certainly didn't do it the last couple of days.' Daphne jumped down from the cart and made a fuss of the dog.

Sal went to harness the horses and left them to put Star in the field. She clicked her fingers and the dog trotted along beside her. He was familiar with horses and the Shires seemed happy to have him around.

Whilst she was checking the harness, the dog had flopped down by the wall, where he was invisible if you didn't know he was there.

The bloke who was Den's mate was suddenly behind her. He reached out to grab her shoulder. His hand was still in mid-air when he was thrown to the ground by the dog. Lazzy was snarling and had his teeth sunk into the man's arm. The bloke was yelling blue murder and people came running.

'Good boy, let him go,' Sal said firmly and, to her surprise, he did as she asked. The man was rolling about on the ground, moaning as if he was half-dead.

'Shut your trap, you ain't that badly hurt,' Sal snarled at him. Lazzy, sensing her anger, was ready to savage him a second time.

Charlie, Daphne, and the other men burst onto the scene. Pickering saw the dog and jumped to the wrong conclusion.

'That bloody dog's dangerous. I'll get my shotgun and put him down.'

Sal and her friends jumped in front of Lazzy. 'Over my dead body, he belongs to Lady Harcourt,' Charlie shouted.

'That man was about to attack me,' Sal said. 'He already threatened me life and Lady Harcourt borrowed me the dog to keep me safe.'

Daphne joined in. 'You'd better get rid of that man before her ladyship gets rid of you.'

One of the other men had wrapped the torn arm in a makeshift bandage made from a grubby hankie. At least the nasty bit of work Lazzy had bitten had stopped moaning that he was bleeding to death.

The farmer changed his tone and beckoned the three of them to one side where they could talk without being overheard. 'Why would he want to threaten you, Sal? He doesn't know you from Adam.'

'He's a crony of a bloke I split up with a while back. Den, me ex, weren't too happy about me going and threatened to kill me if he got hold of me.'

'I see. These men come from London. They're here for the hop-picking next month.'

'They should all be in the services, not shirking down here. I think a visit to the police in Ramsgate is called for,' Charlie said firmly.

'I'll not get the harvest in without them.'

Daphne laughed. 'Too late, they've sloped off whilst we were talking.'

Pickering didn't laugh. 'I won't get the harvest in before the thresher comes next week. God knows what I'll do now.'

'I'll get some extra help,' Charlie said. 'I know exactly who can come. I'll take Star – it'll be quicker across the fields – and I'll ask the twins and Jean if they'll help.'

'I can get some extra hands tomorrow. Right, you get off, Charlie, and we'll get to work.'

With two teams reaping, the field would be finished today. Sal had been told to move on to the next field, not to help making the stooks. The three from Goodwill House had turned up on foot, but quicker than she'd expected. They'd caught a bus to the end of the lane.

Lazzy didn't go far from her all day, and she was glad of his company. She put a brave face on it, pretended that she thought the danger was over, but she knew in her heart that this was just the start.

* * *

John was summoned to the adjutant at nine o'clock with three hours still to go on his shift. He'd only put in his request to become a flyer the day before and hadn't expected things to move so fast.

'There you are, Sergeant Sergeant, you're to get yourself to Hornchurch as quick as you like. You'll get a flip in an Annie to where you're going to be finished off. You don't need to go to Scotland, not with so many hours in your logbook, even if they were on a Tiger Moth.'

'I didn't expect to be going so soon. Do I get the ride from here on a taxi-Anson?'

'No, too dangerous for them to land at the moment. You get the train to London and then to Hornchurch. You've got the afternoon to sort yourself out, but I promised you'll be on your way by this evening.'

'I've got a couple of things to do,' said John. 'I take it I'm not still on shift?'

'Good god, I should think not. Good luck and thank you for volunteering.'

Instead of going to his billet, he headed off the base to the village, where he could telephone Joanna without being overheard.

He was connected quickly and she answered the telephone herself. 'Joanna, it's me. I'm leaving Manston today and wanted to see you before I left. I'm going to become a flyer.'

There was a moment's silence. 'Everybody's out apart from my mother-in-law, who's asleep in the sitting room at the back of the house. Are you coming on your motorbike?'

'I am.'

'Then take the tradesmen's route – I expect you've noticed the track. It's better if nobody sees you. Take the back stairs and meet me in the room you occupied with Percy.'

She put the receiver back in the cradle. He was on his bike before he realised he hadn't reclaimed the unspent coins from the telephone box. The next person who used it would be pleasantly surprised.

He left his bike hidden in the undergrowth and slipped in through the boot room door and up the stairs. Joanna was already there. He'd intended this just to be a sincere goodbye, nothing more. But when he walked in, she was in his arms before he could take a breath.

'I love you, John, and this is the last time I'll see you. I don't want to know if you get shot down, or horribly injured. I want to remember you as you are today and will pray every day that you are one of the lucky ones and survive the war.'

He held her close, too moved to answer for a moment. 'I love you too, Joanna, and I wanted to say goodbye in person. I shouldn't have sneaked off last time.'

'We have until four o'clock, longer than we've had before. I left my mother-in-law a tray with her lunch and a Thermos flask with coffee, so she'll be quite happy.'

'Then we can take our time. Pretend that we're a couple going to spend the rest of our lives together.'

She leaned away from him slightly and her smile was radiant. 'I'd much rather spend the time as if we're on our honeymoon.'

He kissed her, not passionately, but tenderly, and it was all the sweeter for that. Then they took their time undressing each other, enjoying every minute, every touch of naked flesh, until neither of them could wait a moment longer.

They rested for a while, talked about everything but the future, and then made love a second time. There wouldn't be a third – that was the last time – ever.

When they were dressed, it was time for him to go, but he couldn't bear to say goodbye.

'John, my darling, I want you to promise me one thing – well – two, really. Stay alive and when this ghastly war is over, fall in love again, marry someone suitable, and have a family of your own.'

He swallowed the lump in his throat. 'I'll promise if you'll promise me that you won't remain on your own. Find somebody who will love you for your independence, and not wish to take it away from you. Somebody who will love you as you should be loved, and then share your life with them.'

'I promise to marry again if I meet the man you describe. I'll not settle for anything less.' She smiled sadly. 'I don't think such a person exists but, if they do, then I'll take your advice and make my life with him.'

'And I promise never to forget you, but to marry a woman who can make me happy and give me children. I don't regret what happened and I hope that you don't either. We've been given a glimpse of happiness, a taste of how things should be between a man and a woman. Neither of us will compromise on our next relationship.'

He kissed her for the last time and then stood holding her hands, staring at her, hoping to imprint everything about her in his memory.

'Goodbye, be happy and be safe.'

'Goodbye, darling John, and I wish you the same thing.'

He let go and turned away, not wishing her to see the tears in his eyes. He fled through the house and out to his bike. He'd intended to offer it to Joanna for her son but had forgotten to do so. She probably wouldn't have wanted a constant reminder, anyway.

Percy would be happy to have it and that was his next task. He'd find his friend in the mess and would hand over the keys, wish him good luck, pack his kit and take his leave.

An hour after leaving Goodwill House, he was at Ramsgate station, waiting for the train to London. He was going to be a pilot but it wouldn't be up to him whether he joined bomber command, fighter command or coastal command.

Whichever branch of the RAF he was placed in, he'd not let them down. England depended on the flyers and he was excited to be joining them and doing something truly worthwhile. He couldn't be with the woman he loved and living so close would be impossible for both of them. Therefore, he had no option, and if he had to leave, then he'd do it in style and become one of the Brylcreem boys.

20

Joanna remade the bed they'd used and went into her bedroom to wash her face and repair her make-up. It wouldn't do to seem anything but her usual self when she went downstairs to join her sharp-eyed mother-in-law.

John had gone and he'd made the right decision. As long as he was so close, they would find it impossible to resist the temptation of being together. Keeping her promise to him was going to be hard, but she would do her best.

She made tea and took it in to Elizabeth. She was shocked to see the tray she'd brought in earlier was untouched.

'Weren't you hungry? I thought I'd made everything you liked.'

'I've only just woken up, my dear, and didn't even notice the tray. Are the sandwiches still edible or have they curled at the corners?'

'Sorry, you can't eat them now. It won't take me a moment to find you something else.'

'No, I'm quite happy with these biscuits and a cup of tea as long as you share it with me. It's very quiet – where is everybody?'

Joanna explained about the drama at the farm and Elizabeth listened attentively. 'That poor girl, what a dreadful situation to be in. She can't remain here, as her erstwhile man friend will come in search of her.'

'Do you think so? I could ask Mrs Dougherty to transfer her to somewhere at the other end of the county.'

'That sounds a sensible solution. However, I think you'd better discuss it with the girl before you take that step. She might have other ideas. Maybe it would be best if she just vanished – I don't think that being in the Land Army is the same as being in the services, is it?'

'She wouldn't be considered a deserter if she left, although I'm sure she'd be encouraged to transfer rather than leave. I promised Jean that I'd make sure supper's ready for everybody. I'll drink my tea with you, Elizabeth, but then I must get on with my domestic chores.'

'Bring the tray, my dear, and I'll come and sit in the kitchen with you whilst you get on with your work. What are you giving everybody to eat tonight?'

'New potatoes, salad and tomatoes with hard-boiled eggs. Everything's from the garden including the fruit salad for dessert. Even I, with my limited culinary expertise, can manage that.'

'I'm perfectly capable of scraping potatoes, and I can chop the parsley if you wish me to.'

When the girls who worked on the dairy farm returned, Joanna had everything ready. The table in the dining room was laid and jugs of water were standing on the slate in the pantry. There was just the bread to cut, as this had to be done at the last minute or it became stale and unpleasant. The food was plated and just had to be taken in to them.

'No, my lady, it ain't right that you wait on us,' one of the girls said with a smile. 'We know where everything is, we'll just help ourselves.'

Joanna didn't argue, as catering for so large a number wasn't something she enjoyed. The builders had gone for the day and there seemed to be a lull in the need for the squadrons to come and go from Manston.

'Elizabeth, shall we take our meal onto the terrace? I think we could both do with the fresh air.'

'An excellent idea. I was going to suggest it myself. I do miss sitting out there, gazing across the field of potatoes to the woods in the distance.'

'At least we still have the rose garden and the herbaceous borders to enjoy. If you go out, I'll fetch it.'

It was mercifully quiet whilst they ate their supper – an egg salad didn't justify being called dinner – and Joanna was happy to be outside. She wondered if her mother-in-law had suspected about John but certainly wasn't going to ask.

Later, as it was getting dark, she accompanied Elizabeth upstairs and then returned just as everyone who'd been working at Fiddler's Farm got back. The twins and Jean travelled faster on their bicycles but Star wasn't far behind.

She needed to speak to Sal before she retired and thought this had better be done now rather than wait until after they'd eaten. Lazzy had travelled in style on the return journey in the cart, but he jumped out and bounded onto the terrace, obviously delighted to be home.

'Good boy, I'm very proud of you. Come on, you deserve your dinner.' Joe had been shooting rabbits and the dog got the scraps. Rabbit pie was now a weekly treat and even the girls who'd been reluctant to eat it initially were now happy to do so.

'Ma, it was good fun getting in the harvest, but I don't think I could do it every day,' Liza said as she dashed up the stairs, leaving a trail of straw behind her.

'Where's your brother?'

'He's shutting up the chickens and taking care of Star. He'll be in in a minute.'

Jean had caught the sun but looked all the better for it. 'My word, that was hard work, Joanna. Going to have a quick wash and change into something clean and then eat.'

'I'll speak to you later. Thank you so much for helping out.'

'That Mr Pickering was delighted to have free labour – but he's going to have to find other people to do it tomorrow.'

Joanna headed for the kitchen, where she could hear the others. From the noise coming from the downstairs WC, at least one of them was washing there rather than going up to their bedroom.

She found Sal at the kitchen sink, drinking a glass of water. 'There you are, I'm so sorry for what happened today. Do you think you could come with me to my sitting room so we could have a private conversation?'

'Course I can. Your dog was a godsend but I ain't taking him back and risking him getting shot.'

Once they were safely away from eavesdroppers, she invited the girl to sit down.

'I can't sit in one of them posh chairs, I'm that dirty I'll ruin it.'

'It's absolutely fine. Please sit down as there are things we need to talk about.' She waited until Sal was settled and then put forward her suggestions. Having this to think about had kept her mind from John's departure.

'I'm worried this ex-boyfriend of yours won't give up. Which means you're not safe here.'

'I ain't going nowhere until the harvest is in. Charlie's going to do the horses and I'm going to work in the field with the others. I'll be safe enough in a crowd.'

'Good girl, I thought you might say that. Here's what I think would work, but I need your permission to set it in motion. If you dye your hair brown – walnut juice works wonderfully – and change your name, then even if you stay in Kent, I think it very unlikely this man will find you. He'll be looking for a blonde girl called Sal, not a dark-haired girl called something else.'

'Blimey, I'd never thought of doing that. I fancy being called Gracie, after Gracie Fields, as I like her singing.'

'What about a second name?

'Evans – I don't know no one with that name. Gracie Evans seems all right to me.'

'Good, that's one thing settled. You mustn't tell any of the other girls, not even Charlie and Daphne. Finish the harvest, tell them that you're going to leave the Land Army, and then Mrs Dougherty can collect you when everybody's working.'

'I'll have to leave my uniform and that, otherwise they'll smell a rat.'

'I'll get that organised with Mrs Dougherty. Kent's a large county and you could be safely hidden over a hundred miles from here. I'll make sure that you're put in a hostel with dozens of other girls. There's one thing that would help you to hide.' She hesitated, not sure if this suggestion would be considered offensive.

'I reckon if I stop effing and blinding and try and speak proper, that'll help too.'

'Yes, my dear, I think it would. Your East End vocabulary is very recognisable.'

'I can do that. If I says to me friends that I'm pushing off up north, that's what they'll tell anyone who asks. I'll be sorry not to stay in touch with Daphne and Charlie but I ain't that friendly with the others.'

'I'll get Jean to find you some civilian clothes. You can say goodbye to everybody wearing them. They'll know that the area organiser's coming to collect your belongings and has offered to give you a lift to the station.'

'Ta ever so, you've got everything worked out a treat. I'll be sorry to leave Goodwill House but if I stay here, I'll be a goner.'

Den would know by now where she was living, so even with a new name and different hair, he'd find her. If she wanted to stay alive, she had to give up the life she loved and the friends she'd made at Goodwill House.

* * *

Sal collected her salad and afters from the pantry but didn't go into the dining room, as there were now only the three of them left to eat. Jean and the twins were sitting at the kitchen table, and Charlie and Daphne must still be upstairs, so she joined them.

'I don't know how you do that heavy work every day, Sal,' Jean said.

'It gets easier. I ain't going to be doing it for much longer. As soon as the harvest's done, I'm leaving the Land Army. Lady Harcourt's going to speak to the lady what organises things and get me released.'

Her friends walked in and overheard what she said. 'Leaving? Oh, Sal, isn't there any other way you can be safe?' Charlie said.

'No, I'm not risking the lives of any of you by staying around. One of me nan's sisters lives Manchester way. I'm going there to make a fresh start.'

Daphne squeezed her shoulder as she walked past. 'We'll miss you and you're such a good worker.'

'Ta, I'll be sad to go but better gone away than gone in the ground with a bullet in my head.' She had spoken without thinking how the others would take this remark.

Jean dropped the teapot she was holding and it smashed on the tiles, splattering the floor with precious tea.

'Blimey, I'm sorry. I never meant to shock you. I shouldn't have said nothing but it's better you know what he's like. You can't hide from a bullet.'

Charlie recovered first. Daphne was scrabbling about the kitchen floor, picking up the broken bits of pottery. Jean had gone to get the floor mop.

'How absolutely dreadful for you, Sal, I'm not surprised you want to vanish. Do you think he'll come down immediately or do you have a few days before he's likely to turn up?'

'It wouldn't be so bad if it were just him coming, but I reckon he'll bring at least two others. He don't like to be thwarted and I'm the one got away. After what happened today, he'll be even more determined.'

'Why would he want to kill you?' Jean had now recovered enough to ask the sensible question. 'I'd have thought he'd just want to take you back.'

'He did three times and the last time, he said if I ran off again, he'd kill me. He's a man what keeps his word. I would rather be dead than go back to him.'

'You poor thing,' Daphne said. 'I'm not surprised you ran away. Have you got enough to get you to Manchester?'

'I've not thought about it. I'll have me wages and I've not spent nothing this week apart from me board and lodging money.'

Charlie shook her head. 'You won't go empty-handed, Sal, I'll make sure of that. You can take my suitcase...'

Lady Harcourt came in and overheard that last offer. 'Good idea, Charlie. Jean, I was hoping you might be able to alter some of Sarah's frocks and so on, so that Sal can look her best when she departs.'

'I'll be happy to.'

The twins arrived for their supper and Sal was glad the conversation moved on to other things. 'Is there anything left for us? Stacking staves into stooks was hard work.'

'Sit down, I'll get it from the pantry for you. I'm the only one here that's not been doing backbreaking work all day,' Joanna said. 'Whilst you're eating, I'll put the milk on for your cocoa. Jean, would you prefer coffee?'

'That's kind of you, I know how you and Lady Harcourt treasure every coffee bean.'

Sal was so tired she could scarcely drag herself up the stairs later. She nipped into the bathroom and ran herself the regulation five inches of water. It wasn't enough to have a decent soak, but at least she was fresh and clean when she got out.

The light was out when she opened her bedroom door. From the heavy breathing, her friends were already asleep. The good thing about doing farm work was that you were too blooming tired to lie awake worrying.

Pickering had managed to round up four workers from nearby farms and this meant with both teams reaping, the first field was finished mid-morning and the four giant horses went off to start the next huge field.

Sal and Daphne wore their hats, which meant she could tuck all her hair inside so from a distance it would be hard to tell them apart. Den might be a monster, but she didn't reckon he'd risk killing the wrong girl.

The housekeeper at the farm had found a trailer to attach to the back of her bicycle and pedalled to the field with their mid-morning tea and cake. They'd been working since seven, so 9.30 was mid-morning to them.

'Here you are, loves, you need feeding up, the pair of you. Not an ounce of fat on either of you. You'll not get yourself a nice hubby with no womanly curves.'

'We work too hard to put on weight,' Daphne said with a smile. 'Thanks for bringing this up, it makes the day so much easier.'

'I'll be back with lunch at midday.' Mrs Finbarr pedalled off to take the last flask and slices of cake to Charlie and the other bloke with the horses.

'Do we have to give Pickering some of our money back as his housekeeper is feeding us?' Sal asked.

'It's his way of saying thank you after how he behaved when we first got here,' Daphne said. 'It would be nice if Lady Harcourt knocked off a shilling from the sixteen we have to give her, as we don't take sandwiches with us any more.'

'I ain't going to ask. She's been ever so good to me, and to all of us. She ain't doing it for the money but for the war effort.'

She and Daphne dropped down behind a stook, grateful to have a ten-minute sit down. 'Have you noticed, Sal, that the new men and Mr Pickering are sitting in a circle around us? Are they protecting you?'

'We've been told to stay in the middle of the field, not go to the edges where there's bushes and ditches and that. I reckon I'll be safe enough this way until I've finished here.'

She hated to put her friends in danger and wasn't happy about the men having to protect her. Den was to blame and she wished she was brave enough to stay and confront him.

At six o'clock, the farmer came up to them. 'You girls get off, have an early night. To be honest, I don't want you hanging about as it gets dark. I'm going to take over from Charlie and, with the extra four men, we're going to finish in good time.'

'Can these new blokes stay until the thresher comes?' Sal asked, thinking she might be able to leave a bit sooner than she'd thought.

'They can. The weather's perfect, but you never know when that's going to change.'

Half an hour later, they were on their way and caught up with the three girls from the next farm on their bicycles. As Sal turned the horse and cart into the drive, the big, hairy dog was waiting to jump in with them.

'Come on, you big lunk, hop in. I'm going to miss you when I leave. He's a real smasher, ain't he?'

'He certainly is. Lady Harcourt told me she rescued him from the Victorian wing,' Charlie said. 'Talking of which, I can't believe how much they've knocked down in a few days. The roof's gone already.'

'Must be blooming horrible during the day here what with the planes screaming overhead and then builders thumping and banging.' Sal had just finished speaking when the siren at Manston howled and a few moments later, the one in the village went off too.

'I think we'll be just as safe in the field with the horse as we will in the summerhouse,' Charlie said.

The sound of the ack ack guns, of the fighter squadrons taking off, made it impossible to speak without shouting. The drone of the approaching German bombers made Sal wish she was somewhere more protected than just standing in the shadow of the large barn.

The three of them huddled together, the dog had dashed off, and the little horse stood trembling beside them. The poor animal jerked every time a bomb dropped on the base. This raid lasted half an hour and from the amount of thick black smoke coming from Manston, they'd copped a lot this time.

An hour or more after the warning siren, the all-clear sounded. 'I don't reckon as many planes came back as took off, do you?'

'I'm afraid you're right. Those poor boys are all that's between us and the Germans invading. I love this billet, but I'd feel a lot safer further away from Manston,' Charlie said as she soothed the horse.

'I heard one of them blokes on the field today saying them Germans are trying to destroy all the RAF bases and the planes.'

'The boys in blue won't give up. They'll keep Britain safe.'

Sal hoped Charlie was right, but there seemed to be more of them horrible German planes coming every day. That night, they listened to the wireless they had in the ballroom. After *ITMA – It's That Man Again* – which made them all laugh, it was the nine o'clock news.

Sometimes Sal found it hard to follow what the posh bloke said, as he talked as if he had a plum in his mouth. She thought he'd said from today, 21 August, men from other countries could have their own squadrons. Funny old world to have foreigners fighting for Britain in British planes, but she was glad they'd come to help. The blooming Yanks hadn't shifted as yet.

Jean called her over. 'Can you come upstairs with me? I've found a few things that will suit you. I want to see how much alteration they need to fit.'

'Blimey, as long as I'm decent, I don't care if they fit proper.'

'Well, Sal, I do. Lady Harcourt and I agree that you'll leave here looking smart.'

'I wish I didn't have to leave at all. I love it here.'

21

Joanna chaired a WVS meeting in the village hall and then immediately afterwards attended a WI meeting, which was chaired by Mrs Thomas.

'Mrs Thomas, our numbers become fewer every meeting, which is a concern as, when the bombs start falling, we'll need everybody to assist,' Joanna said.

'They also are becoming older, which we've observed before. I believe that we have everything in hand, and I've no doubt that the ladies of the village will step up in any emergency, regardless of the fact that they haven't been attending meetings.'

'How are my land girls getting on at your daughter's market garden?' asked Joanna.

'Splendidly. They work hard, complain about nothing, and are an absolute godsend. How are you finding having so many of them living under your roof?'

'It's working out really well, although it's sometimes difficult to provide them with the hot meal they deserve in the evening as they arrive at such disparate times. Jean – my housekeeper – is managing wonderfully.' She paused and blinked away tears. 'I miss Betty most dreadfully and still can't quite believe that someone so young has died from a childhood illness.'

'The cottage she and her husband occupied is still empty,' Mrs Thomas said. 'I've heard that a young couple who are getting married in a few weeks would like to rent it. I believe it to be the only vacant place in the village presently.'

'If they write to me, then I'll consider their application. It's really for the foreman at Brook Farm but Mr Beattie seems to be managing with just the land girls and hasn't appointed anybody to replace Bert Smith.'

'Somebody told me that the girl who stayed with our doctor is now involved with him. Is that the case? There must be a fifteen-year age gap between them. The girl is obviously hoping to marry above her station.'

This reminded Joanna of her brief but wonderful liaison with John and she looked away, blinking back the tears.

Joanna avoided local gossip, but this was too much to ignore. 'Mrs Thomas, it's none of your business or mine what Dr Willoughby does. However, the young lady to whom you refer, Charlotte, is from an excellent family and is in fact twenty-three years old, so the age gap is considerably less than you stated.'

'I beg your pardon, my lady, I was merely curious.'

'Excuse me, Mrs Thomas, I wish to catch the next bus and it's due in a few minutes.'

The bus conductor took her pennies and handed her a ticket. 'Been a bit noisy up your way, my lady, with all that banging from the builders and the Brylcreem boys landing and taking off every five minutes.'

'It certainly is, but there's a war on and there's nothing we can do about it,' Joanna said.

Since the onslaught from the Germans had begun a few weeks ago, there were rarely any RAF on the local buses. She assumed this was because all leave had been cancelled. Thinking about the base wasn't a good idea, as it just made her think of John and that would do her no good at all.

They were just approaching her stop when she heard the sirens going off. There were half a dozen passengers on the bus, they all needed to get off immediately and find somewhere to shelter. A bus was a very large target for any marauding Luftwaffe.

The bus suddenly lurched to a halt. 'Get down on the floor, everybody, get under the seats,' the conductor yelled.

Joanna didn't need telling a second time and neither did anybody else. She'd just squeezed under a seat when the unmistakable noise of a German plane approaching made the hair on the back of her neck stand to attention. She sent up a quick prayer that this wasn't going to be her last moment.

The hideous sound of gunfire added to her terror. Then this was followed by splintering glass and screams from the other occupants, the vehicle lurched, and then it was over as suddenly as it had begun.

She remained crouched under the seat for a few moments longer, not sure if the plane would return and strafe the bus a second time.

Then the unmistakable roar of two Spitfires overhead made her risk putting her head up to look through the shattered window. She watched in awe as the two brave pilots engaged with the German fighter bomber and successfully chased it away.

She cheered, scrabbled out from under the seat, and looked around to check that nobody had been hurt.

'Bloody hell, that was a close one,' the conductor said as he stood up, brushing off the glass splinters from his uniform.

'Is anybody hurt?' Joanna called out as she made her way slowly along the bus, offering her assistance to the older ladies who were unable to get up. There were a few minor cuts and bruises but thankfully nothing serious.

The driver, in his sixties at least, emerged from his seat and addressed the dishevelled and relieved passengers. 'I can't continue. The engine's damaged, not to mention most of the windows. I'm afraid you'll have to walk from here, ladies.'

'Do you think you can get this bus off the road?' asked Joanna. 'If you could get it into my drive, then it'll not be in the way of passing traffic. You can also use my telephone and arrange for a tow truck to collect it.'

'I'll give it a go, my lady, it might just stagger a couple of hundred yards before giving up the ghost.' The driver gestured to the passengers. 'You need to get off, it's not safe in here with all the glass.'

Nobody argued and soon the six of them, as well as the conductor, were standing on the grass verge. Joanna was amused to see that not one of the ladies had abandoned their bulging shopping bags.

'If you would like to come to Goodwill House, I'll get my son to drive you home. My Bentley will take half a dozen of you and I've got sufficient petrol to manage the journey.'

'That'll be grand, my lady,' one of them said. 'It's over two miles or more to my cottage and I can't carry this bag that far.'

After brushing off glass from each other, they were ready to move. 'I think we'd better let the bus go first, just in case something untoward happens.'

Joanna's suggestion was sensible and nobody argued – but that might be because she was Lady Harcourt. She'd quite forgotten they were still in an air raid and that the all-clear hadn't sounded. A massive explosion in a field the other side of the hedge, no more than half a mile away, caused one old lady to collapse in a heap.

Two of the others attended to her. The bus lurched, and slowly inched its way forward. The conductor, who was taller than Joanna, was staring over the hedge.

'Our boys shot the blighter down. It's crashed in one of your fields, my lady.'

'As long as it didn't crash on any buildings, I don't care where it is. The bus is far enough away for us to continue. We need to get everybody safe before anything else happens.'

They walked in the shadow of the trees that lined the drive on the left-hand side so, if any other German planes appeared, they wouldn't be visible from the air. Members of her household would be in the summerhouse, but she thought there'd be no point in joining them after what they'd been through.

Lazzy must have heard them as he forced his way through the hedge and bounded up to her. His sudden appearance caused further consternation amongst several of the ladies and it took a lot of reassurance from her to persuade them that such an enormous dog was harmless.

'Ma, is that you? Why aren't you in a shelter?' Joe yelled from the summerhouse.

If there was one thing Joanna didn't like doing, it was raising her voice, but she had no option on this occasion. 'Our bus was attacked. We're all perfectly well, but I'm bringing the passengers to the house. I'll need you to drive them home when it's safe to do so.'

'Okay, I'll meet you there. No point in us hiding in here when you're out in the open.'

By the time they reached the front door, even Elizabeth was back. 'Waste of time going down there, my dear, we might as well stay where we are. You notice that the builders carried on regardless – I don't see why we should do otherwise.'

'I expect the all-clear will sound very soon. The Luftwaffe that attacked us has been shot down.'

'Jolly good show. Is that a bus I see parked at the entrance to the drive?'

Joanna explained what had happened and ushered the five ladies and the conductor into the drawing room. Liza had already rushed to the kitchen with Jean to prepare refreshments.

'The telephone's over there; I hope you can get through,' she told the conductor. 'Things don't always work as they should during an air raid.'

An hour later, Joe was on his way, having managed to squeeze all five ladies into the Bentley. He was now confident driving it, as he'd practised several times since the visit to the village a few weeks ago.

The conductor had made his telephone call and then gone to sit in the bus with the driver, so the house was their own again.

'The postman turned up on his bicycle with three letters just before the siren went. I've just had the opportunity to read the one addressed to me,' Elizabeth said as she handed over two envelopes. 'At least, I think it was today – it could have been some days ago. I am getting rather forgetful. My money has arrived at Coutts in London and already somebody there has taken a bank draft to Mr Broome. I imagine that your letters pertain to that as well.'

Joanna opened the first letter and it was indeed saying that the debt to the bank had now been cleared and the account closed. The balance of the money was in their new account and was immediately accessible.

'That's the best news we've had in ages. Goodwill House is safe and our finances secure, thanks to you, Elizabeth.'

'Good, good, but what is in the second?'

Joanna didn't recognise the handwriting and for a horrible

moment thought it might be from John. With some reluctance, she opened it.

The words danced before her eyes. It was from the new Lord Harcourt, a distant relation of her late husband, and what he had written was quite extraordinary.

Sal was working in the centre of the second field when she heard an aircraft approaching. She didn't know if it was a friend or one of the German lot. She leaned on her pitchfork, and then shaded her eyes with her hand in order to squint towards the black shape that looked like a large bird flying towards them.

Daphne did the same. The men also stopped and turned to stare. 'Bloody hell, ladies, it's a German bugger. Run for the ditch. He could kill the lot of us if we stay here,' Pickering shouted. He didn't wait to see if they followed but took off like a rat from a drainpipe, closely followed by the other four blokes.

'Under the staves, Sal, before he sees us,' Daphne shrieked.

There wasn't time to reach the hedge, and anyway, Sal wasn't too happy about being anywhere but the centre of the field. She dived headfirst into the nearest stook and burrowed into it. Her shoes, socks and breeches were brown, and she reckoned they wouldn't show up against the stubble.

It was stifling under the stooks, bits of chaff were getting up her nose and into her mouth, but she ignored it. The drone of the approaching aircraft was closer. Had they been in time? Would the pilot open fire because he'd seen them try to hide?

The sound of machine gun fire echoed across the stubble. She expected to feel the impact of the bullets in her back, but nothing happened. Either he hadn't seen them, or he'd found another target.

As she lay there, she had too much time to think about Den. It had been three days since his cronies had identified her and then run off. More than enough for him to be in the neighbourhood, be lurking somewhere she couldn't see him. He could fire his gun from a distance and she'd never even know she was in danger until she was dead.

Sal snorted, laughing at herself, and was forced to sit up regardless, as she was choking from the straw she'd swallowed. The German plane was firing at something in the road that ran alongside the field. Then two fighters turned up in the nick of time and chased it off. She watched from her position in the staves as the RAF blokes worked together and shot the bastard down.

She cheered and so did the others who'd obviously been watching too. The excitement was over and they had to get back to work. Only Daphne and Charlie knew she wouldn't be coming to work tomorrow, so she couldn't say goodbye to Mr Pickering or his kind housekeeper who'd looked after them over so well since she'd come.

The other girls knew about her plans to leave, so there'd be a bit of a party tonight. She wasn't quite sure when she was going to be able to dye her hair brown, but it would have to be after the girls had gone to work.

Mrs Dougherty had been only too happy to fall in with Lady Harcourt's suggestions and today was Sal's last day at the farm, her last day in the Land Army as far as everyone else was concerned. If she was really giving all this up, she'd be devastated, but she'd still be on the land and there would be other girls to get friendly with.

They left a bit later than the night before, but still a couple of hours before the men finished. Sal looked around, sad to be leaving, as she'd enjoyed being on this farm, getting the hang of everything. She clutched Daphne's arm.

'Did you see that? I think there's someone over there in those bushes.'

'I can see him. Get flat in the cart. He won't be able to shoot you then.'

'No, he doesn't know which one of us is me. We're dressed the same and he can't see our faces from there.' Sal's heart stopped hammering. 'He don't own no rifle, he's only got a handgun and couldn't hit a barn door from so far away, let alone a moving target like what we are.'

She was calmer than the other two. Charlie clicked her tongue and flicked the reins, urging Star into a fast trot. The carriage lurched and bounced over the ruts and potholes, almost tipping her over the side.

Once they were on the road, it was smoother, and they reached Goodwill House in record time. 'You go in and have your bath. Are you going to launder the things you're wearing today, or do you give them back dirty?' Charlie asked as they rocked to a halt in the yard.

'She ain't coming until late morning so I reckon there's plenty of time for them to dry if I do them tonight.'

'Imagine being the recipient of used clothes – we were given everything new. I don't suppose those joining now might be so lucky,' Daphne said.

'Blimey, how many girls do you think bugger off like I'm doing? It can't be more than a handful, can it?'

'Good point, Sal. I'll see you in the kitchen.' Daphne remained behind to help put Star away.

Her friends hadn't mentioned the man lurking in the trees, and she was glad of that. Den knew where she lived – would he risk coming for her tonight? Was he on his own? She hadn't seen

anyone else but then it might not have been Den, but one of
his men.

She rushed indoors and went in search of Lady Harcourt, but
she wasn't anywhere to be found. Lazzy padded up beside her
and stuck his cold nose in her hand. 'I need you to stick by me
tonight, boy, in case we have unwanted visitors.'

'Is that likely, my dear? Have you seen that person?' the old
Lady Harcourt called out from the drawing room and she'd no
option but to go in and explain.

'So, you see, my lady, I ain't sure what's going on or if it was
even him or one of his mates watching us or we just imagined it.'

'Our dog will protect you. He sleeps at the bottom of the
stairs, and I can assure you nobody will get past him without us
being aware of it. What time is Mrs Dougherty calling for you?'

'Late morning, my lady, and I'm to get the one o'clock train. At
least that's what we're telling everybody.'

She didn't like to ask where the younger Lady Harcourt was,
but this old duck seemed to be aware of what was going on.

'I see – at least, I think I do. You leave here in normal clothes,
your brown hair hidden under a hat, are taken to the station and
then go to the ladies' room and change back into your uniform so
Mrs Dougherty can drive you wherever you're going.'

'You've got it in one. It means I've got to take two suitcases, but
I ain't bothered about that. I'll be sorry to leave here, it's been ever
so nice living in this posh house.'

'We'll be sorry to see you go, my dear, but you have no option
in the circumstances. I won't be up when you leave, but I'd like to
give you this to help you on your way.'

The old lady held out her hand and there was a brown envelope in it. Sal took it and almost curtsied. 'Ta ever so, my lady.'

She'd been right to think there was going to be a bit of a do
for her after supper, and she was really la-di-dah in her new

frock. None of the family came in to say goodbye, but that was all right – she'd not been there very long, after all.

Her jodhs, as Charlie always called them, and everything else she'd been wearing had been washed, mangled, and pegged out to dry. There was a good breeze blowing and they were flapping about a treat, and she'd run the iron over them before she packed tomorrow.

The girls had given her a bulging purse full of copper and silver – she reckoned there was about two quid in it. She'd forgotten about the envelope from the old lady and opened it just before she turned out the light in the bedroom.

'Bloody hell! I ain't never seen one of these before. Look at this, you two, it's a bleeding fiver.' Sal spread out the large white note and stared at it in amazement.

'How absolutely spiffing of the older Lady Harcourt to be so generous,' Charlie said. 'That'll pay for your train fare and give you more than enough to get settled in Manchester.'

'It will. It's a blooming fortune. Good night, ladies, ta ever so for being my friend.' She settled down, hiding her wet cheeks in the pillow, not wanting them to know how much she was going to miss them.

22

Joanna had been so disconcerted by the letter she'd had from Peter Harcourt that she'd been unable to think of anything else. She hadn't, as yet, shared the contents with Elizabeth but had continued as if nothing unusual had transpired.

After supper, she retired to the study in order to read it again and make sense of what was in it. She sat at the desk and spread it out in front of her.

Dear Joanna,

Forgive me for my impertinence, but I think of you as Joanna and hope that you will call me Peter when we meet in future.

I know that you thought the worst of me when we met in Ramsgate a few weeks ago and I wish I'd been able to tell you what I was actually doing there.

I have an excellent team working for me and I got them to investigate your late husband's accounts at the bank. I couldn't understand why you were in such financial difficulties that you needed to take in lodgers and immediately suspected there'd been some foul play.

I was correct in my assumption. The bank manager and your previous solicitor were in cahoots and have been systematically defrauding the estate.

It was hard to prove, but I discovered the vital evidence. I thought it better not to act until Lady Harcourt had cleared the debt and you were able to move your account to the new bank.

I have now put matters in motion and have every expectation of the perpetrators being arrested in the next day or two. No doubt you will be anticipating having to give a statement, provide paperwork of some sort, but there's no need for you to do so.

I'll handle everything and you and Lady Harcourt will not be bothered. I am, as you pointed out to me when we first met, now head of the family, and hold the title. Therefore, it behoves me to take care of things for you.

I fully expect you to be refunded by the bank, which will mean that you no longer have to have a horde of unwanted lodgers at Goodwill House.

I remain yours respectfully,
Peter Harcourt

Even his signature was arrogant, Joanna thought. It was larger than his writing and scrawled across the page, demanding attention, just like the man himself. She wasn't sure if she was pleased, horrified or infuriated by what was written.

Obviously, she was delighted to discover that her late husband, David, hadn't been profligate with their money, but the fact that he'd not bothered to investigate the lack of funds was infuriating. He had never spoken to her about financial matters, and she'd just drawn her own conclusions and assumed he'd made some bad investments.

The thought of no longer being dependent on Elizabeth, on the boarders, or anyone else was indeed something to celebrate. She had, at times, wondered if the banks were honest, as the rent from the tenant farmers should have been more than enough to keep the family comfortably afloat.

She was horrified that in the next day or two, everybody in the village, and her erstwhile friends, the ones who had dropped her when David vanished with his regiment to France last year, would be aware that David had been swindled and not been aware of it. The papers, and the gossips, would enjoy pointing a finger and laughing at the family's expense.

This brought her to the other thing that really bothered her. Peter might be the new Lord Harcourt, but that didn't really make him head of the family – he was a stranger, his relationship to her was tenuous in the extreme, and it wasn't his business to interfere in her life.

The more she thought about it, the more irritated and annoyed she became. She would now, of course, have to be polite to him, thank him for spending his own time and money sorting out her affairs. She'd found him arrogant, overbearing and more like David than she was comfortable with.

She was still mulling over how she was going to respond to this letter when she heard the girls going up and realised she hadn't been in to say goodbye to Sal, or to join the impromptu party. Neither had she been there to take Elizabeth to bed, and a wave of guilt washed over her. She had responsibilities to those living under her roof and she had sadly neglected them tonight.

Joanna put the letter in the desk drawer and closed it firmly. Peter had said he wanted to deal with everything, that she needn't be involved, and, on balance, she thought that was probably a good thing. The less she saw of him, the better.

They'd had to go down to the summerhouse twice and although the siren hadn't sounded, the fighters had been coming and going all evening. It was late and even Jean had retired. She felt another flash of guilt that she hadn't spoken to her children but had remained in the study all evening, dwelling on something that was out of her hands.

After collecting the blankets and pillows that would be needed if the siren went during the night and putting them on the kitchen table, she checked the Thermos flasks were filled with boiling water and the tin with the latest batch of biscuits was ready to be taken down to the shelter in the cellar.

At least she could say a proper good night to the dog, who was flopped in his usual position at the bottom of the staircase in the hall. Joe and Liza always checked the windows and doors were locked, so there was no necessity for her to repeat the process as she trusted them implicitly.

Tonight, she didn't knock on any of the doors but just opened them a crack to see if the occupants were soundly sleeping, and they were. She'd become a poor sleeper since John had left and now the contents of the letter, and the writer of it, made sleep impossible.

She heard the girls leave for Brook Farm at dawn and decided to get dressed. Her eyes were gritty, her head ached, but she might as well be up as lie in bed awake when there were things she could be doing.

She met Jean on the stairs. 'Good morning, I'm hoping you can find me something useful to do. I just couldn't sleep...'

She didn't get to finish that sentence as the house shook from the roar of the squadrons leaving Manston. Moments later, the sirens wailed.

'We have to go to the basement – there isn't enough room in the summerhouse for everybody,' Joanna said. 'I got everything ready last night.'

Doors banged and the girls appeared in various stages of undress. Jean had already dashed back to help Elizabeth and the twins arrived at her side. The dog was whining – he just didn't like the noise of the sirens.

A few minutes after the first howl, everybody was making their way to the underground shelter. This wasn't the first time they'd had to go down and everybody knew the drill. However, this was the first time they'd had to come down without having had their breakfast, so the flasks and biscuits would be appreciated.

'Ma,' Joe said, 'I think Lazzy needs to go out. I'll take him down the passageway and let him out into the woods. Don't worry, I won't go with him.'

'Be careful. I'm sure I could hear dozens of bombers approaching. I think today's going to be a really bad one.'

Jean and Liza made the tea and it was welcomed, as were the biscuits. Sal was wearing one of the frocks that Jean had altered to fit and was almost unrecognisable. Joanna was concerned that today might not be a good day for anyone going to Ramsgate station. She was going to miss this lively girl and hoped she would be safe wherever she went.

Joe returned without his customary smile. 'It's really bad, there's bombs dropping all over Manston. I think Hitler must be trying to destroy the RAF.'

'I'm sure you're right, but from the noise I heard just before the sirens, all the planes managed to get off the ground.'

'I can't see that those inflatable Hurricanes are any good at all,' he said as he slurped his tea. 'They're supposed to fool the Luftwaffe so they drop bombs on them instead of the real ones.

They might work if the bombers came in at two thousand feet, but at the height those bombers were, they'd see immediately they were fakes.'

'How do you know they've got these facsimiles, Joe?'

'I've walked the dog along the perimeter a few times. Seems strange that we don't know many people on the base now. The balloon unit's always worth a look.'

'What sort of balloons, young man? Barrage?' Elizabeth asked.

'No, Grandma, little ones that take propaganda across the Channel.'

'How extraordinary – I can't see that dropping leaflets on the enemy is of any use at all.'

* * *

Sal was finding it hard to relax. Not being in uniform set her apart from the others. Though they probably didn't mean to, they were talking to each other and not including her in the conversation.

Lady Harcourt smiled and gestured that she follow her out of the shelter and into the rabbit warren of cellars and passageways.

'You look very smart, Sal, but it must be strange not being in your uniform and having to pretend that you've left the Land Army.'

'It is, I don't belong here no more. Do you think Mrs Dougherty will still come if the place is being bombed?'

'I hope so. Did she tell you when you spoke to her on the telephone where you're to go?'

'The nearest town's Haywards Heath and the hostel's in a village what's called Plumpton Green. If she don't come then I'll catch the bus to Ramsgate station and get a train. I ain't stupid, I've got a tongue in me head and can ask how to get there.'

'Good girl, I'm sure you'll arrive safely. Hopefully the others will be able to get off to work when the raid's over so you can get your hair dyed.'

'I've been thinking about changing me name and all that, my lady. How's that going to work, as I can call meself Gracie Evans but me documents will give me real name?'

'I thought Mrs Dougherty had explained that to you. The hostel where you'll hand in your ration book will be aware of the reasons for this. As long as all the girls know you as Gracie Evans and refer to you by that name, then I'm sure your disguise will work.'

'We thought we saw someone watching us last night, but I reckon we might have been imagining it. It'd be hard for Den to wander about in Stodham, being a stranger like, as he'd stand out like a sore thumb and some nosy parker would ask to see his papers.'

'That's true, but it's better to be away from here just in case.'

'I'm going to nip upstairs to the bog, I ain't using the one in there.' Sal dashed off before Lady Harcourt could object. When she'd finished, she went to the back door, opened it, and hastily shut it again as the racket outside almost deafened her. She scuttled back downstairs and was glad to be in the safety of the shelter with the others.

Joe went to check an hour later, said the all-clear was sounding and they could go up. None of the girls stayed for breakfast as they were already late. The house soon emptied and Sal went out to the washing line to check if her uniform was dry – it wasn't, so she left it.

There was another raid two hours later and this time they went down to the summerhouse as there weren't so many of them. The builders had pushed off and Sal thought they probably wouldn't come back today, it was Saturday, after all. Joe and

Liza kept stepping outside in order to look at what was going on in the sky.

'You can't see Manston because of the smoke and the dust,' Joe said.

'Please don't keep doing that, you two,' Joanna said. 'You never know if a stray Luftwaffe fighter might see you. Remember the bus was shot at yesterday by one of them.'

'I thought civilians were not supposed to be shot at by enemies,' the old Lady Harcourt said. 'There's no honour in war any more. I thought the last one was supposed to be the last one.'

Even the old lady laughed at what she'd said. They were stuck out there for an hour and when the all-clear went, Sal headed for the washing line at the back. She was collecting her laundered garments when Liza came out. 'Mrs Dougherty just called. She said she can't come and collect you but will call in when she's in the area next. There's a bus at eleven o'clock, if it comes, and it will take you to the station.'

'Then I'll get that. Ta for coming out to find me.' Liza might think it a bit odd if she saw her ironing the things she was handing back, so she'd have to wait until the twins were in the study with their tutor.

'I'm not going to colour me hair,' she told Lady Harcourt. 'With it shoved under this hat what you gave me, nobody can see it anyway. I need me uniform so can't leave it here.'

'I thought of that, Sal, and will put a suitcase of old clothes by the front door. Are you going to be able to manage if you have to carry everything, including your gumboots?'

'I'll feel ever so grand having two suitcases – people will think I'm a real toff, owning so much.'

Sal said goodbye and then, proudly carrying both suitcases, set out to catch the bus. The air smelled of burning, there was the constant noise of lorries and that from the base as they tried to put out the fires. She was glad to get away from Stodham, but only because she was taking the danger away from her friends. She'd loved it here and had felt valued for the first time in her life. At least she could pretend that she was really a posh girl setting out for a new life and this would make it a bit easier.

There was only one other passenger on the bus, which she thought a bit odd, but when they got to the village there'd be the usual dozen or so housewives waiting to get on. Going into Ramsgate was worth the ride as there was more choice and they could buy a lot of things cheaper than in the village shops.

She'd never worn a proper hat before and hadn't even owned woolly winter gloves, let alone the white lace summer gloves she was wearing at the moment. Lady Harcourt had insisted on giving her two of her old pairs as her ladyship had said her hands would immediately reveal she was a land girl if anybody saw them.

Nobody got on at Stodham and the other lady got off – now Sal was concerned. The conductor was sitting on the front seat, talking to the driver through the sliding window.

'Excuse me,' she called. 'Where is everyone? Why hasn't the bus filled up? Is it safe to go into Ramsgate today?' She was trying to sound more like Charlie or Daphne and thought she'd got it about right.

'It's the air raids, miss, there's been two already and folk reckon there could be more. You'd be better off going home and waiting till it's over.'

'I can't, I have to catch the one o'clock train.' She took a deep breath, trying to think of what one of her friends might say, what words they'd use. 'I'm going to London to train as a nurse. It wouldn't do to be late.'

'Good for you, miss. I wouldn't want to be in London now for all the tea in China.'

The bus turned into the forecourt at Ramsgate station and the conductor insisted on carrying her suitcases over to the left luggage office.

'Thank you so much, I do appreciate your help.'

To her astonishment, he touched his cap as if she was someone special. She rather liked this pretending lark. The old bloke came round and collected her cases and took them behind the counter and put them in the rack.

'Trains are running a bit all over the shop today, I'd be here half an hour early to be sure.'

'I'll do that. I'm going to purchase my train ticket now.' She said every word clearly, thought she sounded daft, but he just nodded and smiled and handed her the ticket to reclaim her belongings.

Ramsgate looked the same as it had when she'd arrived a few weeks ago. Nobody seemed fussed, they were going about their business as usual. She had an hour and thought she'd treat herself to a bit of lunch in the café, but first she'd better buy her ticket.

The ticket man apologised for not being able to offer her a reservation as these weren't available any more. 'I doubt there will be a lot of people going to London today, miss, so you should get a seat all right. Do you have any luggage?'

'I have two suitcases which I have deposited in the left luggage area.' She sounded stilted, as if she didn't really understand how to talk English properly. She hoped they didn't think she was a German spy.

'Then I'll get your suitcases put into the guard's van. You don't want to be lugging them down the train.' He handed her a single ticket to London and then stamped another one and gave it to her. 'Take this to Albert in the left luggage, he'll stick it to your cases and then they'll be put on the train for you.'

'How kind of you. Thank you so very much.'

She wasn't sure if she should have tipped him a tanner, but too late to worry as the old coot had vanished back into his cubbyhole to read his paper and drink his tea.

The café was half-full and she waited, clutching the handbag that Lady Harcourt had also insisted she took to complete her outfit, until a waitress hurried over to her.

'Are you here for coffee and cake or something hot, miss?'

'I'd like lunch if I can. I won't have the opportunity to eat once I'm on the train.'

'You can't go wrong with our fish and chips. The fish came in this morning off the boat. Customers eating lunch sit with the tablecloths on this side of the restaurant.'

Sal was conducted to a nice table in the window with a white cloth and everything. Good thing she'd learnt her manners while living at Goodwill House. She was enjoying the last mouthful of her lunch when the train steamed in. She was about to leap to her feet and rush out, but the waitress smiled and waved her back.

'It doesn't go until one, whatever time it comes in; you've got plenty of time to finish. You've got to eat your rhubarb crumble and custard before you go.'

Feeling a bit foolish, Sal resumed her seat and sat back as the waitress took away the clean plate. Where she came from in the East End, they prided themselves on the quality of their fish and chips, but this had been the best she'd ever eaten.

She could see the platform from where she was. As she waited for the afters to be fetched from the kitchen, she gazed along the platform to see who might be getting off.

The steam from the engine made it difficult to see but there were definitely three men and two ladies walking towards the ticket collector. Her meal threatened to return. One of the men was Den and he was heading for the café.

23

Joanna had yet to tell Elizabeth of the contents of the letter and with two raids already today, there hadn't been the opportunity. Everywhere was covered in a thick layer of dust that had somehow filtered in through the closed windows – it must have come from the base, as the builders weren't working.

She collected a tray of coffee and carried it along to the small sitting room at the rear of the house where her mother-in-law would be waiting. It would probably be more sensible for them to be in the drawing room, as it was nearer to the summerhouse if the sirens went off again.

'Here we are, Elizabeth, I'm afraid we've eaten all the biscuits. I'm just going to get the letter I received yesterday so that I can share the contents with you.'

'There is no need for me to read the letter, just tell me the gist of it.'

Joanna did so and waited to see the reaction. Instead of being shocked at the news that the bank and the solicitors were fraudsters, Elizabeth laughed.

'My word, how exciting! I never thought my son was particularly bright and this just proves the point. You told me you thought there was something amiss with the finances and how right you were.'

'Things would have been so much easier for all of us if David had bothered to enquire. I always thought he'd made unsound investments, but it seems that wasn't the case. Sarah would have been able to go to study medicine without having to apply for a scholarship.'

'That's true, but we also wouldn't be enjoying the company of the young ladies. If we didn't have them here, then I think it would make sense for us to give the house to the War Office and move somewhere more convenient.'

'I did think of that when things were bleak a few months ago. Although I'm not sure that they'd accept the offer. What possible use could a huge house like this, so close to an active RAF base, be to them?'

'They could use it in exactly the same way that you've been doing on a much smaller scale,' Elizabeth said. 'It would be ideal as an RAF convalescent home. I believe there are a dozen or more bases in Kent.'

'I hadn't thought of that. I certainly have no intention of handing it over at the moment, as these girls are happily settled. That said, Mrs Dougherty might well decide it's far too dangerous for them being so close to an active base and move them somewhere else. If that happens, then I'll certainly make enquiries.'

'This house is far too big for just a handful of us. Once the monstrosity at the far end is demolished and everything made good, this will be a handsome place and ideal to be used in the way I suggest.'

Elizabeth had been conversing as if there was nothing wrong with her mental faculties at all. Joanna prayed this was the case as she would be bereft without her mother-in-law, despite the fact that they'd not got on at all well when they'd first met.

'Have you now changed your opinion of Peter Harcourt?'

'In some respects, my dear, of course I have. He's obviously not a villain and has our best interests at heart. I don't think, however, that it was any of his business to interfere. From your expression, you agree with me.'

'I certainly do. Why is it that men of his type immediately think women need protecting, are incapable of making sensible decisions for themselves? My dilemma's that I really must respond to this letter and at the moment, I'm far too cross to write anything polite.' She poured the coffee and sat down opposite Elizabeth with her own drink.

'You do realise, Elizabeth, that when these men are arrested, there'll be headlines in the *East Kent Times* and everybody at the WVS and WI will be talking about it.'

The old lady chuckled. 'As I don't attend either, it makes no difference to me what they say. In fact, the whole world can be talking about us and it won't matter to me as I don't go anywhere. Now I can't get to church on Sunday, I see no one at all apart from family.'

'It's a shame that we can't use Star to take you. Mr Evans does come most Sundays after church, so you can take communion.'

'He does, and I'm grateful. It's very kind of Joe and Liza to take it in turns to remain behind with me. I thank God every day that they came into our lives.'

'As do I. This is another reason why we must continue to host the land girls. The twins are learning so much from being around other young people. If they were to be moved elsewhere, then I'll find somewhere else for us, somewhere you can walk to church and have more visitors.'

'I do hope it's safe for Sal to go to Ramsgate today. If that woman isn't prepared to come because of the raids we've already had, then perhaps it might be better if the girl remained here until tomorrow.'

'She left half an hour ago, Elizabeth, and will be on the bus by now.'

'Did she? I thought she might have said goodbye and thank you before she departed.'

Joanna quickly explained the reason for Sal's having to leave without saying goodbye.

Elizabeth liked to sleep before luncheon, so Joanna left her in the sitting room and went to the study to compose a letter to Peter Harcourt. His address was embossed on the thick, expensive paper, so she had no excuse not to reply.

He lived in an expensive area of London, Kensington, which she supposed was close to his place of work. He might be overbearing and interfering, but she was quite certain he was brave and wouldn't move out of the city when the bombs started to drop.

She thought it might be wise to compose a letter in her notebook first and not waste either ink or headed paper. It took her several attempts but eventually she had a version she was satisfied with and managed to copy it out without either blotting the page or making any errors.

Dear Lord Harcourt,

Thank you so much for writing to inform me of the result of your investigation.

As you are aware, I had already moved the family bank account from this bank and changed solicitors. Therefore, it comes as no surprise to me to hear that not only were these people incompetent, but they were also dishonest.

Mr Broome, my solicitor, was already in the process of

finding out why there was so little money coming in and it was only a matter of time before he too would have made the same discovery.

Lady Harcourt and I would like to thank you for your interest in our business but would respectfully request that you desist from this practice forthwith.

Yours sincerely,

Lady Joanna Harcourt

She wrote his name and address on the matching envelope and put on the required stamp. One of the twins was bound to be going into the village to visit their friends in the next day or two and could post it then.

It was approaching midday – Jean would be serving luncheon soon and the children would be finishing their studies. They ate in the breakfast parlour as Elizabeth refused to eat in the kitchen, which would be more sensible. She insisted that standards had been lowered quite enough already.

It was unusual for the tutor to come on a Saturday morning but, as he was unable to come on Monday, he'd come this morning instead. The five of them were sitting at the table enjoying yet another egg salad when the sirens wailed for the third time that day.

'I refuse to rush off to the summerhouse before I have eaten my meal,' Elizabeth announced and short of picking her up and carrying her kicking and screaming, there was nothing Joanna could do about it.

'In which case, Elizabeth, we'll all have to remain with you and therefore you're putting us all at risk, not just yourself.'

'I'm not asking you to stay, so it's nothing to do with me if a bomb lands on you too.'

Joe dropped his cutlery and rushed off to see just how bad

this raid was going to be. He was back moments later, his face white.

'There's hundreds of them – bombers and fighters. They've not stopped at Manston but are dropping their bombs on Ramsgate.'

* * *

Sal wanted to run away but was unable to move. Then the siren howled into life and suddenly everything changed. The waitress slammed the tray down and yelled to those in the restaurant.

'Quick, follow me out the back. There's an entrance to a tunnel. We'll be safe down there.'

Chairs were crashed back, voices were raised, and in the general chaos, Sal was able to grab her handbag and hide herself amongst the dozen or so customers rushing for the exit somewhere at the rear of the building.

As soon as they stepped into the sunshine, she glanced up and saw the sky was black with approaching bombers. The RAF were swarming around them. The air was filled with the scream of fighter engines and the sound of machine gun fire.

She'd no idea about any tunnels but anywhere underground would be safer than staying in the open. The waitress pointed to a long flight of steps.

'Down there. Just keep going. Our mayor got the tunnels built for us.'

There were a dozen or more staff from the café heading in the same direction as well as the customers who'd been eating there when the siren went off. Sal daren't look back to see if those from the train were part of the crowd.

As long as she kept her back to Den, he'd not recognise her, dressed as she was. With a hat and gloves on, smart shoes and a real leather handbag, he'd think she was a posh bird.

It seemed like there were hundreds of steps leading down to the tunnel and she was glad of the railing to cling onto. She didn't have a torch and wondered how they'd be able to stumble around in the dark without breaking their necks.

The first few yards were gloomy, but then there were light bulbs hanging from the walls. She thought it was blooming marvellous and was finally able to catch her breath. She wasn't sure if she was more terrified of the bombs about to fall or of the man pursuing her.

She could hear voices ahead. Around the corner, there were benches all along the wall and many of them were already occupied. She wasn't sure if it would be safer to get deeper into the tunnel or sit before her legs gave way.

People were still pouring in behind her – she could hear their voices and the sound of running feet – and decided it would be safer to keep going. If Den actually walked past her, he might very well recognise her, and god knows what would happen then.

But what could happen in a tunnel during an air raid? He certainly couldn't shoot her, he couldn't drag her off, so she was safe enough for the moment. Her fingers had been clenched so hard it took a moment for the feeling to come back into them.

The seats were filling up, so she flopped down on the next one; immediately a stout lady and an old bloke with a flat cap and a long straggly moustache sat next to her. The final space was taken by a different waitress to the one that served her earlier.

Another thirty or so people went past but she was fairly sure Den hadn't been one of them. Even so deep in the ground, a lot of people were still uncertain they were safe. Bits of dirt kept falling from the roof of the tunnel, the ground shook, and it sounded as though there were a lot of bombs being dropped on Ramsgate.

She turned to the lady next to her. 'I thought the Nazis were trying to destroy Manston. Why are they purposely bombing here?'

'The last raid made so much smoke and dust, I don't think they could see the base so have decided to flatten us instead. And I thought towns and civilians weren't supposed to be targeted.'

The bloke with the long moustache chimed in. 'You can't trust that Hitler, he'll do whatever he wants. After all, there's a war on, so I suppose we must expect such things to happen.'

'But if Mr blooming Hitler thinks he can put the wind up us by bombing women and kids – well, he's got another think coming, that's all,' the lady said.

'I didn't know about these tunnels. Are they big enough for everybody to shelter in?'

'I reckon we might be living down here after this.' The old bloke pointed at the roof of the tunnel. 'Every time a bit of dirt falls on us, that's a bomb dropped on the surface. Ramsgate's taking a pasting, that's for sure. Churchill won't stand for it – those Germans will get what's what.'

'Live down here? I'm not sure I'd like that,' Sal said. She was already feeling a bit uncomfortable not being able to see any daylight. Being shut in a small space had always bothered her.

They sat and chatted about rationing, the blackout, the weather and the Germans for an hour or more before word spread from those nearest to the exit that the all-clear had gone.

'It's been nice talking to you. I'm supposed to be going to London, but I don't suppose there's any trains running now,' she said.

'The trains will run regardless of the Huns,' the old bloke said firmly. 'It'll be London cops it next. You'd be better off stopping here.'

'After today, I don't think it'll make much difference. I hope my suitcases survived the bombing.' Sal stood up and smoothed down the front of her frock, checked her stocking seams were straight, her hat not crooked, and was ready to follow the others to the surface.

The waitress who'd been sitting on the end of the bench was walking next to her. 'I wonder if my rhubarb crumble and custard will still be waiting for me. I was so looking forward to it.' She was proud of the way she managed to keep swearing out of her sentences and sound ever so posh.

'Don't see why not, miss, I shouldn't think anybody was hanging about in the café. It'll be just as nice cold, and I'll get you another pot of tea to go with it.'

'I've not paid for my fish and chips either so have to come back anyway.'

'That's good of you. I doubt many will do the same.'

Talking about her missing afters kept Sal's mind off who might be waiting for her. All thoughts of Den vanished as she reached the top step and, from this vantage point at the top of the town, was able to look around at the scene of complete devastation.

'Blimey, half the town's been flattened,' she said without thinking.

Flames could be seen rising from the middle of the town and there were dense volumes of smoke coming from the gasworks. The waitress pointed to the hundreds of houses with broken windows.

'Bad time to be a window cleaner in Ramsgate,' she said with a grin.

There were holes in the road three feet deep, whole walls were missing from houses, in fact whole houses seemed to have been plucked from the row in some places. The station appeared undamaged and she wasn't the only one making her way towards the café in the hope of getting a much-needed cuppa.

The waitress grabbed her arm. 'Don't go that way, miss, come in the back with me.'

'Do you think there've been many casualties?'

'I should think so. Not everybody's close enough to the tunnel to get in quickly.' The girl waved her hand at the ruined town.

'There'll be people dead as well as injured and hundreds made homeless. The WVS and WI will have their work cut out sorting all this, that's for sure. Look over there, some poor blighter's kicked the bucket.'

Sal didn't want to look but something made her do so. Her eyes widened. She recognised the fancy shoes sticking out from under the tarpaulin thrown across him. Den was dead – she was almost certain he was. She had to know as then she'd be free and wouldn't have to leave Goodwill House after all.

'Excuse me, I need to see if my suitcases are still there. Someone could have gone in and taken them whilst we were in the tunnel.'

'You do that, I'll have your tea and pudding waiting. You were sitting at the table for two by the window, weren't you?'

'I was. I won't be long.'

Somehow, she forced her feet to move towards the covered body. She was approaching it when an ARP warden called out to her.

'I shouldn't go any closer, miss, not for the likes of you to see a dead man.'

'I think I might know who it is. I recognise the shoes.'

He looked at the feet and didn't think her answer strange. 'They're certainly a bit different. The poor sod was gunned down by a fighter. He came out of hiding too soon. I reckon over five hundred bombs dropped in five minutes. It'll take months for us to recover from this.'

They were now a few feet from the corpse. 'Could you pull the cover down a bit so I can see his face?'

'He was shot in the chest, so he don't look too bad.' The man lifted the tarpaulin.

'Yes, it's a man called Dennis Taylor, he's a very bad man, an East End villain, and the world's a better place without him.' Instead of being shocked at the sight of a dead person, all she felt was overwhelming relief that she was finally free of him.

The bloke didn't ask how someone who looked like her knew somebody like the stiff on the ground. 'Thanks for the information, miss, very helpful.'

Sal walked away, happy for the first time in years. She could carry on and pretend to be someone she wasn't, Gracie Evans, or give Lady Harcourt a ring and ask if she could come back.

First, she was going to have a pot of tea and eat her cold rhubarb crumble. Her stomach rumbled as if she hadn't eaten fish and chips just a couple of hours ago. She was about to go in the café when she remembered her suitcases. She didn't want them put on the train if she wasn't getting on it herself.

The old bloke wasn't back behind the counter, so she nipped round and removed them herself. Then she went to the ticket office and this time it was occupied and she asked for a refund for her ticket.

'Changed your mind?'

Sal wanted to say it was bleeding obvious or she wouldn't have asked for a refund but smiled sweetly and stayed in character for just a bit longer. 'I have, I don't think I want to go to London to be a nurse if we're going to have bombs dropped on us every day. I'll do something else instead.'

She was handed her coins with bad grace but as long as she

got them, she wasn't bothered how they were given to her. She still had the five pound note given to her by old Lady Harcourt and that would be returned, as would the money in her purse.

There was a telephone box just outside the station and by some miracle, the lines were still working. She asked to be connected to Goodwill House and the operator knew the number.

Sal was ready with her pennies and dropped them in the slot. She had her finger poised over button A, ready to push it when someone answered.

24

Joanna had just settled Elizabeth on a chaise longue in the drawing room when the telephone interrupted the conversation. 'Excuse me, I must answer that. Lady Harcourt speaking.'

'My lady, the most dreadful news. Oh, I beg your pardon, it's Mrs Reynolds, your counterpart in Ramsgate. The town has been dreadfully bombed, a murder raid, people are calling it. Hundreds of houses are destroyed and hundreds of families are homeless.'

'I feared as much, Mrs Reynolds, when my son saw the bombs dropping an hour ago. How can we help?'

'We're going to need everything you've got put by for this eventuality. Heaven knows where we're going to put everyone. I think it quite likely some of them will move into the tunnels until alternative arrangements can be made.'

'I'll contact Mrs Thomas in the village and get the word out,' Joanna said. 'Do you need us in person or just the furniture, bedding, crockery, clothes and so on?'

'We need as many ladies as possible to make tea, sandwiches and take them round. There is little point in coming today – far too dangerous, as there are fires burning and until the fire brigade has put them out, we've been told to do what we can for those who are already in the tunnels or congregating in the park.'

'Shall we say nine o'clock tomorrow morning outside the station?' Joanna said.

'Excellent, thank you so much. I don't know how many people have been killed or injured, it's too soon to tell. I thank God that our mayor and his engineer had the foresight to dig the tunnels and make them ready, as there could have been thousands of deaths.'

Joanna had just replaced the receiver in the cradle when it rang again. With a sigh, she picked it up.

'Lady Harcourt speaking.'

'Lady Harcourt, I'm the adjutant at Manston. No doubt you are aware that things are absolutely dire here. The base is out of action, the water cut off, so we can't put out the fires. It's going to be emergency use only until things can be rebuilt.'

'I thought that might be the case and I'm so sorry. I won't enquire about losses, as I know they will be appalling. How can I help?'

'We're evacuating the WAAF and wondered if you have capacity to take them?'

'I'm sorry, I don't. I have a full contingent of land girls.'

'I thought it was worth asking, as they enjoyed being with you before. I suppose the silver lining, as far as you're concerned, is that it will be much quieter at Goodwill House for the next few weeks.'

'Will the base be reopened at some point?'

'Yes, it's a vital part of the coastal defence,' the adjutant said. 'It's rare that a base is so badly damaged it can't be back in action within a day or two, but we're temporarily abandoning it. I can assure you by the end of the year it'll be fully functioning again and better than before.'

'Thank you for informing me and I'm sorry I couldn't be of more help.'

Half an hour later, she contacted Mrs Thomas and promised to get word around to all the members of the WVS and WI that were available. The fact that it would mean missing church and working on a Sunday was unimportant. She then sent Joe to find the builder and see if he could be persuaded to transport the furniture and other items to Ramsgate tomorrow morning – her son could also post the letter to Peter Harcourt.

When the telephone rang for a third time, Elizabeth complained. 'Good heavens, will that wretched thing ever be quiet? The constant jangling is upsetting my nerves.'

Joanna ignored her and rushed to pick it up. 'Lady Harcourt speaking.'

'My lady, it's me, Sal. Den's a goner so I don't have to leave. Can I come back?'

'Of course you can, I know that Mrs Dougherty will find it far more convenient to have you remain here and not have to find a replacement. I was very worried about your safety and am so relieved that you're unharmed. I was concerned that you might have been injured in the bombing.'

'Someone's banging on the door, there's a queue waiting to use the telephone. I'll tell you what happened when I get back.'

The line went dead and Joanna smiled. When she went in to give her mother-in-law the news, she was asleep. Liza and Jean were in the kitchen, cobbling together something for lunch.

'Sal's not leaving?' Liza asked. 'That's smashing news, Ma, I was worried she might have been hurt with the bombs dropping on Ramsgate like that.'

'It seems that the man who was threatening to harm her is

dead. There wasn't time for her to explain how this happened, but that's why she can now remain with us.'

When the sirens went off later in the afternoon, nobody went down to the summerhouse. They didn't even bother to go to the shelter in the basement but carried on as if there wasn't a battle raging somewhere in the skies above them.

Joe returned unscathed and was full of what he'd seen. 'Our boys sent them packing. I don't think more than a couple of the Luftwaffe got through. Nobody bothered to go into the shelters in the village.'

'We didn't do so either and I think that was unwise. We mustn't become blasé just because no bombs have dropped on Goodwill House so far,' Joanna said. 'Manston has been evacuated; you must have seen the cars and lorries and so on whilst you were out.'

'I was about to mention that. It doesn't matter how many bombs they drop on the base now that there's only a handful of people there.'

'You've got smudges of black all over your clothes and face, Joe, it must be from the fires on the base. Did you manage to find the builder? I should have asked that first, as that's the main reason you went into Stodham.'

'I did and he's happy to help. He'll be back here Monday as usual.'

* * *

The first girls, the ones working at the dairy and the market gardens, returned full of stories about hiding under hedges during the raids, of cows refusing to give milk and two pigs escaping from their field which were still loose somewhere in the neighbourhood.

'I've got news too,' Joanna said. 'Sal isn't leaving after all and should be back sometime today. I'm not quite sure how she's going to get herself and two large suitcases from Ramsgate station, but she's a resourceful young lady and I'm sure will manage it somehow.'

'I don't think the buses are running, my lady,' one of the dairy girls said.

'Then she'll have to walk and will just have to hope there are no more raids today.'

'Golly, we've had five. That has to be a record,' Jean said.

Joe was helping himself to a slice of rabbit pie – he should have waited until the meal was served, but today wasn't a day for sticking to rules.

'I could go and fetch her in the Bentley, Ma, I don't suppose there's any constables going to be taking notice.'

'You're right, Joe, and you look a lot older than almost fifteen. Anyway, I think it highly unlikely the local police are going to stop someone in the Harcourt Bentley.'

He grinned as he helped himself to a second slice. 'They might think I've pinched it.'

Liza had been taking food in to the girls who were here and immediately asked if she could accompany her brother. 'Nobody will think you're stealing if I'm sitting next to you.'

'If you put your hair up, wear one of Ma's hats and then sit in the back, they'll think I'm your driver. I don't suppose you've got a peaked cap hiding anywhere, Ma?'

She laughed. 'As a matter of fact, I know exactly where one is. Run upstairs and do something with your hair, Liza, and there's a suitable hat on top of my bureau.'

Her daughter ran off and she and Jean exchanged a smile. 'I don't want them to dwell too much on what's happened today, so this adventure will take their mind off things.'

The twins would definitely pass for chauffeur and passenger if nobody looked too closely. Joe was now a competent driver and she had no worries about him having an accident.

Jean had taken a tray into the drawing room for Elizabeth and there was another one laid up for Joanna. She collected it and walked through. The sound of an approaching car made the tray tilt, and she almost lost her precious supper on the floor.

It couldn't be the Bentley, as they'd only just left. She rushed back to the kitchen, put the tray on the table and went to the front door. She stood, out of sight of anybody who might be driving, to see who it might be.

It was an army staff car, driven by a girl in the uniform of an ATS. Her stomach lurched. It could only be Peter Harcourt, come to get a response to his letter in person. A little odd, as she'd only had the letter yesterday.

She moved into the doorway of the drawing room so Elizabeth could see her. 'How long have you had that letter from Peter Harcourt?'

'I've no idea, perhaps a week, you know I forget things. I did say I thought it was yesterday but wasn't really sure. Does it matter?'

'Actually, it does, as he's just arriving.'

Sal returned to the café and ate her cold crumble and drank three cups of tea before she was ready to think about how she was going to get back to Goodwill House. There was a bus in the fore-court outside the station, but the windows were broken. That wouldn't be going anywhere today.

As she was paying her bill, the sirens went again. This time, everybody knew the drill and she hastily pushed her suitcases under the table and covered them with the cloth and then followed the others into the tunnel.

This time, they were only there for half an hour. The ARP warden shouted down the tunnel that the RAF fighters had driven the bombers back. Everybody cheered and then trudged back up the long staircase. Sal noticed some of the people stayed where they were on the benches and thought maybe they were the ones whose houses had been destroyed so they had nowhere else to go.

Her suitcases were where she'd left them. She picked them up and set out down the main road heading towards Stodham, praying somebody might stop and give her a lift. Nobody did – in fact, no cars drove by at all.

After walking for an hour, her feet were sore as the shoes she'd been given, which had once belonged to Sarah Harcourt, were pinching something rotten and she reckoned that the blooming cases had stretched her arms by several inches.

Then she had an idea of a way to make things a bit easier. If she changed into her uniform, put the gumboots round her neck like she had when she'd travelled before, her feet would be more comfortable in her shoes and the cases would be lighter.

There was a gap in the hedge she was able to push through and ten minutes later, she was back in the clothes she preferred, her old self again and not some posh bird who wasn't her. She smiled – that wasn't quite true, as she'd changed a lot since she'd left London, and Sal the land girl was a different person to Sal the bit on the side of an East End villain.

Despite the fact that her feet were no longer hurting, and the cases were definitely lighter, after walking another mile, she was done in. She didn't own a watch so had no clear idea of the time but, by looking at the position of the sun, she reckoned it was getting on for six o'clock. She was still too far away from Fiddler's Farm to be able to get a lift in the cart.

Sal put the cases one on top of the other and then sat on them. Maybe if she had a bit of a breather, she'd be able to walk another mile. She was sitting, feeling fed up, when she heard a car approaching from the wrong direction. Not much use to her but she looked up and, to her delight, she recognised the driver.

Joe brought the car to a smooth standstill beside her. 'Blimey, that's a turn-up for the books. I'm going to go home in style, then.'

Liza was dressed up like a proper lady on the back seat and jumped out and hugged her. 'We're all so pleased you haven't got to leave. Quickly, let's get your cases into the back. It's a shame you didn't stay in your smart clothes as then we could be two grand ladies sitting together whilst our driver takes us home.'

'Joe can get out and put the cases in the car if he's acting as our chauffeur – that's only right – ain't it?'

The young man grinned and touched the peak of his cap. 'Fair enough. Leave them there and I'll put them in the boot, madam.'

They had to go in the wrong direction for a bit until Joe found somewhere he could reverse the large car and then they were heading towards Stodham as easy as you like. Joe was a good driver and Sal was enjoying every minute of the ride. She couldn't remember ever being so happy. Goodwill House was the best home she'd ever had and everyone there was like a big family.

When they turned off the road, she saw there was a big car, painted brown and green, outside Goodwill House. Standing beside it was a girl in a smart soldier's uniform.

'Whose car is that, do you think?' Liza asked her brother.

'I've no idea, but I think it would be wise for me to take the car to the barn and then stay out of sight. Only a very high-ranking officer turns up in a staff car like that.'

* * *

Joanna closed the drawing-room door so Elizabeth wouldn't be aware of what was said by the unwanted visitor. She wouldn't invite him in any further than the hall and intended to make it abundantly clear he wasn't welcome.

She lurked out of sight until he knocked loudly on the door. She waited a few moments and then took a deep breath and walked across.

'Good evening, Lord Harcourt. I am surprised to see you here so late.'

He was dressed in his uniform, and even she had to admit that he looked quite magnificent. She hadn't intended to step aside and allow him to come in but did so involuntarily.

He nodded and moved past her before answering. 'Good evening, Lady Harcourt, I apologise for arriving without invitation. I was in the neighbourhood and needed to speak to you urgently. Is there somewhere we can go?'

'The study.'

She was aware of him prowling along behind as she walked briskly ahead of him. He closed the door firmly and she felt a faint flutter of unease. Not because she thought for one minute he had some ulterior motive, but because his reason for coming was urgent and probably bad news of some sort.

'My mother-in-law didn't give me your letter until yesterday. Therefore, my response was only posted today.'

He sat without being asked to, so she had no option but to follow suit. It would be quite ridiculous to remain flapping about in the middle of the room whilst he lounged in the nearest armchair.

He looked directly at her and smiled. 'I imagine that your reply was to tell me to mind my own business.'

'Good heavens, how could you possibly know that?'

'I don't know you well, but you certainly aren't exactly delighted to see me. I'll get to the point. I don't wish to leave my driver standing outside too long – I have to be back in London tonight.'

'Just a moment.' Joanna left him on his own and dashed to the kitchen. She explained to Jean about the girl outside and arranged for her to be invited in and to be given a cup of tea and something to eat.

'I suppose you'd better make coffee for us, Jean, and put a few of the biscuits you made this morning on a plate. I didn't ask the wretched man in, but he's here now and I can hardly continue to be inhospitable.'

'I'll see to it right away, Joanna.'

She'd half-expected him to be on his feet, looking cross, but he was leaning back, his legs stretched out and his eyes closed. Like all military gentlemen, he seemed able to sleep anywhere at any time.

'I apologise for abandoning you, Lord Harcourt, but I was just making sure your driver was looked after. Refreshments will be brought to us once that's been done.'

'Thank you, that was kind of you. I should have asked you do to that myself.'

'Now, please tell me what brought you here so urgently.'

'The bank manager and the solicitor involved in defrauding the Harcourt estate have been arrested but unfortunately a lot of the papers that will be essential to prove the case have been destroyed in the bombing today.'

'My solicitor has all the necessary paperwork,' Joanna said. 'I explained this in the letter that I wrote to you. I was aware of the discrepancy in the accounts, but Mr Broome thought it more sensible to wait until the debt had been cleared and the account formally closed before submitting the evidence to the police.'

'I should have realised you didn't need my interference.' He smiled and then continued. 'You know absolutely nothing about me. Would you allow me to tell you, it might help to explain my actions, whilst we wait for the refreshments you promised?'

Joanna nodded for him to continue.

'I was an unexpected and late arrival and my mother died in childbirth. My father, predictably, blamed me for the loss and I don't believe he spoke more than a few words to me my entire life. I was brought up by a succession of nannies and packed off to boarding school at seven.'

Joanna wasn't exactly sure why she was being given his family history but was sad to think how lonely and unhappy he must have been as a child.

'I became a professional soldier straight from school and discovered when my father died fifteen years ago that I was very wealthy indeed. I've been on my own all my life and to discover that I have a ready-made family – however distant the connection – meant more to me than you could possibly realise.'

'Forgive me for asking such a personal question, but you must be in your forties, why do you not have a wife and children of your own?'

'I married in my twenties, had no children, and Delphine ran off with a wealthy American and as far as I know she's still alive, so I'm probably still married to her. I've never bothered to enquire.'

'How unfortunate – I was married to David for eighteen years and don't regret the marriage because it gave me Sarah, my daughter, who you met at the memorial service, and then put me in a position to adopt Joe and Liza. You didn't answer my question about your age. I'm thirty-six.' She wasn't sure why she was sharing these personal details but something about what he'd told her had touched a chord in her.

'I'm forty-five. I'm told that I'm the youngest Lieutenant Colonel in the army – not that it makes any difference to me. The reason I became involved in your affairs is simple. I am an investigator – a spook, if you like. If something seems wrong, then I have to find out why and put it right.'

'I begin to understand. Sarah's vaguely linked to you by blood, but we all share the same second name. I'm astonished that you've never bothered to get a divorce – I'd suggest that you do so immediately so you can find yourself a suitable wife and produce the necessary heir. Then the title can continue after your demise.'

If she'd suggested that he did somersaults across the carpet, he couldn't have been more shocked. 'I've no intention of doing any such thing. As no doubt you have already observed, I'm an arrogant, selfish sort of fellow and am much better off living on my own. Do I have your permission to use your given name?'

'Yes, Peter, you do. I was being ridiculous refusing to address you informally. You're quite right, I do think you arrogant and irritating but not selfish. If you want to be part of the family, then so be it.'

Jean came in with the tray and put it down with a smile but said nothing. He waited until they were alone again before responding to her offer.

'Thank you. I give you my word that I'll not interfere again in the way that I have done. However, I hope that you won't hesitate to contact me if you do need my help.'

She poured the coffee, which he accepted gratefully and wolfed down most of the biscuits. 'When did you last eat, Peter?'

'About six o'clock this morning. Sorry, is it that obvious?'

'It is.' She was about to go in search of Jean and ask her to make him a sandwich or two, but this proved unnecessary.

'Here, my lord, I've brought you a couple of sandwiches. Your driver said you'd had nothing since breakfast.'

'That's astoundingly kind of you, ma'am.'

'She also made it very clear that you'd insisted she didn't miss out on her lunch.'

Jean smiled warmly at him and then turned to her. 'Joe's back with Sal and the girls are celebrating. The first thing Sal did was return the money she'd been given – Lady Harcourt was insistent that she keep it, but Sal doesn't want to and has asked me to give it to you.'

Peter was now demolishing the sandwiches whilst listening with interest.

'I'll put it somewhere safe. Did she tell you how that horrible man met his end?'

'He arrived at the station whilst she was eating her lunch and then, when those wretched Germans started bombing Ramsgate, he was machine-gunned.'

Jean then left them to return to the noisy impromptu party going on in the ballroom. Joanna's opinion of her distant relative was now more favourable.

'What an exciting life you lead here, Joanna, I'd love to hear more about it but as soon as I finish these delicious sandwiches, I must make a move.'

'I apologise for being less than polite when you arrived. Thank you for coming and for wishing to be part of the family. We're having a celebration for my children's birthdays in September – circumstances allowing – as the twins will be fifteen and my daughter, Sarah, eighteen. I'll send you an invitation if you like. Obviously, you must stay overnight.'

He smiled. 'Circumstances allowing, I'd be delighted to come and be able get to know you all better. Goodbye, Joanna, I'm so glad we can be friends.'

She stood in the open doorway, watching the car until it turned onto the road. What a strange day it had been – Sal's murderous ex-boyfriend had been killed in an air raid, enabling her to return to Goodwill House, where she belonged. Manston had been all but destroyed and all those working on the base had been evacuated heaven knows where, so it was going to be quieter and safer for all of them until it reopened in a few months.

But the most surprising thing of all was Peter's arrival and the fact that she now viewed him as a member of the Harcourt family and not a potential threat. She'd never feel about him in the same way she had for John, who was undoubtedly the love of her life, but from now on, Peter would be a friend.

ACKNOWLEDGMENTS

I want to thank Team Boldwood for inviting me to join their company. Best decision I've ever made. My books wouldn't be bestsellers without the input of so many people but especially my editor, Emily Ruston. She makes a good book an even better one. Thank you all.

Fenella J. Miller, November 2022

BIBLIOGRAPHY

Chronicle of the Second World War edited by Jacques Legrand and
Derrik Mercer
A to Z Atlas and Guide to London, 1939 edition
Oxford Dictionary of Slang by John Ayto
Wartime Britain by Juliet Gardiner
How We Lived Then by Norman Longmate
The Wartime Scrapbook by Robert Opie
Land Girls at the Old Rectory by Irene Grimwood
Ramsgate, August 1940 by D. T. Richards
The Land Girl Manual 1941 by W. E. Shewell-Cooper
Land Girls and their Impact by Ann Kramer
Land Girl by Anne Hall
The Women's Land Army by Bob Powell and Nigel Westcott
A Detailed History of RAF Manston by Joe Bamford and John
Williams with Peter Gallagher Fonthill
Old Ordnance Survey Map, Ramsgate 1905, the Godfrey Edition
BBC Archives: World War II

MORE FROM FENELLA J. MILLER

We hope you enjoyed reading *The Land Girls at Goodwill House*. If you did, please leave a review.

If you'd like to gift a copy, this book is also available as an ebook, digital audio download and audiobook CD.

Sign up to Fenella J. Miller's mailing list for news, competitions and updates on future books.

https://bit.ly/FenellaMillerNews

The War Girls of Goodwill House, the first in the Goodwill House series, is available now.

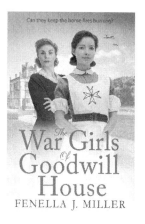

ABOUT THE AUTHOR

Fenella J. Miller is the bestselling writer of historical sagas. She also has a passion for Regency romantic adventures and has published over fifty to great acclaim. Her father was a Yorkshireman and her mother the daughter of a Rajah. She lives in a small village in Essex with her British Shorthair cat.

Follow Fenella on social media:

 twitter.com/fenellawriter
facebook.com/fenella.miller

Sixpence Stories

Introducing Sixpence Stories!

Discover page-turning historical novels from your favourite authors, meet new friends and be transported back in time.

Join our book club Facebook group

https://bit.ly/SixpenceGroup

Sign up to our newsletter

https://bit.ly/SixpenceNews

Boldwood

Boldwood Books is an award-winning fiction publishing company seeking out the best stories from around the world.

Find out more at www.boldwoodbooks.com

Join our reader community for brilliant books, competitions and offers!

Follow us
@BoldwoodBooks
@BookandTonic

Sign up to our weekly deals newsletter

https://bit.ly/BoldwoodBNewsletter

Made in the USA
Columbia, SC
22 December 2022

74857931R00159